"Like it or not, you need me, Shamus."

Abby smiled at Nick's familiar endearment—but she wasn't about to admit how right he was. "What makes you such an expert on me?" she inquired as they drove along the bumpy road.

"A lot of studying," Nick replied with a sexy grin. "I think about you day and night . . . and I think you've forgotten how to share. How to trust. Abby Shay, you're in a rut."

"I am not!" *The man had gall.*

"Hey, with a little work, we'll get you out of there," Nick said, reaching over to stroke her cheek.

"And how do you plan to save me?" Glancing in the rearview mirror, Abby frowned.

"By joining forces. You want me as much as I want you. You're just not sure how to handle us as a couple yet."

"I think we should call a truce," Abby warned.

"Why—because I'm winning the argument?"

"No, because someone is after us," she answered wryly, aiming her thumb at the back window.

Leandra Logan makes her debut at Harlequin Temptation with a fun, suspenseful, action-packed romantic comedy. An avid reader of detective stories, she felt it was time to write one herself. As for the setting, she confides she's never been to Mexico. Her mother, though, took a trip there, and Leandra made her promise she'd come back with tons of notes—never mind having a good time! Leandra plans to write more stories in exotic locales, but she hasn't revealed her mom's next destination....

This talented author of four young-adult romances lives with her husband and two young children in Minnesota.

Cupid Connection
LEANDRA LOGAN

Harlequin Books

TORONTO • NEW YORK • LONDON
AMSTERDAM • PARIS • SYDNEY • HAMBURG
STOCKHOLM • ATHENS • TOKYO • MILAN

Published October 1990

ISBN 0-373-25420-2

Printed in U.S.A.

1

"STOP THE CAR, ABIGAL! Stop the car!" Her hair swirling around her shoulders in a bright red cloud, Blanche Shay abruptly shifted her gaze from the windshield to look at her daughter behind the wheel.

"Stop where, Mother?" Abby clearly had doubts about halting her maroon Cutlass Supreme in the middle of the street, but she obediently began to pump the brake pedal anyway. When the old cumbersome car was rolling at little more than a crawl, she turned to Blanche, pulling off her large sunglasses to reveal alert green eyes and a heart-shaped face full of curiosity. "Are you sure Charles Farrell lives here on Blue Spruce?"

"Of course I'm sure about Blue Spruce!" Blanche replied with annoyance.

"But you thought it was Green Spruce a few minutes ago. We drove up and down, up and down. For nothing!"

"Give me a break! I was here only once and it was dark then. That house on the other street looked a lot like Charlie's—until I saw that Saint Bernard loping through the rosebushes. Charlie doesn't have a dog."

Abby set her glasses on the dashboard and peered out at the stately homes of Evergreen Estates, one of Minnesota's wealthiest communities nestled twenty miles south of downtown Minneapolis. It was Abby's first visit to the elite suburb and she was a little in awe of the velvety lawns, the huge tudor-style mansions, and the massive oaks and evergreens gracing the yards and boulevards. Her well-honed instincts had warned her that they were out of their league the very moment they'd crossed through the community's ivy-covered gates. But Abby knew that instinct and common sense fell to the wayside when Blanche Shay was on a rampage. Abby knew from experience that it was best to ride the crest of her mother's wave of fury instead of trying to stop it. So once again she found herself in the center of a funnel cloud, hanging on to Blanche's shirttail, trying to keep her mother out of trouble.

"Pull over by this two-story brick place with the white shutters and long winding driveway," Blanche ordered, jabbing a crimson-tipped finger out the open passenger window. "That's where the geriatric gigolo lives. I'm certain of it!"

Abby brought her car to a stop at the curb and switched off the engine. "Geriatric gigolo?" she repeated, tossing a thick curtain of auburn hair over her shoulder and confronting Blanche with a look of amazement. She reminded Abby of a small tigress about to pounce on its prey, in her black dress of polished cotton, and her vibrant red hair in disarray. "Is this the same man you said danced like Fred Astaire, crooned like Frank Sinatra, and dressed like George Hamilton? Before this last trip to Mexico, you claimed that Charles Farrell was your perfect match, a cuddly new Cupid Connection."

"Quoting me verbatim is one of your more annoying habits, Abigal," Blanche chastised, wagging her manicured finger at her daughter.

"I'm merely trying to get the facts straight," Abby asserted, her large eyes taking on a stubborn glitter identical to her mother's.

"There's no need for me to clarify the facts. They're crystal clear. That man stole my emerald brooch! He caressed me under the Mazatlan moonlight and—"

"And his nimble fingers caressed our heirloom right off your blouse," Abby cut in dryly, straightening the collar of her pink and white floral shirt. She'd barely had time to dress properly before Blanche hauled her off on this crazy caper.

"He's a nimble-fingered crook!" Blanche agreed, oblivious to her daughter's gibing tone. "He thought he could hoodwink me by replacing my beautiful brooch with a cheap replica."

"If you recall, I was against your getting involved with the Cupid Connection right from the start." Abby couldn't resist lecturing her mother. She'd been wondering where Blanche's dating service dabbling of the last several months would lead. Hanging around with that swank Cupid Connection crowd, lunching and brunching with wealthy ladies like Verona Vickers and Penelope Belmont. "Didn't I tell you that computerized hanky-panky had a phony ring to it?"

"Charlie handled the hanky-panky part quite well," Blanche protested, a wistful smile crossing her face. "I may not have immediately recognized the fact that the gem was an imitation, but I certainly would've spotted a phony—"

"Mother, really!" Abby ran a hand through her long thick hair, expelling an exasperated breath. Her mother's cavalier attitude about sex was a bit hard to handle at ten o'clock on a Monday morning. Especially before coffee! Oh, what Abby wouldn't have given for some steaming caffeine. Just a single cup to take the edge off Blanche's shrill cry for vengeance.

Upon her return home last night from a trip to Mexico sponsored by Cupid Connection Blanche had discovered that the genuine emerald brooch that had been in the Shay family for over a hundred years was gone. A glass imitation now resided in her small velvet jewelry box. In a panic she'd called Abby shortly after midnight, babbling on about one Charlie Farrell, perfect match turned jewel thief.

"It's too bad she didn't catch the thief red-handed," Abby murmured dolefully as she watched a uniformed gardener in a neighboring yard trim a lilac bush with precise, rhythmic clips.

"I heard that, Abigal," Blanche exclaimed indignantly, her turned up nose in the air. "I would've immediately spotted the botched up job on the inscription if I'd had my reading glasses on anytime during the trip. But quite frankly, dear, Charlie and I had no spare time for reading."

"I can always count on you to be frank, Mother," Abby said with a long-suffering sigh. A Cadillac passed by from the opposite direction, the elderly female driver glaring at them with undisguised contempt. "I'll bet that woman disapproves of my ancient Cutlass littering her street," Abby guessed, sinking a bit lower in the driver's seat.

"Hah!" Blanche snorted. "In my book anybody that would dye her hair a hideous shade of blue doesn't have a lick of sense."

"I was just thinking the same thing about dyed redheads," Abby shot back. "During one mad fling you managed to lose a piece of jewelry that the Shays have kept under lock and key for over a century!"

"I'm trying to make up for my bad judgment now," Blanche insisted defensively, toying with the handle of her purse. "This stakeout was my idea. And a good one, too. I'm sure we'll catch Charlie doing something illegal."

"Police handle stakeouts," Abby corrected firmly. "This is nothing more than a little impulsive surveillance. And a foolish waste of time," she added, glancing at the gold watch on her slender wrist.

"But time is of the essence, Abby. Oh," she lamented, "what good is it to have a private detective in the family if she isn't prepared to handle a crisis when it arises?"

"I can handle this crisis, Mother," Abby objected. "I make a living at helping people in trouble. And as an expert, I can tell you that this is the wrong approach. It's foolish to begin an investigation blindly. As it stands, I know nothing about Charles Farrell—aside from that coy message you wrote on the back of that postcard you sent me from Mexico."

"A postcard hardly has the space, nor does it afford the privacy for one to bare one's soul." Blanche's thin penciled brows rose as she cast Abby a pathetic look.

"Little old impetuous you rarely has trouble communicating," Abby retorted, not about to fall for the damsel-in-distress routine.

"You wouldn't understand. You're never impulsive, Abigal. Everything you do is always by the book." Blanche pounded her fist into her hand like a judge pounding a gavel. "You tread along life's path, calculating every step, noting every detail."

"Just give me the chance to understand the situation, Mother." Abby urged in a tone full of challenge. "Tell me more about Charles Farrell. Tell me more about the rich man who swooped down from his evergreen lair to romance my middle-income mother for a single piece of jewelry."

"Well, we met at the first Cupid Connection gathering that I attended at Christmastime. Oh, he was so charming and—"

"You've known him since Christmas and didn't mention him until this trip?" Abby interrupted, totally aghast. "It's April tenth!"

"We were already quite an item back in February, when I went to Mazatlan for the first time," Blanche confided.

"How could you keep this from me?"

"Oh, you know how you are." Blanche murmured with a dismissive wave. "Charlie's rich, divorced, loves to play the ponies. You would have disapproved of him from the start, doled out all sorts of unsolicited advice."

"Unwanted advice truly can be a pain." Abby agreed, casting a wry look at the queen of meddlers seated beside her.

If Blanche caught her daughter's pointed look, she didn't let on. "Like me, Charlie's lived in Minnesota his whole life. And he was hungering for a thrilling romance—just like I was." Blanche shook her head sorrowfully. "Of course you wouldn't understand that hunger, being a workaholic."

"Mother, this is no time to discuss my love life. Yours is causing enough havoc." Abby rubbed her temples, straining to keep her tone steady. But she was weary of her mother's constant pressure for a son-in-law to fix her leaky pipes, and grandchildren to take to the playground. She knew exactly where her life was headed and was managing quite nicely without a husband.

Abby had decided long ago to earn her degree in law enforcement and pursue a career in private investigations. At twenty-nine, she considered her ambitions fulfilled. After four years of college and two thousand hours of apprenticeship, she'd become a licensed private detective.

And she'd paid her dues. At times the road had been quite rocky. Apprenticing for the huge Compton Investigations had proven gruelling. The hours were hideous and she'd been at the beck and call of every cocky private eye in the place. Then there had been her yearlong partnership and relationship with an investigator named Roy Stark. He was killed while working on one of their biggest cases, leaving Abby alone in a sterile office high rise with cool, impersonal clients to deal with.

Eventually she closed up shop in Minneapolis, fortified with a new dream and a new perspective. She opened up Wildcat Investigations in suburban St. Paul, content to work alone. Though Roy had been gone for three years, and business was steady, the scars left behind still ran deep. She'd been hurt badly enough to know better than to ever mix business with pleasure again.

Ironically, all the traits Blanche criticized in her were the very ones that helped her survive.

"I say we confront Charlie right now!" Blanche declared with sudden vehemence, her delicately lined complexion flushing to an attractive pink.

"You're too agitated to face this man now," Abby protested, putting a restraining hand on her mother's forearm.

"But that was the plan," Blanche shot back. "I brought you
along for moral support—to help me through this!"

"We can't accuse Charles Farrell of anything without any
concrete proof to back up our claim," Abby told her mother
adamantly. "Something just doesn't add up here," she added
reflectively, once again looking across the velvety green lawn
and through the trees at the two-story brick house. Why
would a man living in Evergreen Estates, one of Minnesota's
most exclusive neighborhoods, want to steal an emerald
brooch? He even had a fountain in the center of his circular
driveway, for Pete's sake! "Let's go, Mother. We never should
have come rushing over here in the first place." Abby moved
her hand to the ignition, but Blanche intervened.

"Wait. Let's sit here for a while," Blanche coaxed, "just to
see if anything develops."

"All right," Abby relented, glancing once more at her
watch. "But my time is limited. I have a luncheon appointment today with a prospective client."

"I won't hold you up much longer, dear."

"Don't expect snap results. Charles Farrell isn't likely to do
anything incriminating out on the front lawn within the next
thirty minutes."

"Never can tell about old Charlie," Blanche murmured,
smoothing out her disheveled hair.

"SOMEONE'S WATCHING THE HOUSE, Dad." Nick Farrell's angular features narrowed to a scowl at the sight of the decrepit
maroon car parked at the curb.

"You sure, Nick?" Charlie Farrell asked, eyeing his tall,
broad-shouldered son from his favorite recliner. The gray-
haired man set his coffee mug down on the end table, sprang
out of his chair, and purposefully crossed the length of his

cedar-paneled den. He joined his son at the bay window, which offered a clear view of his wide sloping front yard.

"Do any of your poker buddies drive a '79 Cutlass?" Nick asked, his blue eyes reflecting suspicion.

"No, none of them." Charlie fished in the pocket of his yellow knit shirt for a cigar. "If one of 'em was that bad off, I'd be inclined to buy him a new car," he said reflectively.

"You going to light that thing up?" Nick asked, wincing at the cheap cigar clamped between his father's teeth. Charlie struck a match to the pungent tobacco in affirmation. Even though Charles Farrell had long been the master of a large financial empire, he still insisted upon smoking the same foul-smelling cigars year after year.

"These stogies remind me of my poorer days. They keep my values in perspective. Besides, they're comfortable, like an old shoe."

"Smell like an old shoe, too," Nick observed, his heavy dark brows drawing together disapprovingly. "They'll no doubt kill you one day."

"That's pretty conservative talk coming from a man who earns his living driving a little car around in a circle at speeds in excess of two hundred miles per hour. As a matter of fact, I'll bet the occupants of that junker out there are here to see you." Charlie grinned slyly, his pale blue eyes twinkling. "Probably female fans from the racetrack. Probably want a Nick Farrell tune-up."

Nick ran a hand through his coarse black hair and glared at his father with the handsome face that had made him a racing circuit favorite. Though his good looks hadn't changed, his circumstances undeniably had. His accident at last year's Indianapolis 500 had ended his triumphant career and almost his life. "You know very well that my racing days are over, Dad," Nick said, his voice rough with emotion. He glanced down at the black metal cane that was propping up his right leg. "The female fans are part of the past, too."

Charlie also gazed at the cane. "That leg will be back in commission in no time. True, with the ligament damage you sustained, you may never regain top standing on the track. But any woman who would've loved you exclusively for your status on the circuit really wouldn't have made much of a wife anyway."

Nick grunted in protest, his blue eyes darkening with his mood. "You manage to wangle women into every conversation we have. My accident at Indy and the loss of my standing on the circuit have nothing to do with my love life."

"The hell you say!" Charlie ran a hand through his thinning gray hair. "Women have something to do with everything. You're thirty-five. I figured that by now you'd know that much."

"Look who's talking," Nick shot back. "While you were busy wooing and cooing in some redhead's ear on the shores of Mazatlan, she stole your pocket watch while you had it with you."

"Touché, lad." Charlie surrendered with reluctance.

"Where are your binoculars, Dad?" Nick inquired, turning his attention once again to the Cutlass.

"Someplace around here." The cigar clamped between his teeth, he growled as he pawed through the deep bottom drawer of his rolltop desk. "Blanche Shay did indeed try to get the better of me, stealing my watch right out of my pants pocket. Would've gotten away with it, too, if she'd known that the damn watch hasn't kept the correct time in thirty years. Her mistake was to replace my broken pocket watch with one that really worked! Ah-ha. Here are the field glasses, under my fishing guide," he said a moment or two later.

Nick took the binoculars from Charlie and raised them to his eyes.

"Yup," Charlie continued, flicking ashes into the huge amber ashtray on his desk. "I knew something was wrong when that watch read ten o'clock at ten o'clock! Almost missed my flight out of Mexico because I figured it was barely past eight." Charlie moved back to the window. "Say, you recognize anyone in that car?"

"No," Nick replied meditatively. "But then I don't know many redheads in their fifties . . ."

"What?" Charlie wrenched the glasses from his son's grip and focused them on the Cutlass. "It's *her* dammit! The flamin'-haired pirate!" Charlie's breathing accelerated causing smoke to billow from the cigar still clenched between his teeth.

"You look like a steam locomotive amidst all that smoke," Nick observed, breathing shallowly to avoid inhaling too much of the rolling cloud of gray. "The little engine that could."

"Shut up."

"I can't believe that she has the nerve to show up outside your house after lifting your watch."

"Blanche has more brass than a three-foot urn," Charlie muttered, his tone laced with sardonic admiration.

"Sounds like the type that would turn your head all right," Nick said with new understanding.

"Probably thinks I'm a pushover," Charlie ranted, waving the binoculars in the air. "She's probably come to clean out the safe."

Nick wondered if Blanche Shay actually knew about the safe concealed behind the original Picasso in the den, but said nothing. Charlie was already riled to the limit.

"Wonder who her wheelman is." Charlie mused with a grunt, tilting the binoculars in different directions in an attempt to see through the cluster of trees obstructing his view of the car.

"From this angle it's impossible to tell," Nick replied. From his six foot three stance, he watched the scene over the shorter man's shoulder.

"Well, maybe we'd better change our angle then," Charlie bit out with a ferocious glare.

"I still think the police should be notified immediately," Nick asserted.

"No police!" Charlie roared, turning to carelessly toss the high-powered binoculars onto the small leather couch behind him. "I can see the headlines now—'Chairman of the Board Snookered by Redheaded Bombshell.'"

Nick groaned deeply. Charlie had rousted him out of his apartment at seven o'clock in the morning to report the theft, then proceeded to sputter about Blanche Shay for the next two hours over breakfast and two pots of coffee laced with Irish whiskey. Even now, when the woman seemed to be on the verge of trespassing on Farrell property, and was obviously up to something, Charlie refused to call in the law. Nick's patience was spent. "Tell me something. Are you hung up on this Blanche Shay?"

"Hanging's too good for her." Charlie eluded his son's probing gaze by turning to his desk and carefully grinding out his cigar in the ashtray.

"I believe I'm beginning to understand." A mirthless smirk formed on Nick's firm mouth. "You're in love with a crook."

"Hah!" Dismissively, Charlie waved a hand through the air. "I just don't want to be responsible for sending a delicate lady to prison."

"I thought she was brassy," Nick objected, circling the desk to meet his father's evasive eyes. "I'll wager she could withstand prison chow and an uprising or two in the laundry room."

"If you want to help me, forget about the cops. I intend to handle this matter myself from start to finish."

"Sort of like Kojak, Perry Mason and Judge Roy Bean rolled into one," Nick chided, his square chin set in rigid disapproval.

Charlie's pale blue eyes gleamed as he struck a match to another cigar. "Right you are, lad. Right you are."

"MOTHER, CAN WE GO NOW?" Abby tugged at the hem of her white A-line skirt and shifted uncomfortably on the cracked vinyl car seat. "It's almost eleven o'clock."

"I'm bored too, you know," Blanche said pouting, raising a faintly freckled arm up over the back of the seat. "If your radio didn't make that tinny sound, we could've been entertaining ourselves with a little music."

"You're too fussy," Abby accused, rotating her ankle to revive her sleeping foot. Abby had a transistor radio in the glove compartment that she often listened to while on surveillance, but she was too proud to admit to Blanche that her car radio was as decrepit as the rest of the Cutlass. "We've fished. We've failed. It's time to cut bait."

"Please be patient a little while longer," Blanche implored, her eyes full of emotion.

"Every gust of wind passing through the car is like a spray of pine-scented air freshener," Abby complained with a sneeze. She dabbed her nose with a tissue and rolled up her window.

"I'm sorry about your allergy, but naturally Evergreen Estates is likely to boast a few evergreens," Blanche pointed out.

With a sniff Abby placed her sunglasses back on her watering eyes. "This street alone could qualify as a Christmas tree farm."

"Look!" Blanche exclaimed suddenly, gesturing toward the house. "One of Charlie's garage doors is opening."

Abby gazed through the windshield just as a silver Ferrari backed out of the third stall, the automatic garage door immediately closing behind it. The car rolled to a stop at the front door and a thin gray-haired man of average height came jauntily down the front steps, slipping his arms into a tweed coat. He got into the passenger side of the Ferrari and the sports car began its journey down the long ribbon of black-top to the street.

"That's Charlie, all right," Blanche squealed like a school girl, giving the maroon dashboard a triumphant slap. "Probably going to meet his fence."

The car shot out into the street and headed off in the opposite direction.

"I suppose you expect me to follow them," Abby declared, starting up her engine with obvious reluctance.

"I do. Charlie looked real shifty coming out of the house, don't you agree?"

"Since he wasn't wearing a ski mask or carrying a limp bundle over his shoulder, I'm tempted to give him the benefit of the doubt."

"ARE THEY REALLY BEHIND US, Nick?" Charlie twisted around in the tight confines of the leather-upholstered Ferrari, excitement illuminating his weathered face.

"Yes. We just can't see them yet." Nick shook his dark head in amusement as he cruised the wide, curving streets of Evergreen, just a couple of miles over the conservative speed limit. "I don't understand it, Dad. Why would Blanche Shay be following us around?"

"Hard tellin'," Charlie replied, stroking his narrow chin thoughtfully.

"And who is driving that piece of junk?" Nick wondered. He'd caught a fleeting glance at the woman behind the wheel as he left the driveway. Her profile followed lines similar to those of Blanche Shay, but she was considerably younger and had only a trace of red in her thick brown hair.

"I figure it's the gumshoe daughter," Charlie replied, surprising Nick with his ready answer.

"Gumshoe?"

"Yeah, yeah, you know. Private eye, shamus. Gumshoe."

"Wonder if she packs a heater," Nick contemplated, beginning to enjoy the situation. After spending months in the hospital struggling to regain his strength, he was due for just such a diversion.

"Packs a what?" Charlie barked in surprise.

"C'mon, Dad," Nick said with a chuckle. "Piece, rod. Heater."

"Don't mock me, lad. That watch is priceless. Don't forget, it was presented to my great-grandfather by Abe Lincoln back in 1865—three short weeks before he took the bullet. That's a slice of history, son. A silver slice of history."

Nick was well aware of the watch's worth—from a financial point of view as well as from a historical one. A long while back he'd had it appraised for insurance purposes and had found its estimated value staggering. But did that stop Charlie from swinging the timepiece around on ten yards of silver chain—not on your life! "History's a living thing," Charlie always said whenever Nick tried to lock up the watch. "Touch this watch and you're touching Abraham Lincoln."

"They're still back there," Charlie observed, breaking into his son's thoughts. "Think they'll be disappointed when they find out we're having lunch at the country club and then you're going on to the hospital for physical therapy?"

"I don't think they'll last that long," Nick drawled with assurance.

"SPEED UP, ABIGAL, you're going to lose them," Blanche warned anxiously, stomping her size 6 black patent leather pump down on an imaginary accelerator on the passenger floor.

"That's a switch," Abby teased. "When I was sixteen you stomped on an imaginary brake. Now that I'm twenty-nine and really know what I'm doing, you're hitting the gas."

"Our roles have sort of reversed over the years. You've grown conservative and I've assumed an attractive bohemian style."

"Bohemian or not, I am in control of the situation. I follow people for a living, remember?"

"But they are picking up speed. And they have the advantage of knowing their way around this neighborhood."

"As it is, my old car is conspicuous enough in this high-rent district. Besides, if I ride his bumper, he'll no doubt recognize you immediately.

"Just don't be too cautious," Blanche insisted. She was silent for a moment or two, then slanted her daughter a bewildered look, "Abigal, why are you grinning?"

"Must be a muscle spasm," Abby claimed, focusing on the road with renewed concentration. It was true that Abby was upset over Blanche's loss of the valuable brooch that she herself was supposed to inherit, but the circumstances did amuse her in a way. It wasn't every day that a male got the better of Blanche Shay. Up to the time of his death three years ago, Abby's father had been totally under Blanche's spell. Abby was certain that her mother missed him terribly, but that hadn't stopped Blanche from rebuilding her life as a single woman. She indulged in everything from gambling in Monte Carlo, to parasailing in Miami Beach, to her recent fling at a Mazatlan resort. Blanche felt she had the magic touch with men that Abby so sadly lacked. Well, Abby thought smugly, she had to tip her hat to Charles Farrell. He'd certainly taught Blanche a thing or two!

"We've lost them!" Blanche's shrill accusation jolted Abby out of her reverie.

"They headed south at the next street," Abby said calmly, peering at the corner sign. "They have to be on Norway Pine." Abby turned in pursuit moments later only to find the wide well-kept street deserted, with the exception of a shiny brown mail truck backing down one of the long driveways.

"They're gone, Abby." Blanche turned to Abby with an I-told-you-so frown. "You blew it."

"They can't be far," Abby insisted confidently, pushing her slipping sunglasses back up the bridge of her nose. She proceeded to roam the neighborhood, zigzagging through similar-looking streets each named after an evergreen, but found no trace of the Ferrari. In the meantime, Blanche rummaged through her purse and pulled out a large round compact.

"This is neither the time nor the place to apply makeup," Abby scolded.

Blanche opened the compact and held the mirror up near the windshield. "With this spring action, I'd say you're right." As they bounced along, Blanche scrutinized her fair, faintly freckled complexion in the reflection.

"I just can't afford a new car right now," Abby said answering the unasked question she knew was hovering on her mother's lips.

"You should try to arrange something. This beater rides rougher than the dirt bike I rented in Nevada last summer."

Abby released a frustrated sigh as she turned around in a cul-de-sac and headed back in the direction of Interstate 94. "I give up. We've really lost them."

"This is no time to throw in the towel, Abigal!"

Abby's mouth dropped open and her tone took on an incredulous edge. "Don't you realize that I'm giving in? Admitting that you're right for a change? Charles Farrell ditched us."

"But I think we're really on to something," Blanche persisted with a feline smile.

"How so?"

"I've spotted them."

"Where?"

"In my compact," Blanche answered triumphantly.

Abby flashed her a puzzled look. "Mother—"

"I mean in my mirror, dear. The Ferrari is right behind us. Just turned off Ponderosa Pine. Or was it Douglas Fir?" Blanche pursed her lips, trying to identify which street it had been.

One glance in the rearview mirror confirmed Blanche's claim. "Damn!" Out of sheer panic Abby pressed down on the accelerator. "That driver's good. I didn't spot him once along the streets—not even the glint of a fender. Not just anyone can pull such a neat maneuver." Abby glanced at Blanche, then again in the mirror. "Who do you suppose he is?"

Abby took a quick inventory of the driver. His head of thick black hair, the dark outline of his face and the tan-sleeved arm angled out of the open window may have given her a limited view, but it left a sharp impression. He was intimidating. And it wasn't a professional observation, Abby realized to her own chagrin. It was an earthy instinct that females have respected since the dawn of Time.

"Oh, it's probably Charlie's son, the race car driver," Blanche ventured airily, snapping her compact shut.

"A professional driver?" Abby nearly exploded over the news. The sleek sports car was now aligning itself on her back bumper with the accuracy of a heat seeking missile. She felt a surge of adrenaline as her foot locked on the gas pedal and her fingers squeezed the steering wheel. "This could get very sticky," she muttered ominously.

"Not to worry," Blanche said soothingly, her expression guileless.

"Not to worry, not to worry. With you, trouble always seems to hover just beyond those very words, Mother."

"I really mean it this time," Blanche hastened to assure her.

"I've been forced off the road before." Abby inhaled shakily. "I believe that's what this man has in mind."

"Oh, no boy of Charlie's would do a thing like that," Blanche scoffed, wrinkling her turned up nose.

"You're certain that the Farrell family draws the line at bodily harm," Abby clarified with as much sarcasm as she could muster, while trying to steady the playing steering wheel of the oversized car. Abby thought the Cutlass was like a grand old ship, heroic, regal-looking, but when speed and efficiency were at stake, it was definitely past its prime.

"Of course I'm certain about the Farrells," Blanche insisted. "Charlie may be a thief, but he isn't dangerous."

"Do you love this man or hate him?" Abby cast Blanche a quick narrow-eyed look before snapping her attention back to the street.

"For the time being, let's just say that I love to hate him!"

"I never should have agreed to this," Abby lamented in self-disgust. Blindly she'd come running to help her mother in what she'd thought was an emergency. Why, it was nothing more than a game of cat and mouse! Abby didn't like the setup. In her line of work she was accustomed to being the cat that took chase. Not the nervous mouse skittering for cover.

"What shall we do now?" Blanche asked exuberantly.

Noticing her mother's mood swing dramatically from furious to downright cavalier. Abby suddenly gained new insight into the situation. Blanche was thoroughly enjoying this crime, savoring her outrage at her roguish lover. Did her quest for thrills have no bounds? Why, she didn't even seem all that concerned about the brooch anymore!

As she jockeyed past a parked car along the sloping thoroughfare, Abby experienced an unexpected stab of envy over her mother's uninhibited zest for life. But envy was swiftly superseded by suspicion as Abby recalled some of Blanche's past escapades. "This isn't another one of your schemes, is it, Mother?" she asked, gritting her teeth as she took an especially sharp corner onto Evergreen Road. The gates to Evergreen Estates and the freedom of Osborn Avenue were just ahead. Thank God, a street not named after a tree! Interstate 94, her escape route back to St. Paul was within three blocks of Osborn.

"Steady," she coached herself, glancing in the mirror. The silver Ferrari was still bearing down on her ponderous Cutlass mile for mile, just as the shadowy features of Charles Farrell's son bore down on her breath for breath. Surely he would back off once she was out of Evergreen's boundaries.

"Scheme?" Blanche questioned with wide-eyed surprise. "Whatever do you mean"

"Matchmaking, of course," Abby responded tensely, easing onto Osborn. He was still behind her! He was obviously not content with just chasing her through Evergreen. "Remember the carpet cleaner you sent over to my office to shampoo my threadbare rugs?" Abby shook her head and clenched her teeth. "Just because he had nice buns!"

"He had a future, too." Blanche beamed proudly. "His own company truck."

"Then there was the time you bought a piano on trial just so I could get free lessons from the handsome salesman."

"The double-crosser was gay." Blanche socked her palm. "Can't trust anybody anymore."

"He couldn't trust you, either. You returned the piano!"

"What would I do with a piano? I'm tone-deaf."

"Try to understand this, Mother. I'm happy on my own."

"Not to worry. After you were so cool to that charming lip sync performer at the Lucky Lounge, I decided to give up on trying to fulfill your fantasies."

"Oh, no!"

"What's the matter now, Abigal?"

"Look for yourself," Abby said grimly as she looked through the rearview mirror. The silver Ferrari had disappeared. Instead, a blue and white patrol car, its red bar over the roof flashing, was now in hot pursuit. Abby had no choice but to pull over to the curb. She suspected he'd done it purposely. Got her revved up where he knew the police routinely set up a speed trap, then dropped back to let the radar take its course. "Son of Charlie is a son of—"

"Abigail!" Blanche cried. "Watch your language."

"Sorry, but I've just been nabbed by Minnesota's finest and I'm steamed," Abby said, already digging through her purse for her driver's license.

Blanche's face brightened with inspiration. "Let me do the talking, Abigail. I'll pretend I'm having a heart attack."

Abby ripped the sunglasses off her face, her delicate features about to explode with fury. "Sure, then they'll be more than willing to give you a police escort to the hospital."

"Then tell them you were speeding because you have to go to the bathroom. Always works for me."

"That's because you look like you have a weak bladder," Abby retorted, rolling down the window as the officer approached.

"Did you know that one of your brake lights is out?" the officer asked, pulling out his ticket pad. "And you were exceeding the speed limit by ten miles an hour . . .

WHEN NICK FARRELL PULLED UP on a side street along Osborn Avenue a short time later, he saw Abby and the policeman standing near the rear bumper of her Cutlass, examining the blinking taillights while the mother sat in the driver's seat, obviously pushing on the brake.

"It's plain to see now that Blanche's daughter Abby isn't carrying a concealed weapon," Charlie noted with a chuckle.

"Abby?"

"Yes, didn't I mention her name before?"

"No, I believe you called her a gumshoe." Nick had to agree that the smooth molded lines of Abby Shay left spare room for a firearm of any size. Her pink floral blouse wrapped neatly around her straight back and full breasts, and her narrow white skirt followed the curves of her rounded hips, revealing a glimpse of stockinged leg through the front slit.

Although she was of average height, her legs were unusually long, giving her a sleek, graceful posture. He felt almost sorry he'd prodded her on that merry chase, then forced her to gun the engine within the speed trap. He could think of some physical games that would have satisfied him much more than this mental challenge had.

"Looks a lot like Blanche," observed Charlie in an admiring tone. "The hair's not near as red, but the sunlight picks up a gleam of the pirate's flame."

"Figure they're in on the theft together?" Nick pondered, fascinated by the way the gentle April breeze stirred Abby's long auburn hair like a caressing hand.

"Don't know," Charlie murmured, resting his gaze on Blanche.

"This would be an ideal time to involve the police," Nick asserted without much enthusiasm.

"Told you no." Charlie replied absently.

"Maybe I can get satisfaction from the daughter," Nick mused.

"I'm willing to bet you can do just that, lad."

2

Shortly after two o'clock that afternoon Abby reached her office. It was located in the Crestview shopping center in the St. Paul suburb of Oakdale. As usual, all the parking spaces in front of Wildcat Investigations were taken. Customers from Barney's Supermarket next door and Value Rite Drugstore beyond that, had overflowed into Abby's territory on the blacktop, leaving their shopping carts in her parking stalls and in front of the plate glass window of her office. Abby circled the lot three times before a man with a station wagon full of children vacated one of her spaces.

"Hello, Gloria!" Abby called out cheerfully as she pulled her briefcase out of the Cutlass.

"Well, hi, Abby." The middle-aged woman leaving the grocery store waved, then paused to wait for the private detective. "Isn't it a beautiful spring day?"

"Lovely," Abby agreed, joining Gloria Paulson amidst the people on the concrete walkway spanning the storefronts. The continuous onslaught of shoppers in the L-shaped center didn't bother Abby one bit. True, the neighborhood setting didn't evoke a Sam Spade atmosphere with which to impress her potential clients, but it made up for it in economy and convenience. Rent was low in comparison to the office space she'd shared with Roy downtown and Abby's two-bedroom rambler on the shores of Crystal Lake was within walking distance of Wildcat Investigations. This proved especially convenient whenever a client called after hours with an urgent problem. Abby could be at the office in no time with hot coffee and a sympathetic ear.

"I want to thank you again for finding my girl," Gloria said in a grateful tone as she shifted her grocery sack from one arm to the other. "Tracking her across three states couldn't have been easy. But convincing her to come back home was nothing short of a miracle."

"I'm just glad Judy agreed to return home with me," Abby said with a supportive smile. Tracking Gloria's runaway teenage daughter to a small town in Illinois had been an exercise in old-fashioned legwork—interviewing Judy's friends for leads, checking her savings account, distributing her picture all across the Twin Cities. When Judy had called home from Chicago, Abby caught the first plane to the Windy City and traced the girl to the small town of Waverly, where according to her notes, Judy's best friend's sister lived. Abby had been determined to locate Judy as swiftly as possible, before she got into any serious trouble. She knew the girl was fairly naive and was running away from wounds that would easily heal with help from Gloria.

"I hope you realize that I intend to pay you every cent I owe." Gloria promised as she stepped off the curb.

"The monthly installments are working out just fine," Abby insisted with feigned indifference. Actually, Abby didn't feel quite as lighthearted as she may have appeared. Putting clients like Gloria on a payment plan was seriously delaying her plans to buy some necessities. She desperately needed a new car, and a washer and dryer. But Abby knew the score when she set up shop in this neighborhood. Aside from a dappling of insurance fraud claims, Abby didn't attract many high-powered business accounts. Her clientele often burst through the office door carrying a brown sack or a plastic jug of milk, without an appointment and without an expense account. Her clients usually reported a missing spouse, a runaway child, or a relative out to cheat them somehow. On a good day, her next-door neighbor, Barney, would call her over to assist his security personnel with an overly ambitious shoplifter. So much for the Charlie's Angels image. Though Abby was every bit as attractive as the television detectives, her life-style lacked the glitz and cash that Hollywood scripts provided.

"Where have you been, Abby?" Donna Clark looked up from her typewriter as her boss glided through the glass doors of Wildcat Investigations.

Abby smiled at the eighteen-year-old blonde seated behind the reception desk and looked around the sparsely furnished room. As usual, the area was spotless, with the molded plastic chairs pushed up against the wall and Abby's outdated magazines stacked neatly on the square glass-topped table. It wasn't surprising that the most expensive things in the room were Donna's red print dress and matching red leather shoes. Donna still lived with her parents and spent most of her income on luxuries. Why, the girl even had a new car. But Abby didn't begrudge Donna her life-style. She was an efficient secretary and a good friend—not to mention the fact that she worshipped the ground Abby walked on, longing to be a detective herself one day.

"My lunch with Mr. Simpson took longer than I expected it to," Abby explained. Setting her briefcase on the carpet, she hiked her skirt up slightly and rested her hip on the edge of Donna's steel desk.

"He hired us—er, you?" Donna's hazel eyes widened in anticipation.

"He's considering it," Abby replied, tucking stray strands of russet hair behind her ear. She picked up the mail and began to thumb through the envelopes as she spoke. "It would be a break all right. Mr. Simpson believes one of the employees at his print shop is dipping into the till. Could mean a large retainer and future referrals." Abby gave the girl a sober look. "Remember, Donna, all client information is confidential."

"Oh, nothing ever leaves this office," Donna assured her solemnly. "Whew, have I ever been busy since you called this morning. Got lots of info on the Farrell boys."

"You make them sound like outlaws." Abby laughed, dropping two flyers into the wastebasket. *Which may be quite accurate,* she added silently.

"Oh, they both appear honest enough," Donna said, flipping open her steno notebook. "Charles Farrell is the chairman of the board of a company he began over thirty years ago, Farrell's Vacuum Supplies. I don't do much vacuuming myself, but apparently Farrell rates right up there with Hoover. I called Mom and she says we have a Farrell vacuum. Guess I never noticed."

Abby held back a smirk. "Very good. Continue."

"Mr. Farrell doesn't play an active role in the company anymore. He serves on the board, pokes around the plants once in a while, and leaves the rest of the business to his other son, Jonathan." Donna looked up from her notes. "You only cared about the foxy son, right, Ab?"

"Right," Abby agreed without thinking. "I mean, I'm only interested in the racer," she amended. "As far as I know, he is the only one involved in this situation."

Donna blew at her long pale bangs and again referred to her notes with avid concentration. "Nick Farrell, incredible hunk—"

"Does it say that?" Abby interrupted, leaning over to scrutinize Donna's notebook.

"Of course not." Donna sighed dreamily. "*I* say that."

"Only the facts, please, Donna."

"That is a fact," Donna objected softly before continuing. "Anyway, he had a terrible accident at Indy last year. He was lucky to have survived. Another driver clipped the rear end of his car only fifteen minutes into the race. Nick lost control of his car and careened into a concrete retaining wall. The impact was so violent, it tore the car in half, broke Nick's shoulder harness, and sent him skidding along the track in his cockpit."

"Sounds awful." Abby felt a rush of sympathy for the man, then remembered the way the cagey creep had treated her on the road.

"It was awful," Donna affirmed, returning to her notes. "He fractured his right leg in three places, broke his left hand and five ribs. His body was covered with bruises and he was in the hospital for almost four months. It was a terrible blow, especially because he was a favorite to take the checkered flag. It would've made him a three-time winner at the Brickyard."

"The Brickyard?" Abby inquired, looking perplexed.

"Sure, it's a nickname for the Indianapolis Speedway. It used to be paved with bricks in the old days. Don't you know anything about the Indianapolis 500?"

"Not really," Abby admitted sheepishly.

"Well, Nick Farrell was a big shot, a front row starter."

"Is that good?"

"Of course, Abby," Donna replied with mock exasperation. "He clocked over 215 miles per hour to qualify for the front row."

"Wouldn't you know I'd be the one stuck with the speeding ticket," Abby grumbled under her breath.

"Did you say something?"

"Nothing." Abby avoided Donna's inquisitive stare by studying her fingernails. "What else did you find out?"

"Well, it seems he was something of a celebrity on the circuit. He appeared on the Johnny Carson show regularly, spoke at fundraising benefits, made a lot of personal appearances. Now it looks as though he may never race professionally again. There was extensive damage to his right leg." Donna pulled a *People* magazine out of her desk drawer. "I went to the library today on my lunch hour and borrowed this. It gives a clear account of the man."

Abby took the magazine and began to flip through it.

"Don't lose it. I used my library card to withdraw it."

"I'll be careful," Abby promised with an indulgent smile.

"You know," Donna said thoughtfully, resting her chin in her hand, "it's hard to believe that Charles Farrell would risk sullying his reputation by stealing your mother's emerald brooch."

"Yes, it's puzzling," Abby agreed, staring down at a full-face photo of Nick Farrell. Donna was right. The man was a hunk. His dark blue eyes seemed to leap off the page at her, sending an erotic message, beckoning, disturbing. His jaw had a strong, square line with just a hint of five o'clock shadow. His black hair was thick, with a tight natural wave. She wondered, to her own surprise, if the hair on his chest was just as dense.

"Maybe the old guy is a compulsive thief—a kleptomaniac." Donna suggested, her excitement mounting.

"Donna, there was nothing compulsive about this theft. Somebody went to a lot of trouble to have a copy of the brooch made in advance."

"Oh, yeah, that's right," the secretary conceded with conspicuous disappointment.

"Even though I don't believe that Mr. Farrell is a kleptomaniac, I haven't ruled out the possibility that he's lost some very necessary marbles," Abby asserted vigorously. "If so, his hotshot son should be seeking professional help for his father." *Instead of terrorizing innocent victims with his behind-the-wheel technique*, she thought with a grimace.

"He really got to you, didn't he?" Donna observed with an impish grin.

"You sound like Blanche when she's trying to pair me off with an eligible man," Abby retorted.

"Under the circumstances, Nick Farrell is probably the last man she'd want you to become involved with," Donna speculated with wicked delight.

"That knowledge alone would almost make it worthwhile." Abby slid off the desk and reached for her briefcase. "I'll be in my office if you need me. Oh, yes, pull the file we compiled on the Cupid Connection Corporation when my mother decided to join the ranks of the lovelorn."

"Do you think it may be involved in the swindle?"

Abby paused. "I really don't know what to think right now."

"Did you ever tell Blanche you checked that place out before she joined?"

"Are you kidding?" Abby hooted. "She's not happy unless she thinks she's pulling all the strings."

"Hey, look!" Donna exclaimed, nearly leaping out of her chair as she pointed out the plate glass window. "The hood of your car is open! A man is leaning over the motor."

Abby's briefcase thudded to the floor as she snapped her attention out to the parking lot.

"Who could it be?" Donna asked in wonder. It was hard to believe that anyone would be interested in examining the Cutlass with such concentration.

"Nick Farrell." Abby instantly recognized the head of coarse black hair and tan jacket straining against his broad shoulders. She watched avidly as he rose to his full height to wipe his large hands on a handkerchief, then duck his head under the hood once again. His Ferrari was out there too, parked over in Barney's section of the lot. A sleek silver bullet amongst the more prosaic economical vehicles.

"Those jeans could never fit anyone else like they fit him," Donna observed in an admiring tone, pressing her nose nearly flush on the window to check him out.

Abby was startled by Donna's off-the-cuff remark, but she had to agree. Nick's lean, muscular legs laid undeniable claim to those snug, washed-out denims. Abby had the uneasy feeling that Nick could lay undeniable claim to anything or anyone he wanted. That feeling rankled her independent soul to the core. But at the same time it set some overactive butterflies loose in the pit of her stomach. It had been a long time since Abby had stood so boldly by a window, mentally stripping a man of his clothing, layer by layer. Privately amused, she realized the routine came back with ease. Rippling muscles under smooth taut skin . . .

"So, whatdaya say?" Donna asked with a giggle.

"Exceptional bod."

"Better buns than the rug shampoo guy."

Better than a whole lot of people. "Wonder if the Farrell boys are after our silver-plated tea set now," Abby gibed, attempting to hide the fact of her awakened libido.

"Maybe stealing is a family curse," Donna suggested, sparing Abby an amused smirk before turning back to the window.

"If he's not cursed yet, he will be in a minute," Abby vowed, her eyes narrowing to slits of green fire.

Nick spotted Abby in his peripheral vision the very moment she burst through her office door. Even though his view was no higher than waist level, he had no trouble identifying Abby's sleek legs pounding the blacktop in her open-toed sandals. Those strong, trim ankles and feet atop those feminine shoes blew Charlie's gumshoe description all to hell. No sensible oxfords for this lady sleuth. No way.

Her stride was purposeful as she made a beeline toward him through the menagerie of shoppers pushing carts and strollers. The breeze tugged at the front slit of her skirt, causing it to flap back and reveal an alluring hint of firm thigh. A jolt of lust and longing that no bikini-clad racetrack groupie had ever triggered caught Nick in the gut, temporarily throwing him off balance. He was nothing less than amazed that a subtle, teasing glimpse of stockinged leg and toe could affect him so strongly.

"What are you after now, Mr. Farrell?" Abby demanded, standing defiantly in front of the front fender of the Cutlass, her arms folded across her chest. "My car?"

"Surely you're joking," Nick replied with a low amused chuckle.

"Perhaps my battery interests you," Abby sputtered, his roguish attitude enkindling her temper.

"Your battery charged?" Nick met her gaze directly, challenge in his dark, mocking eyes. He really didn't need a verbal reply. Abby Shay was charged all right. Sparks flew between them like a live wire swinging over a puddle. This lady PI was a mass of contradictions, standing before him with miles and miles of leg and the firmest bottom he'd ever seen on a well-rounded woman. A lady, yet a hellion. Furious, yet controlled. And all of this in the damn parking lot! Nick could only speculate with lustful curiosity what sort of passion would ignite between them if they were to move their duel from the blacktop to bedsheets. It was a rotten shame that the mother had swindled Charlie. "A rotten shame . . ."

"A rotten shame?" Abby repeated Nick's articulated thought none too cordially. "Mr. Farrell, we have a bit of a problem here. I don't think we're on the same wavelength."

Nick smiled, thinking how easily such a problem could be solved. But he knew he had to resist temptation. He had to respond to the job at hand: recovering the watch. "I certainly didn't track you down to steal your car. I spotted it in the lot on my way to your office and couldn't resist opening the hood to examine the magical shoestring that keeps it together. As long as I did have the chance to diagnose it, I strongly advise you to have it towed away to a proper burial ground."

"Not everyone has the option of replacing their car as easily as they would a tattered sock."

"I'm only warning you that you may find yourself stranded one of these days."

"Thanks."

"Look, I didn't drive all the way over here to discuss rust buckets. I was hoping we could get together to reach an agreement."

"You're willing to cooperate?" Abby inquired with undisguised surprise. She never dreamed it would be this easy. She thought she'd have to press hard to get through to any of the Farrells.

"Of course I am," Nick contended in a voice insinuating accusation. "I figured you'd be expecting me—or dad to make a move."

"Not really," Abby admitted in her usual candid way. "Though naturally I am eager to settle the matter of the theft."

It was Nick's turn to be surprised. "Perhaps together, you and I can work this out for the folks." He straightened up and slammed the hood of the car shut. He smiled pleasantly, his blue eyes gleaming. Abby noticed that a dot of grease had smudged his square chin. It gave his otherwise angular face a boyish charm.

"I think we both realize that older people—often lonely people—behave in an eccentric fashion on occasion," Abby offered generously.

"Yes, I'm certain that the theft wasn't financially motivated," Nick added, hooking his thumbs in the front pockets of his faded, tight-fitting jeans.

"Or that real harm was intended." Abby's eyes traveled the length of him, appreciatively noting that every muscle of the man's body seemed perfectly developed. If his injuries at Indy were as extensive as they sounded, Nick Farrell must have put strenuous effort into rehabilitation.

"But an heirloom is an heirloom, Miss Shay—"

"Call me Abby."

"Yes, and I'm Nick. Now, as I was saying, an heirloom certainly holds sentimental value. But in truth, it's also worth a lot of money. Stealing is a crime punishable by law—"

"Of course no charges will be filed with the police if the jewelry in question is returned." Abby interceded charmingly.

Nick continued to smile despite his rising indignation. Saucy broad. "You drive a hard bargain, but all right. No charges will be filed."

She drove a hard bargain? Abby bristled at the man's nerve, anger swiftly making its presence known on her small, delicately shaped features. "Considering the spot your father is in, Mr. Farrell, I'd say your bargaining power is zero!"

"My father is nothing more than a victim of Blanche Shay! A pawn in her game to love'em and fleece'em!" Nick shook his head pityingly. "Poor duffer didn't even know what hit him until it was too late."

"Poor duffer? Charles Farrell?" Abby sputtered, her outrage nearly out of control. "He's entirely to blame for this unfortunate episode!" Abby paused to push back strands of wind tossed hair from her face, noticing to her chagrin that shoppers were stopping to eavesdrop, forming a ragged circle around her Cutlass. "Perhaps we should continue this conversation in my office," she suggested coolly.

"Perhaps we should've gone there in the first place," he retorted, snapping his metal cane open. Only months ago he'd relished publicity, welcomed the attention of the crowds at the racetrack, enjoyed the appearances he'd made. But everything had changed. The thrill of victory was gone. Nick Farrell was out of the winner's circle and therefore wished to be out of the public eye.

Abby fell into step beside him, as he stomped in his boots with a confident step on the blacktop, his cane beating out an intermittent tattoo. They were interrupted as they waited for a slowly moving car to pass.

"Hey, mister, you used to be Nick Farrell, didn't ya?"

Nick turned around and pinned the voice on a young boy in the center of the dispersing crowd. The kid was a mess in a dirty striped T-shirt, tattered twill pants, and dishevelled brown hair. Nick smiled in spite of himself. After all, how could he expect a boy of approximately ten years of age to recognize an insensitive question, when adults three and four times his age asked the same heartless thing.

"Didn't ya, mister?" he repeated with wide eyes.

"I am still Nick Farrell," Nick responded with quiet firmness. "And I intend to be for a long time."

"Are those real snakeskin boots you're wearin'?"

"Yep."

"You gonna race again?" the boy asked. "Ever?"

"Ah, probably not." Hell, what was happening to him? In the course of an afternoon he'd been dazzled by a con artist's slit skirt and had stuttered at a kid with a chin full of acne. He was losing the Nick Farrell touch. It was gone. Kaput.

"Maybe I should get your autograph. Might be worth something someday—after you're gone."

"Timmy Baker!" Abby gasped in shock. Even a crook like Farrell had to have feelings.

"What's the matter, Abby?" Timmy whined in confusion.

"Never mind," Nick interceded, laying a restraining hand on her arm.

Abby didn't like the way the brush of his lightly calloused fingers against the tender skin of her forearm sent a delicious quiver down her spine. Sexual tension could too easily distort the issues at hand. She reminded herself of her steadfast rule not to mix business relationships with personal ones.

Nick reached into his jacket pocket and extracted a pen. "Where do you want me to sign, kid?"

Anxiously the boy looked himself over from head to toe. "How about my shirt?"

"I don't think your mother would appreciate that, Timmy," Abby declared.

"'Spose it might come out in the wash anyway. How about my grocery bag?" He thrust the bag with a loaf of bread and a box of cereal in it up to Nick's face. "I can hold your cane," he offered.

"I can handle the cane," Nick assured him wryly. Using the cereal box as a prop, he scribbled his signature on the brown paper.

"Sorry," Abby blurted out as the boy darted away and ran through the lot between the rows of parked cars.

"I've sure come a long way from signing embossed autograph books for heads of state," Nick remarked with regret. The accident at Indy had had many repercussions, emotional as well as physical. Nick's leg wasn't the only thing on the mend. His ego had suffered just as serious a blow as his body. The taste of fame and the thrill of gambling with his life at two hundred miles per hour, were hard to set aside for a tame existence. He wasn't certain if he could do it. He had the urge to confide in Abby, feeling that behind those intelligent green eyes was a wealth of sensitivity. But it was neither the time nor the place for an exchange of confidences. If she was a party to the theft of the pocket watch, she could hardly be considered a trusted confidante.

Once inside her office, settled in her comfortable executive's chair, Abby felt she could set the appropriate tone of the meeting. The arrangement was now businesslike—as it should have been from the start, with Nick seated on the other side of her massive oak desk. It was like a wooden shield between them. Abby only hoped that it was dense enough to ward off the sensual signals Nick seemed to emanate, signals that were like a huge neon sign flashing Take Me. Donna had nearly swooned when Nick had stomped into the place in his snakeskin boots and had greeted her with a sexy grin.

"Now, let's see, where did we leave off?" Nick pondered thoughtfully, stroking his square stubbled chin.

"We were talking about the poor old duffer," Abby supplied with an edge of sarcasm, rapping a pencil on the top of her desk.

"So true," Nick assented, slipping off his jacket to reveal his well-developed torso. "Quite frankly, Abby, I'm a bit confused over the mixed signals you've been sending me."

"Oh, really, Nick?" she inquired tersely, tossing aside the pencil. "I'm a trifle confused by your attitude, too. You chase me through the streets of Evergreen Estates like a demon on the loose. You come here to offer a truce. Then, when I agree with what you say, you turn on me in anger." Abby threw her hands up in a helpless gesture. "Hardly the actions of a level-headed individual."

"Wait just a minute . . ." Nick growled, his face clouding over in a dangerous-looking scowl.

"My only concern in this matter is the brooch," Abby interrupted in an effort to maintain her cool facade.

"Brooch?" Nick snapped, taken aback by the sudden change of subject. What was she trying to pull?

Abby extracted the brooch from her skirt pocket and set it before him on the desk. "Of course this is a copy," she supplied matter-of-factly.

"Of course." Nick agreed mockingly, holding the oval emerald up to the fluorescent ceiling lights. He tilted the stone above him, examining the ornate silver leaf design in which it was set and comparing the many facets of the emerald to the shifting green lights of Abby Shay's eyes.

"In case you're curious, it was the engraving that tipped us off," Abby taunted, pressed to the limit by his insolent attitude. Great buns didn't make up for bad manners.

"Turly yours, Ashly," Nick read, squinting at the tiny inscription on the back of the brooch below the pin.

"It should read, Truly yours, Ashby."

Nick returned the emerald to Abby. "That's all fine and well, but I don't follow you." If Abby was trying to evade the issue of the pocket watch with these tactics, she wasn't going to get away with it.

"Somebody's a lousy speller," Abby accused.

"Somebody's a lousy thief!" Nick roared, losing his patience over the exchange of banter. He was up on his feet in a shot, leaning over the massive desk until his face was only inches from hers. "Time to cut the games."

"What do you want from me, Mr. Farrell?" Abby swallowed hard, meeting his piercing stare as steadily as she could. This was no time to inhale his masculine scent. No time to gaze at the corded muscles of the arms that could so efficiently keep a steering wheel under control at breakneck speeds. To be encircled in those arms would most likely be an extremely gratifying experience. In sheer self-defense she wheeled her chair away from the desk and jumped to her feet. She started moving around the room, hoping to escape the thrall of his overwhelming sexuality. She had to keep a clear head!

"I want to hear you say that the pocket watch is not yet in the hands of a collector. That," he warned, spinning around to pursue her with his penetrating glare, "is the only way you can satisfy me."

"Don't try to bully me," Abby shot back defiantly. "I know nothing about a pocket watch. My only concern is for—"

"Can it, Abby," Nick interrupted sharply. "There is only one response that can satisfy me."

"The pocket watch is not yet in the hands of a collector," Abby replied sweetly. "Satisfied?"

"Hand it over and this whole thing will be forgotten." The open hand thrust in Abby's direction was large and unyielding. "It wouldn't be my policy to handle such a serious situation in so lenient a manner, but I intend to respect Charlie's wishes, no matter how much it pains me. Or you."

For the first time, while staring at Nick's open palm, Abby felt that she had perhaps pushed this man too far. They were definitely on different wavelengths and he was extremely angry. Handling civil suits and tracking runaways hardly prepared her for an enraged man with violence in his eye.

"Let's call a truce," Abby said on a long sigh. "When I said I knew nothing about the watch, I meant it. My only concern is for the brooch someone stole from my mother. That is why I was at your father's house this morning. Mother has it in her head that Charles Farrell took it during their holiday in Mazatlan."

Nick looked deep in thought for a moment, then began to rumble with deep, jovial laughter. "Don't glare at me that way, Abby. Apparently both of our parents have been swindled. Dad firmly believes that Blanche lifted his pocket watch. He doesn't know whether he should recover it by throttling her or marrying her!" Nick's face, now alight with humor, was utterly charming.

Abby fingered the brooch as the revelation began to sink in. She found that she wasn't as jovial about the circumstances as Nick Farrell. "As amusing as the day's adventure was, I am still stuck with a forty-dollar traffic ticket," she informed him stiffly.

"You don't blame me, do you?" Nick asked incredulously, his clear blue eyes reflecting pure disbelief.

"I most certainly do! You harassed me with your driving skills." Abby poked her index finger inches from his chest to underscore each accusatory word.

Nick had an overwhelming urge to grab that little finger of hers and nibble his way to heaven. But he knew he'd have to bide his time before reaching for a sample. Besides, he was looking forward to the chase. He needed a challenge to test his timing, to regain his confidence. This charming, uptight woman was exactly what the doctor ordered. Literally.

"Well, do you intend to make good on the damage you've caused?" Abby demanded impatiently, her foot tapping on the threadbare carpet.

"You can't blame me for your brake light." Nick retorted.

"I weasled out of that one," Abby said with a dismissive wave.

Poor cop never had a chance, Nick thought with empathy. "Tell you what, I'll split it with you, fifty-fifty," he dickered.

"All right, it's a deal," Abby agreed, feeling small and weak-kneed as he towered over her. Seeing his cane still propped up against the desk, she felt the urge to grab it for support. She was certain that at that moment of confrontation, she needed it far worse than he did.

Nick pulled a crisp twenty out of his wallet and tucked the bill into the pocket of her pink and white floral blouse. "Just don't make a habit of tearing around Evergreen in that hunk of junk. I may not bail you out next time."

Abby's pulse quickened the moment Nick's knuckle sank into the soft flesh of her breast. The layers of fabric may just as well have been gauze for all the protection it afforded against the bold, lingering pressure of his touch. "Why, you!" She jerked back, nearly taking his finger along with her. "Look what you almost did," she scolded breathlessly, smoothing the fabric in search of damage. "You almost ripped my pocket off."

"You're the one who moved," Nick reasoned, his lips curving playfully.

"I can see you may become a very costly acquaintance," Abby complained, hoping to hide the rattling effect he was having on her. "Tickets. Pockets."

"I may have to start up a tab with you, Shamus." Nick eyed her with delight.

"Shamus?"

"Dad calls you a gumshoe. But that term doesn't quite fit," he decided with a twinkle in his eye.

Suddenly the inner office door swung open and Donna sailed in with a file folder under her arm. One look at Abby's flushed complexion and Nick's crooked grin caused her mouth to open in wonder.

"What is it, Donna?" Abby asked, clearing her throat to strengthen her voice.

"I have that file on Cupid Connection." She strolled past Nick in her clingy jersey dress, her wide-set hazel eyes never leaving his.

Nick smiled in return. She wiggled a lot, but those big flirtatious eyes of hers betrayed her innocence. Donna was wearing some very fine feathers, but she was still a chick fresh out of the nest. Abby flashed him a disapproving look. Surely she couldn't think he'd hit on a child! Her line of work certainly bred suspicion.

"Goodbye, Mr. Farrell," Abby said, dismissing him curtly.

"I'd like to see that report," he countered, standing his ground.

"I'd be happy to give you a condensed version," Donna offered eagerly.

"Donna!" Abby's tone was nothing less than aghast. Whatever happened to all the confidentiality the office was supposed to boast?

"Oh, I don't mind, Abby," she said, positively glowing. "After all, we're all on the same side, aren't we?"

"How do you know that?"

"C'mon, Ab. The walls in this place are paper-thin." Without waiting for a response, she opened the file on Abby's desk. "Cupid Connection is a video dating service chain with locations all over the country. I called their headquarters in New York and pretended that I was a reporter doing a feature on their operation," she confided proudly. "They gave me all sorts of information."

Nick winked from his position against the wall. "Clever move."

"There are lots of specific rules. The decor is standard. The staff ranges from six to ten people, depending on the size of the city. Romantic trips to exotic spots are commonplace. Mexico is a popular location, especially with the northern states. The trips are scheduled on a monthly basis from September to May, and can last anywhere from four to seven days."

"Well done, Donna." Nick grinned.

"You can leave the file with me," Abby instructed, settling back in her squeaky chair. "And you, Nick, can just leave," she added the moment Donna was gone.

"Just like that? After all we've been through?"

"What have we been through?"

"We've shared more thrills in one day than some married people do in twenty years!"

"Get serious!"

"Like you?" Meditatively, Nick shook his dark head with regret. "I believe I'll pass. Thanks for the information, though," he added, heading for the door.

"Happy hunting." She opened the file and began to pour over the top page.

"Excuse me. Shamus?"

"All right, consider it done." Abby smiled and lowered her eyes.

"No," he objected, crossing back to her desk. "I mean I'd like to offer you a bit of advice."

"You?" Her mouth pursed in disbelief.

Nick leaned over the wooden desk and turned the file completely around in her hands. "Reads twice as fast right side up."

Nick's deep resonant chuckle filled the room and echoed through the outer office. Abby threw the file across the room in frustration. She just wouldn't do it! Not only did he turn her on, but he also turned her right side up! He stomped into her world arrogantly and juggled her emotions like a handful of oranges. It had to stop. Her life was perfect—calm, predictable and wonderfully systematic.

Nick Farrell was the wrong man for her.

Ah, but what a man!

3

CHARLIE OWED HIM ONE. Nick made that decision as he crossed the lobby of the Mutual Trust Bank Building in the heart of downtown St. Paul. It was close to noon on Tuesday and the lobby's worn marble floor was teeming with business types making the most of their lunch hour. As eager as Nick was to recover his father's stolen pocket watch, he dreaded the task that lay ahead of him. Never in his wildest nightmares did he envision himself paying a visit to the Cupid Connection dating service—for any reason. But under the circumstances, he had no choice. When Charlie's theory that Blanche Shay was the culprit hadn't panned out, the next logical step was to investigate this place.

Nick entered one of the crowded elevators and pushed the button for the tenth floor, the home of Cupid Connection. Though appropriately dressed in a lightweight gray suit, oxford shirt and striped tie, Nick felt uncomfortable in his surroundings. He wasn't the nine to five type, pure and simple. Even hard-nosed Charlie had finally acknowledged that fact. During Nick's early years on the racing circuit, when he often slept in the back seat of his car to cut expenses, Charlie had tried to lure him into the family business with promises of a hefty salary and many fringe benefits. But racing was already in Nick's blood, and Charlie eventually learned to accept the fact that the hot business deals that got his adrenaline pumping didn't challenge Nick one bit. Charlie did a complete turnabout at that point and volunteered to join Nick's sponsors. He even regularly visited the pits with crocks of homemade chili for his son's crew.

Although they viewed some things differently, the bond between father and son was extremely tight. Nick wanted to see Charlie happy again and if having his pocket watch back would do the trick, Nick would find the broken hunk of silver and glass—presented to the Farrells by Abe Lincoln way back in 1865, three weeks before he took the bullet!

The elevator was still fairly crowded when it reached the tenth floor. A group of young women in bright spring dresses preceded Nick out of the car, laughing and complaining about the supervisor of their typing pool. When Nick started toward the Cupid Connection suite, he caught them exchanging amused glances and giggles. He knew that they were speculating about his love life, wondering why he couldn't find a woman on his own.

Hell, he grunted to himself as he stepped through the dating service's entrance, Charlie didn't just owe him one. He owed him one—and a case of his best Irish whiskey besides!

"Can I help you, sir?" A dark blonde in her mid-twenties was smiling at him from behind a glass and chrome reception counter. Her name tag read Corki.

"I'm Nick Farrell. I have an appointment with Phillip Barone."

"Oh, yes, Mr. Farrell," she said, picking up the phone. "I'll tell him you're here."

Nick wandered around the room, noting that everything was just as Charlie had described. The furniture was modern, the carpet was a plush burgundy, and the receptionist named Corki had an incredibly large bust and wore far too much makeup. Leave it to Charlie to notice her, Nick thought, shaking his dark head with wry amusement. Maybe Blanche Shay was just what Dad needed after all. True, she was a bit exuberant, but she was Charlie's age and a better match for him than the younger girls he tended to admire in recent years.

Thoughts of Blanche and Charlie's relationship led to thoughts of Abby. Nick had to admit that Abby was never far from his mind since their confrontation at her office yesterday. He found her totally captivating, from her brilliant green eyes, to her quick wit and stubborn insistence that her junker car should have the right to bear a Minnesota license plate. Oh, how indignant she would be if she knew he viewed her as a henna-haired wildcat. But time had a way of changing everything, even wildcats. He'd most likely trap her in a compromising position one day soon, and she would most likely like it!

"Mr. Farrell."

"Yes?" Nick turned to face the man who was now standing beside the reception desk. Tall, slender and blond, he was dressed in an expensive blue suit and was impeccably groomed. Nick wasn't surprised to find him so carefully groomed from his tawny thin moustache, right down to his manicured fingernails. Whenever his father described a man as prissy, it usually meant that he had clean fingernails. Good old Charlie.

"I'm Phillip Barone, owner of the Cupid Connection." Nick shook the hand Barone extended in greeting.

Unlike his father, Nick never judged a man by his fingernails, but he did judge him by his handshake. Barone's sent him contradictory messages. His palm was as smooth as a baby's bottom, as if the most energy he ever expended was to comb his hair. Surprisingly, though, his fingers held a viselike strength. His eyes also sent out confusing signals. They were serenely gray in color, but held a distinct steely quality. Nick intended to watch this character closely.

"Come along to my office," Barone invited, leading Nick down a cool spacious corridor dotted with large potted plants.

The burgundy carpet continued into Barone's office, as did the contemporary decor. Barone sat down at his glass-topped desk and Nick moved over to the floor-to-ceiling window across the room. He looked out at the panoramic view of the Minneapolis skyline across the Mississippi River.

"Nice view," Nick remarked smoothly, though the throbbing pain in his leg was beginning to bother him. He'd been forced to park his Ferrari in an outside lot several city blocks away from the Mutual Trust building. He'd been so preoccupied with his plan to question Barone, he'd forgotten his cane in the car.

Barone nodded his blond head. "On a clear day like today the scene is spectacular." He gestured to a chair made of curved tubular steel and rough tweed upholstery. "Please, have a seat."

Nick grimaced as he eased into the uncomfortable looking chair. Normally he did fifty laps at the Esquire Athletic Club at this time of day. He found it ironic that he was sitting on a Herculean death trap instead of going for his therapeutic swim. But Charlie was in such a state about the missing watch that Nick felt obligated to take immediate action. Posing as a lonely single looking for a Cupid Connection introduction was the only course of action that had come to mind.

As Phillip Barone went through the social amenities, Nick surveyed the room, looking for some sign of Abby's presence. Disappointingly, there was nothing. Not even a hint of her light, sweet perfume. But Nick had no doubt that if she hadn't yet been to the Cupid Connection today, posing as an applicant, she'd make it here before closing time. Even yesterday, when she strongly suspected Charlie might be the culprit, she had told her secretary to pull the dating service's file from her records. She was thorough—that much he could count on. He wanted to count on so much more.

"Your father is one of our most respected clients." Barone was saying as Nick tuned in on the conversation.

"Yes, he feels very strongly about his affiliation with your dating service," Nick responded, unable to resist the cryptic dig.

"I'm so pleased that he recommended our service to you, Nick." Barone's narrow face expressed concern. "We cater to each individual's needs the best we can. And as I understand from the newspapers, you are suffering from extenuating circumstances."

"How so?" Nick inquired, lifting a heavy black eyebrow.

Barone eyed Nick's right leg significantly. "Women can be a fickle lot," he intoned sympathetically.

"Details of my dating habits haven't been reported in reputable papers like the *Dispatch* and *Tribune*," Nick countered firmly. That sort of speculation was strictly scandal sheet dirt. Nick was surprised that some of that dirt hadn't gotten under this guy's fingernails.

Barone's expression still exuded pity despite Nick's objections. "Once a man is out of the spotlight, females often move on to other game . . ." He trailed off on a heavy sigh.

Nick ran a finger beneath the buttoned collar of his oxford shirt, resisting the urge to lunge forward and dim this jerk's spotlight. But Nick knew full well that he couldn't afford to indulge his temper. He was there to find a lead on the pocket watch, and Phillip Barone had to be handled with kid gloves if he was going to get anywhere.

"Did Charles enjoy his last trip with us to Mazatlan?" Barone asked, moving on to safer ground.

"Yes, I believe so," Nick replied, grateful for just such a chance to draw Barone out.

"Blanche Shay is a fine woman," he said as heartily as his evenly modulated voice would permit.

"I hope so. I wouldn't want Dad to be the victim of a female fortune hunter." Nick gazed at him with pointed interrogation. "I wouldn't want one of Cupid's little connections to dazzle Dad and lure him to Las Vegas for a quickie wedding."

"No need to be concerned for Charles—or for yourself, Nick. We carefully screen our prospective clients to weed out any riffraff." Barone leaned forward on his desk, setting his carefully folded hands on the glass. "After all, our sterling reputation is our trademark."

If only he knew what a sterling silver reputation he was acquiring, Nick mused. "At your prices, Phillip, I doubt many undesirables slip into your organization." Nick counteracted his cutting remark with a broad smile.

Phillip Barone cleared his throat and stroked his moustache with a loving caress that would very likely send a cat into ecstasy. "I hope you'll be joining us Friday night for our monthly party here in the suite. We encourage dancing and small talk at these functions. It's especially nice for our newer members. Gives them a chance to meet some of the people they view on the videos without first setting up a date."

Charlie had filled Nick in on the parties already. Barone used them to push the trips. "I wouldn't miss it for the world. It sounds like a wonderful way to get acquainted." Nick shifted uncomfortably in his chair, acutely aware of the pain in his leg. He couldn't stand it or Barone much longer.

"Naturally, the videotapes are the main vehicle to bring most of our clients together," Barone explained. "If you have time today, you can sign the necessary forms and then make your video." Barone's tone was smooth, but Nick could sense the eagerness in his voice, like a salesman about to get the customer to sign on the dotted line.

"I'm ready," Nick replied. "Perhaps I could watch some videos today as well."

"Certainly! I will put you in my sister Candace's capable hands then. We're partners in the business and she handles the tapes." He picked up his phone and summoned his sister.

"She will be here momentarily," he said, setting the receiver back on the console.

The door opened moments later and a tall, striking woman in a bright blue knit dress entered the room.

"Ah, Candace. Allow me to introduce you to our latest client, Nick Farrell."

Nick stood up, relieved to be on his feet. "The pleasure is all mine." Nick had a practiced eye for sizing up beautiful women. With a swift, noncommittal glance, he took in short black hair, brown almond-shaped eyes and a carefully painted face. Her lips were on the thin side and she'd tried to compensate for it by outlining them with red pencil. Her skin was lined at the temples and mouth, but she'd done a fair job of filling in the grooves. Nick wagered that she was attempting to project a soft, kittenlike look. But Candace Barone had been around the block too often to make it work.

"Nick would like to make his video and view some from our extensive library."

"Wonderful," Candace said enthusiastically, throwing Nick a flirtatious smile. Linking her arm through his, she guided him to the room next door. "Our cameraman will tape your interview in here, and then you can step across the hall to the screening room, where you can look for your perfect Cupid Connection."

"You and Phillip certainly don't show any family resemblance," Nick observed as Candace sat him down on a small set complete with a velvet chair and bookcase.

"Nor do you and Charles," Candace tossed back lightly, apparently not intimidated by his question. Nick didn't know what kinds of questions he should ask. Abby probably knew just how to handle these matters. She was trained to poke into other people's business. He just drove cars around in a circle for a living.

Nick spent the next forty-five minutes making his video under Candace's direction. It was horrible. What kind of cologne did he wear? Did he like a woman who made the first move? Would he be willing to share a bubble bath with just the right lady? Hell, she even asked him if he liked to eat crackers in bed! He wondered how his father had handled Cupid Connection's ludicrous interview. He made a mental note as he crossed the hall to the screening room to view Charlie's tape sometime.

To Nick's relief, Candace left him alone in the screening room to look at the tapes on his own. Though it may have seemed odd to her, Nick requested to see the service's most recent applicants. With a guileless smile, he'd explained that he wanted a first crack at any new prospects. Candace looked slightly surprised by his request, but Nick didn't care. If Abby had made a tape, he was determined to see it.

The tapes were identified only by a six-digit number, so Nick had no way of knowing if Abby's was among them. Nor did he know if he was being watched. To be on the safe side, Nick went through the motions of putting each tape into the videocassette recorder, patiently viewing them with feigned interest. He was amazed by the number of lonely women he came across. Young and old in all shapes and sizes. The only thing most of them had in common was a decent income, which was no surprise considering the high fee that Cupid Connection exacted.

Nick's diligence finally paid off. Tape number 761658 was Abby. Seeing her face suddenly appear on the twenty-five inch screen was startling. And not simply because he was losing hope after having viewed six other women in succession. He was looking at Abby Shay, and yet, he wasn't. This was a vamp, dressed in a low-cut sweater with a pear-shaped jewel nestled in her bosom. The businesslike private eye was playing the part of Abby Walters, a wealthy, carefree divorcée looking for action.

The wildcat had gone undercover!

Watching conservative Abby Shay chatter on about her zodiac sign, and describe her idea of a romantic interlude on a velvet-covered waterbed, all with a low seductive laugh was more than his libido could bear in public. He knew she was putting on an act. That this was all in the line of duty. Still, there had to be many many layers of Abby waiting to be explored. Hidden fires burning beneath that cool facade. She had every quality Nick found intriguing in a woman. Smart. Shy. Aggressive.

Stunning.

"YOU LOOK STUNNING, ABIGAL!" Blanche exclaimed with pleasure from her living-room doorway. In a way, it was a lot like the first time Blanche had admired her daughter in a black silk dress on a Friday evening before a dance. But in a way, it wasn't. Abby was hot on the Cupid Connection case and she wasn't going to let her mother forget it. The teenage sparkle of anticipation that had lit up Abby's green eyes twelve years ago in that same living room, was now replaced by a mature gleam of efficiency.

Abby slipped into her silver pumps and in one fluid motion rose from her mother's floral velour sofa. "Is everything in place?" she asked, performing a pirouette in the center of the cozy, lamplit living room. Abby's knee-length silk dress was a perfect fit. Its scooped neckline fell in soft folds at her full rounded breasts, displaying them to advantage, and the back V plunged daringly to the base of her spine, baring a generous amount of shoulder and back. Her thick hair was swept up in a rich auburn chignon, which accentuated her lovely heart-shaped face.

Blanche sailed into the room for a closer look, her gold jersey caftan and shoulder-length red hair flowing in her wake. "Basic black brings out your finest features, dear," she murmured proudly. "Always has."

"I've bared my assets for one reason and one reason only, Mother." Abby reminded her firmly. "To call attention to Aunt Sybil's jewelry at the dance. If the thief saw her pear-shaped diamond and matching earrings on my video, he may be just dying for a closer look tonight."

"I know," Blanche admitted grudgingly. Reaching into the pocket of her caftan, Blanche produced the pendant on a silver chain and two large earrings. "Seems like such a waste to get dressed up only to lure a crook to your side."

"Consider the dress a mere disguise," Abby needled playfully, as she took the earrings from Blanche one by one and clipped them on. "Tonight, I am posing as Abby Walters, Cupid Connection number 761658. A lively divorcée with a lot of money, an overactive sex drive, and a penchant for fine jewelry."

"I don't see why you can't mix a little business with pleasure tonight," Blanche persisted, standing on tiptoe to fasten the pendant's clasp at the nape of Abby's neck. "Get a line on the brooch, get a line on a man."

"Mother, we're both really out on a limb, me borrowing Sybil's jewelry, you investing in my Cupid Connection membership—"

"I know, I know."

Abby couldn't help but be concerned over her mother's current spendthrift ways. True, she'd received some insurance money when Dad died, but her vacations and dating service fees had quickly depleted her extra cash. Blanche was in the middle-income bracket and probably always would be. "It's very important that you take this situation seriously. Charles Farrell can throw money around trying to catch the thief, but we can't."

"You don't have to chase the men around the room, just keep your eyes open for prospects," Blanche persisted.

"I think not," Abby said gently but firmly, wondering why it was satisfying, even as an adult, to rebel against her mother's wishes. Mothers and daughters never seemed to surrender certain rituals.

"Perhaps I should go along with you tonight," Blanche suggested, the sudden inspiration lighting up her green eyes.

"Absolutely not!" Abby countered. "If you wish to find a replacement for Charles Farrell, I suggest you hit the church socials."

"I was thinking of helping you in your investigation," Blanche explained with dignity. "And," she flared, "there is nothing wrong with my Charlie!"

"Nothing..." Abby's mouth gaped in surprise. It was the first time the Farrell name had passed between them since the chase through Evergreen Estates four days ago. Abby had given Nick Farrell plenty of thought since their meeting, but she had assumed his father was out of Blanche's life for good. "You thought the man was a crook," Abby reminded her.

"So I was mistaken," Blanche shot back defensively. "He thought the same thing about me, so I figure we're even."

Blanche's skewed logic grated at Abby's practical nature. "This should be more than a case of keeping score, Mother. Your mutual distrust should tell you something."

"Like what?" Blanche demanded, the golden hem of her caftan airborne as she flounced around the small room in a flurry of activity.

"That your relationship with Charles Farrell must've been on pretty shaky ground right from the beginning." Noticing Blanche's aggrieved expression, she softened her tone. "Isn't trust a big part of what love is all about?"

Blanche retaliated with a fiery comeback. "You may be an expert on business matters, but I win hands down on romance!"

Abby's reddish lashes dropped to her cheeks as she struggled to remain calm. "Please promise me you will consider your position in this relationship, Mother. Lust is not enough."

"Not to worry," Blanche cooed with a guileless smile.

Abby rolled her eyes, her tone full of resignation. "Whenever you say that, that's just when I do begin to worry."

Blanche followed Abby around the house as she retrieved her evening bag and silver shawl. "Remember what I told you. Keep an eye on Candace Barone. She always tags along on the Mazatlan trips."

"And brother Phillip."

"He's as innocent as a newborn babe," Blanche gushed.

As smooth as an eel, Abby thought with a grimace. He'd been oozing with charm the day Abby taped her interview. Though he was very handsome and elegant in a contrived way, his attentiveness somehow struck a hollow note with her. She couldn't quite identify the reason for her wary response to the man, and eventually attributed her feeling to instinct. "Anyone else who takes the trips regularly? What about that guy who likes to dance?"

"Oh yes, George Merdel." Blanche's voice was laced with disgust. "As I told you over dinner, he's always hanging around the Cupid Connection suite. Makes every trip to Mexico."

"Is there anything about him that would make it easier for me to pick him out of the crowd?"

"Let me see . . ." Blanche tapped her finger against her chin in contemplation. "Barrel-shaped body. More hair on his knuckles than on his head. Wire-rimmed glasses. Tacky suits."

"I believe that's enough to go on. I'll find him."

"He'll find you! As I've told you, he loves to dance. He also loves to cut in on everyone."

"Wonderful," Abby replied dryly.

"It wouldn't hurt to loosen up a bit tonight," Blanche suggested. "Maybe Charlie's son will be there."

The thought had occurred to Abby, but she didn't want to give Blanche the satisfaction of knowing it. "Maybe he will be, it's a free country."

Blanche shrugged her narrow shoulders and stared into space. "I guess he really isn't your type anyway."

Although Abby knew that Blanche was goading her, she found the temptation to respond impossible to resist. "Why not, Mother?"

"Because the man is a pleasure-seeking animal," Blanche squeezed her eyes shut, smiling dreamily.

"Judging from his struggle to regain his health after the accident at the Brickyard last May, I hardly think he's been whooping it up much lately," Abby countered with a teaser of her own.

"The Brickyard?" Blanche repeated with a puzzled look.

"The Indianapolis Speedway," Abby supplied matter-of-factly. "Don't you know anything about racing?"

"Not much." Blanche murmured, her interest waning. "And since when do you?"

"I had Donna do a little digging when you thought the Farrells were behind the theft of your brooch." Abby explained. "But I assure you, when I reach that party, the last thing on my mind is going to be Nick Farrell." Tossing the shimmering shawl over her shoulder, Abby headed for the front door. "When I'm on a case, I stick strictly to business."

"You know best, dear."

NICK FARRELL WAS NOT THERE.

That was Abby's first observation an hour later as she stood on the fringes of the crowd at the Cupid Connection party. Scolding herself for drifting away from the business at hand, she scanned the room once more. This time she made certain that her delicate features radiated the kind of insolence she needed to display for the part. Wearing pear-shaped diamonds just cried out for a heavy dose of insolence.

The atmosphere of the spacious party room was nothing like the cool burgundy and chrome so prevalent in other parts of the Cupid Connection suite. Abby surmised that once his fees were paid, a client was whisked into more romantic surroundings. The walls were papered in gold foil and a cut glass chandelier sent shards of light glancing off the walls and hardwood floor. A long buffet table loaded with tempting dishes and a champagne fountain flanked a side wall. A four-piece band was set up in a back corner, playing a ballad heavy on the soulful tones of the saxophone. Many couples were dancing, most with a comfortable familiarity. Abby reckoned they solidified their relationships on Cupid junkets, just as Blanche and Charlie had. Unfortunately, no one in particular looked like a thief on the prowl for expensive jewelry.

"Good evening." Candace Barone was at Abby's side, looking stunning in a floor-length red gown, an orchid pinned in her short cap of black hair. "You're Abby Walters, aren't you?"

Time to go to work. "Yes, I am."

"I'm delighted that you decided to join us tonight."

"I wouldn't have missed it for the world," Abby gushed charmingly.

"You'll have your chance to mingle tonight," Candace assured her. "And we have a wonderful presentation planned about our next Mazatlan trip. Perhaps you'd be interested in coming along. Phillip and I make an effort to accompany our people on every one. The romantic atmosphere seems to strengthen the relationships started at our service."

"Perhaps a trip is just what I need," Abby declared dramatically. "Getting away from it all sounds very inviting after suffering the pains of a messy divorce."

Candace's heavily shadowed brown eyes flashed with sympathy. "Was it really tough?"

Abby sniffed, her nostrils flaring in indignation. "Bert was a real dog."

"I am so sorry," Candace purred.

"Don't be," Abby said, tossing her carefully coiffed head. "Bert may have been a mischief maker during our relationship, but he agreed to a very equitable settlement in the end." Abby fingered her large earring, flashing Candace a sly smile. The opportunity to play a role as dramatic as this one made up for the dull hours Abby often spent on surveillance with warm sandwiches and cold coffee, or digging for facts and figures at city hall. She had learned through experience that whenever setting up a cover it helped to stick as closely as possible to the truth. In this case, Bert did actually exist. He was the poodle Abby had had as a child. And he was indeed a mischief maker. Chewed the toes right off her fuzzy pink slippers! The handsome settlement was in the form of a loving, cold-nosed nuzzle.

Candace was spirited away by some new arrivals moments later, and Abby was left wondering if Candace's attentive look at her jewelry was anything more than polite interest.

Abby wended her way across the room to the long windows spanning the opposite wall. The night was inky black, speckled with the white lights of the city. Suddenly, she felt herself shrink to the size of one of those lights, lost in the dark vastness of the sky. What if she were to get caught in the Cupid Connection fold indefinitely? True, the undercover position was fun in small doses, but what if she were forced to linger for months, waiting for the thief to target her? Blanche would have a fit if the brooch wasn't tracked down soon.

"Allow me to compliment you on your nicely shaped pears," a husky masculine voice murmured in Abby's ear.

"I beg your pardon!" Abby gasped, turning smack into Nick Farrell's broad chest. Instinctively she jumped back a little, taking in his navy blue suit, snowy-white shirt and red tie.

"I'm referring to your jewelry, of course," Nick said hastily, an infuriating grin splitting his face. He had a cleft in the center of his chin, Abby observed suddenly, wondering how she could have missed it the other day.

"What are you doing here?" Abby demanded in an angry whisper.

"Ah-ah-ah," Nick chided, enveloping her fist in his large hand. "Any detective worth her salt would hold tight to that spitfire temper. After all, we're supposed to be strangers trying to make a Cupid Connection."

He was right. But it was hard for Abby to admit it—even inwardly. She was determined that this man should never get the better of her again, as he had during the chase through Evergreen Estates. Reluctantly she allowed him to courteously shake her hand.

"I kindly suggest you keep your nose out of my investigation," Abby said tightly, smiling for the benefit of a happy young couple passing by arm in arm. After they had gone, Abby pulled back her hand as if she'd been suddenly bitten.

"You don't sound kind at all," Nick accused in a wounded tone, taking two glasses of champagne from the tray of a passing waiter.

Abby accepted the stemmed glass Nick offered and together they sipped their bubbly drinks.

"Cheap stuff," Nick muttered, though maintaining a tranquil expression. "Probably just stomped on some grapes out back in an old bathtub and hurried it in here."

Abby laughed in spite of herself. "You'd make a heck of a con artist."

"That's part of your job description, Shamus, not mine."

"I take my job very seriously."

"Yeah, I know. Saw your video the other day." His eyes gleamed suggestively. "Hot stuff."

Abby felt a blush tinge her cheeks. "I'm only trying to attract attention. Only trying to catch a thief."

"You shouldn't have any problem—attracting attention, I mean."

"Nick, exactly what is your game plan?" she asked, hoping to throw some heat back at him.

Nick's heavy brows rose in surprise. "I too intend to catch our light-fingered lonely heart."

Abby's emerald eyes flicked over him from head to toe. "And what are you planning to use as bait?"

Nick's sigh was heavy with regret. "I'm afraid I don't have any yet. Wearing a pear-shaped pendant with a set of matching earrings might be just a bit too obvious in my case." Nick made a display of examining the clear stone nestled in Abby's cleavage. "Are they genuine?" he asked, his seductive gaze rising to eye level.

"Can't you tell?" Abby asked with wide-eyed wonder. Her heart was knocking at jackhammer speed over his amorous innuendo. "A man of the world should know such things at a glance."

"I'm just a poor boy who has spent the better part of his life tinkering around with engines." Nick slanted a boyish smile at her, his dark blue eyes sparkling with mischief.

"Hah!" Abby erupted, despite her vow to keep a rein on her emotions. "I've read all about your exploits in *People* magazine!"

"Oh, really," Nick drawled, his expression behind the rim of his glass a maddening combination of delight and triumph. "Were you spying on me, or do you just happen to have a subscription to *People*?"

Abby blushed profusely, pinching the stem of her glass so hard she thought it would break in half. "My interest is purely professional. When someone rides my bumper for several miles, I make it my business to track him down."

"Then I really must ride your bumper more often," Nick said quietly, as if making a mental note of it.

"Now, if you will excuse me . . ." Abby tried to walk away from the window, but Nick reached out for her arm.

"Speaking of riding bumpers, would you give me the pleasure of this dance."

"No thanks, Nick," Abby declined, acutely aware of his fingers sinking into the tender skin of her forearm, sending several separate trails of heat through her body.

"Just one dance."

"I'm here to mingle. And so are you!"

A waiter paused to take their empty champagne glasses. Before Abby could stop him, Nick was whisking her off to the square dance floor, which was roped off with thick cords of purple velvet.

The band was playing a slow, soulful version of *Misty* as Nick encircled her in a snug embrace, capturing her slender hand in his.

"Just relax and let me lead, Abby," he murmured in her ear. "It may be the first and last time I have control of our relationship."

"I'll get you for this," she threatened, finding it impossible to control her responses. Nick's roughened palm was pressing into the soft bare skin of her back, sending tantalizing shivers along her spine.

"I'd like to suggest a merger," Nick proposed, his cheek resting on the satiny pillow of Abby's upswept hairstyle.

"What do you mean?" Abby whispered, resting her head against the smooth lapel of his suit. She drew a ragged breath as Nick's thigh brushed against her hip, causing the black silky fabric of her dress to tighten over the roundness of her bottom.

"I want to join forces with you to recover the stolen jewelry." Nick raised his head, forcing himself to avert his gaze from the stress point of the black silk. Perhaps it would have been less distracting if he'd arranged a meeting with Abby in the Crestview Shopping Center's parking lot. But then he remembered that tight white skirt of hers. Any breeze would have caused the front slit to flip open and he would have been aroused in much the same way as he was now. He suspected even her telephone voice would rattle him to the core.

Abby could have sworn she felt his chest shudder under her hand, but could hardly believe it. After all, Nick Farrell was accustomed to holding women close. A lot of women. "I work alone," Abby stated flatly.

"Let me hire you, then," Nick offered. "Just consider me a helpful client."

"My mother has already hired me, Nick." Abby sighed softly as Nick's thumb rotated sensuously at the small of her back.

"I'll double your fee if you take on the Farrells, too," Nick bargained.

"The arrangement I made with my mother is a bit unorthodox," Abby explained, lifting her head from his chest and meeting his bemused gaze with a sparkle in her eyes.

"I don't get it."

"Mother is paying my expenses in cash, but my retainer has no monetary value. She has agreed to butt out of my affairs for six whole months."

His black brows bunched in a scowl and his voice grew husky. "A price far too high to pay, Shamus. Too high a price for me."

4

ABBY FOUND HERSELF LOCKED IN the deepest blue depths of Nick's eyes as they moved around the dance floor. Her heart picked up in an unsteady beat as she watched him lower his black lashes, heavily weighted with desire.

It was happening, she realized with panic. Nick was awakening a sexual yearning that she'd buried long ago beneath a heavy caseload of clients.

As Nick skillfully guided her to the darkest corner of the floor, Abby's hand traveled from his shoulder to the tender skin at the back of his neck. She felt his arm tighten around her in response. In a distant corner of her mind, Abby knew they were no longer dancing to the tempo of the music, but merely swaying to the erotic rhythm of lovers.

A disturbing fire ignited within her as Nick's knee slipped between her thighs. An involuntary gasp escaped her lips as he slid his hand along her spine and suddenly drew her up his leg with one quick thrust.

"Nick!" Her passion-hazed expression belied the protest in her tone.

With a barely audible moan, he placed a light kiss on her temple. Abby arched into him—a compliant kitten nestled in the cocoon of his arm.

"Nick, this isn't a good time . . ." she protested weakly.

"I'm having a good time," Nick argued softly.

"I mean it isn't a good time to get so close," Abby jerked away, falling back on the velvet rope behind her.

Nick shook his head in bewilderment. What was the matter with her? When had the music stopped? And what was Abby scowling about?

Abby's scowl was actually focused on the bald head bobbing behind Nick's shoulder. A bald head with a knuckle's worth of hair sprinkled on it.

"Evening, folks. Good evening."

Nick whirled around at the sound of the jubilant voice, almost knocking over the rotund man behind him.

"George Merdel here." He extended a pudgy hand in Nick's direction.

"Nick Farrell." Nick shook his hand and turned to Abby. "And this is Abby Walters."

The moment George captured her hand, Abby realized he had no intention of returning it. Her fingers were trapped. Trapped in a soft pad of flesh.

"You're new, m'dear."

"Trying to make a Cupid Connection," Abby responded with a light laugh. She glanced at Nick's disappointed expression and then forced herself to return her attention to George. She had no right to feel so put out about the interruption. This was just the kind of break she needed—a suspect approaching her out of the clear blue.

Damn Nick Farrell for making her want him!

"Do you cha-cha?" George asked, his shifty eyes devouring her as though she were a delectable pastry.

"Well, do you?" Nick asked, matching George's expression over the shorter man's rounded shoulder.

"Perhaps later, when the music picks up," Abby stalled.

Suddenly, the band began to play a lively tune.

"What a lucky coincidence," Nick said, trying to maintain a sense of humor.

George nudged Nick conspiratorially. "Not on your life. Slipped the pianist a fin for this little number." With that, he swept Abby into his arms. "Never leave anything important to chance I always say—especially Cupid's arrow."

Nick moved off the dance floor, his gaze never leaving Abby. He had to admit that the chubby man in the tan drip-dry suit was amazingly light on his feet, his shiny black shoes gliding back and forth with grace and efficiency. Abby followed his lead with a brave expression on her face. He knew it was crazy to feel that a part of himself was suddenly ripped away and in the arms of a plump man named George.

George's timing had been incredibly awful. Abby had just begun to respond to his overtures, eagerly softening against him in a way that made him feel an indispensable part of the investigation. No matter how much she protested to the contrary, he knew he turned her on. It was a beginning. It was all the encouragement he needed.

LATER THAT NIGHT Abby looked around the nearly deserted parking ramp from the front seat of her Cutlass and groaned in weary frustration. It was after midnight and most of the Cupid Connection party-goers were long gone.

For the fourth time she turned the ignition to start the engine, and for the fourth time the engine replied with grinding protest. She had to face it—the grand old vehicle that had seen her through many a surveillance, that had seemed to automatically find its own way to city hall, the police station, and her office, had finally died of old age.

The perfect end to a perfect evening. No clues. No leads. No Nick. After their erotic dance together, Abby hadn't come within a foot of him again all evening. But, she reminded herself, she had attended the party to work and not to indulge her desires. She shouldn't let the fact that Nick had just the right touch for just such indulgence distract her so easily.

The low efficient rumble of a much healthier engine interrupted her thoughts. She turned to find Nick's silver Ferrari rolling to a stop in the angled space beside her. With practiced grace he unfolded his large frame from the low-slung car. He still looked amazingly unrumpled in his blue suit. Abby rolled down her window as he walked around the Ferrari and toward her car.

"Just passing through the ramp," he said, greeting her amiably. Resting an arm on the maroon roof of the Cutlass, he leaned over, bringing his face close to hers. "Having problems, Shamus?"

"Yes, I am," Abby griped, her russet eyebrows raised in two wide arches, giving her a vulnerable, helpless look. "Phillip Barone's watch got caught in my mother's shawl, and now there's a long snag. Someone in the row behind me constantly kicked my chair during the Mazatlan film presentation. And my feet hurt. They hurt a lot."

Nick stroked her cheek with his finger. "The cha-cha can be brutal," he said consolingly. "Especially in the clutches of a fanatic like good old George. How many dances did he tie you up for? Six? Seven?"

"Six cha-chas. Two rumbas."

"Think of all the fins he invested in the band to get just the right mood music. He was in hot-footed pursuit."

Abby was in no mood for being teased, even though Nick's gentle stroking motions on her face were surprisingly soothing. "Don't let me hold you up, Nick."

"Don't think a thing of it." His dark blue eyes twinkled. "How's the Cutlass running?"

"It's not. And you know it!" she added as he opened his mouth to respond.

The chuckle he'd been suppressing behind his sparkling eyes overflowed richly, echoing off the concrete walls. "I plead no contest. I merely—"

"Don't you dare say, I told you so."

"I'd say no such thing. I merely wanted to offer you a ride," Nick declared. He opened Abby's door and extended his hand.

Abby collected her belongings and allowed him to take her arm.

"After all, there's no point in dwelling on the obvious at this hour of the night," he continued, shoving her door shut with his free arm. "We both know I advised you to junk this heap."

"Do women always end up paying such a high price for a simple lift home?"

"Odd," he replied thoughtfully. "I was just wondering how difficult a passenger you would prove to be."

"If my feet weren't on the critical list I'd hike down to the taxi station on the corner."

"And hurt my feelings? Why—"

Nick and Abby turned as a spotless white Lincoln Continental stopped behind them. The front tinted window lowered and Phillip Barone eyed them with open curiosity. "In need of assistance?"

"No, Barone." Nick's refusal was polite but adamant.

"It seems a bit chilly for standing around a parking ramp," Barone pressed, flashing Abby a charming smile of even pearly teeth.

"My car's stalled and Nick has generously offered me a ride," Abby hastened to explain, amazed at how quickly she turned down the chance to question a prime suspect. But her decision made sense, Abby told herself. She was cold, tired, and in no mood to continue the investigation any further that night.

Phillip drooped in disappointment and continued on his way. Nick swiftly got Abby settled in the Ferrari, fearful that she would change her mind again.

"Take off your shoes," he invited minutes later. He switched on the heater, then he backed out of the space.

Abby slipped off her silver pumps, wiggling her toes in the hot rush of air rising from the floor. "Mmm . . . Simple pleasures are the best."

"Yeah." He inhaled deeply as Abby's perfume sweetened the warm air circulating around them.

"Playing a flamboyant divorcée with money to burn is more strenuous than I'd anticipated," Abby admitted.

Nick watched her out of the corner of his eye as he guided the car through the winding, multilevel ramp. Pulling a few strategically placed pins from her chignon brought what seemed like reams and reams of thick auburn tresses tumbling to the creamy skin of her exposed shoulders.

"Nick, look out!"

Nick jerked his attention back to the concrete tunnel ahead, braking on a dime as they approached a car in front of them. "What's the matter?"

"You were cutting it pretty close," Abby protested, pointing at the taillights beyond.

"You're just a little jumpy because you're tired," Nick asserted.

"Maybe," Abby conceded with a tinge of doubt in her voice. "It's been a rough night."

"But worthwhile, I'd bet," Nick wagered with admiration. "Tolerating twinkle-toes George must've really paid off."

"How so?"

"Because you let him put you through your paces." Nick explained matter-of-factly. "You two really cut the rug out there tonight. Sturdiest legs I've seen in a long time."

"Mine?"

"His. Can you imagine carrying around that spare tire dance after dance?"

"To be honest, I can't imagine it." Abby shrugged, staring out the windshield. "Of course I did expect to get some leads from George. Blanche strongly suspects he's involved in the theft. You have to understand, Nick, sometimes detective work takes a lot of time and can be very monotonous. And painstaking," she added, curling her toes in the plush floor mat.

Nick stopped at street level in front of a wooden gate blocking their path. He handed his ticket to the attendant in the glass booth at his left. "All of that bustling back and forth was for nothing?" His question was weighted with a mocking amazement that bruised Abby's pride.

"Not necessarily. He seemed extremely interested in my pear-shaped pendant. That could mean he's an expert on gems."

"Six dollars, please, sir," the attendant requested.

Nick handed him the right change and the gate lifted. "On the other hand, it simply could mean that he's an expert on a pair of another kind. And that, Shamus, would make George Merdel nothing more than a mediocre rumba dancer with good taste in women." Nick shot out into the one-way traffic along Carver. "Where are we headed?"

"My mother's house in west St. Paul. I'm sure she'll loan me her Skylark for a day or two, until I find another car. Just follow Carver to Robert Street and hang a left."

Nick complied, trying to keep his attention focused on the road rather than on his passenger. Abby Shay had the annoying habit of making him feel like an easily distracted high school boy on his first date.

"So what did you turn up?" Abby challenged with a haughty smirk. "I saw Candace Barone cozying up to you during the film. Did she let anything slip?"

"Only that she likes to cozy up, I'm afraid," Nick admitted with regret.

"See, investigating isn't as easy as it looks."

"What about brother Phillip? Everybody saw him leave with you. Is he a suspect with secrets to spill or just another admirer?"

"He insisted upon taking me to my car. And yes, he definitely is a suspect. Robert Street is just ahead," Abby said, as they rolled by empty, dimly lit storefronts.

Nick smiled as he swung left at the corner. "I believe we're having our first fight, darling."

"We had our first fight over the speeding ticket," Abby tossed back without thinking.

"That doesn't count. We weren't a team back then."

"We are not a team, Nick."

"How can you deny it?" Nick's voice was thick and dreamy, his eyes sparkling in the shadows.

Abby knew he was reliving their erotic dance, just as she was. "One dance a team doth not make."

"Try telling that to Fred and Ginger."

"ARE YOU SURE YOU WANT to disturb your mother at this hour?" Nick asked ten minutes later, easing the Ferrari up to Blanche's gray stucco rambler. "It's nearly one in the morning."

Abby glanced up at the house. The rosy glow of Blanche's mauve ginger jar lamp still lit the living room. "Mother's a night owl. She won't mind."

When they emerged from the car, Abby paused on the boulevard to throw Blanche's silver shawl over her shoulders in an effort to ward off the late night chill. Nick was instantly behind her, adjusting the shimmering fabric over her bare skin.

"Your mother must be quite a woman," he said, his hand lingering on her shoulder. "Charlie sure fell hard for her."

"And she for him," Abby responded as they strolled arm in arm up the walk. "But of course their feelings for each other were far too impulsive and impulse is not a strong enough foundation upon which to build a lasting relationship. First the thrill of two romantic interludes at a posh resort in Mexico. Then the rage of a lover scorned. Surely not a very stable beginning."

"Charlie has been very unpredictable since his semiretirement eighteen months ago," Nick confided, sounding puzzled himself. "In the old days, he ran Farrell Vacuum with an iron fist. He was notorious for his sharp business acumen. In recent years his life has really changed. First my mother grew weary of his workaholic ways and filed for divorce. That was back in 1985. That slowed him down some."

"I'm sorry, Nick."

"Oh, it was coming on for a long time. They simply grew apart. Anyway, Dad developed kidney problems in '87, which cramped his style even more. He eventually learned to appreciate his leisure hours and put my brother Jonathan in charge of the company, stepping into the board of directors chair himself. His present focus centers around smoking cheap cigars, winning poker games and hanging around the Cupid Connection suite."

"Unbelievable," Abby whispered, amazed by Nick's story.

"Unfair," Nick countered, as they climbed Blanche's front steps. "Nobody deserves to have that much fun."

Abby pushed the doorbell, but Blanche didn't answer immediately.

"That's odd," Abby said, pushing the doorbell a second time.

Eventually the lock clicked and the door opened as far as the security chain would allow.

"Oh, it's you, Abigail!" Blanche exclaimed breathlessly, peeking through the narrow opening.

"Yes, and Nick is with me. Here's your chance to meet him."

Blanche scrutinized Nick through the narrow opening. "Pleased to meet you, Nick."

Nick moved closer. "Yes, I—"

"To tell you the truth, dear," Blanche interrupted sweetly, "I got the lowdown on you from that lovely article in *People* magazine. Now if you two will excuse me . . ."

Abby quickly put a hand on the door before Blanche could close it. "Mother, I wouldn't be here if it weren't important. Please open up."

"Oh, all right," she relented huffily. The door closed, the chain slid back, and Blanche allowed them to enter.

Abby examined her mother as they stood together in the tiny front alcove. Somehow Blanche wasn't quite herself. Her bright red hair was in mild disarray and her satiny gold caftan was slightly out of kilter, pulled high at the neckline.

"Abigal, I wasn't expecting you to come back here after the dance." One of Blanche's brown-penciled brows twitched and her front teeth were firmly planted in her lower lip.

"Is it all right if we come in and sit down a minute?"

"You're actually staying?" Blanche demanded incredulously. "You snagged a man with your basic black and you bring him home to meet your mother?"

The merry matchmaker strikes again, Abby thought as a hot blush spread across her cheeks. "My car stalled in the parking ramp downtown," she explained evenly. "I was hoping to borrow yours for a day or two."

"Very well." Blanche sighed hard and stepped aside, motioning them into the living room.

Abby looked around the cozy circle of furniture bathed in a welcoming rosy light. Nothing seemed out of the ordinary here. The velour sofa and wing chair were still in place on the worn oriental rug, and the large console television was still on, the volume lowered to a hum.

"Sorry about the intrusion," Nick said politely, joining Abby on the sofa.

"It's all right," Blanche said, looking slightly disconcerted.

"Were you sleeping on the sofa, Mother?"

"When? Now?"

"Yes."

"No. I'll get the keys."

Abby watched her mother scoot into the kitchen. "There is definitely something different about her..." Abby said, thinking out loud.

"Abby, it's late." Nick ran an arm along the back of the sofa, giving Abby's shoulders a brief squeeze.

"Yes, but I was here a few hours ago and she was in an entirely different frame of mind. She's definitely up to something..."

"She tells everybody that, Nick," Blanche said, returning with a key ring. "Don't lose this set, Abigal. It's the only spare one I have to the Skylark—and quit staring at me! It's unnerving."

"I've got it!" Abby said triumphantly. "Your caftan is on backward."

"It can't be!"

"But it is!"

"Funny I didn't notice it hours ago," Blanche laughed, resting an elbow on the wing chair.

"But it wasn't on backward hours ago."

Blanche shook her head. "See what the mother of a private investigator has to endure, Nick? Every detail poked and prodded."

Nick laughed, thinking how inviting that sounded.

"I suppose we'll leave," Abby said, rising with a sigh. Nick followed her lead, handing Abby her purse.

"Come back soon, Nick. We'll have a nice chat."

"I smell something burning," Abby said suddenly, sniffing the air with renewed interest. "I wonder if you have an electrical short."

"Oh, for Pete's sake!" Blanche put a hand on each of them and began to nudge them toward the alcove. "Just skedaddle. Everything's dandy."

"Are you cooking something, Mother?"

"No."

Taking an interest in the odor as well, Nick stopped in his tracks—a fact swiftly noted by Blanche.

"You know, children," Blanche proclaimed, clapping her hands together. "I completely forgot. I'm baking a cake."

Abby turned to Blanche, casting her a baleful look. "That would be a first. Besides, this smell doesn't have a tinge of sweetness to it."

"This isn't a multiple choice question on the *Hollywood Squares*." Blanche fumed. "I say I'm burning a cake!"

"Let's go, Abby," Nick coaxed, taking her arm.

"But—" Abby was poised in protest, but reconsidered when Nick winked at her.

"It was wonderful meeting you, Blanche," Nick intoned, capturing her hand in his. "And I'd like to apologize for my father's idiotic suspicions about the pocket watch."

Blanche's eyes grew wide. "There's no need to apologize, Nick. Truly no need."

"I want to," Nick insisted smoothly. "I only hope Dad's sophomoric pranks on Monday didn't upset you unduly. Chasing you and Abby into that speed trap was his idea of fun. You are so fortunate to be rid of that cantankerous, old—"

"Hold on right there!" Charles Farrell thundered, marching into the living room in a gray cloud of cigar smoke. He confronted the threesome near the alcove, dressed in a blue terry cloth robe, a burning cigar clamped between his teeth.

"Oh, Mother!"

"Oh, Father!"

"Oh, brother." Placing her hands on her tiny waist, Blanche rolled her eyes.

"Didn't take you long to rise to the bait, Dad." Nick laughed uproariously, clapping him on the back.

"So you knew," Blanche grumbled with resignation.

"Dad's cheap cigars are his trademark," Nick told Blanche in an apologetic tone. "I couldn't resist digging at him a little."

"Might as well tell 'em," Charlie urged.

"We've made up, children," Blanche announced all aglow. "Isn't it wonderful?"

Nick and Abby exchanged doubting looks.

"From accusation to consummation in one short week," Abby mumbled.

"Nothing wrong with being flexible, Abby," Charlie said, a twinkle in his pale blue eyes.

"You two should know what you want," Nick declared in an uncertain tone.

"So, did you get our stuff back?" Charlie asked, his weathered face anxious.

"No, not yet," Abby replied patiently, accustomed to handling clients who expected instant results. "Perhaps this would be an ideal time to report them to the police."

"No, no," Blanche protested. "The cops will steamroll their way into the Cupid Connection Corporation and question a lot of our friends. They'll embarrass them."

"Blanche is right," Charlie agreed. "We want this thing handled delicately."

"Delicacy takes time—and money," Abby pointed out.

"I'll pick up the tab for the entire investigation," Charlie announced, exuding as much authority as a knobby-kneed man in blue terry cloth could. "Do whatever it takes. We want action."

Abby looked to her mother questioningly.

"It's all right if Charlie wants to pay." Blanche rested her head on his shoulder. "We move as one."

"At least we were trying to, until you two showed up." Charlie grunted bluntly, planting a kiss on Blanche's fiery-haired head. "And now we bid you a fond adieu."

"That's French for scram." Blanche ushered them out the door, promptly closing it on their heels.

"Can you believe those two!" Abby exclaimed. They stood together on the doormat, with only inches between them.

Nick chuckled. "Dad did have one valid point."

"About the cops?"

"No, about being flexible."

Abby sighed softly as Nick wrapped an arm around her and drew her close. Grasping her chin, he tipped her face up to meet his gaze. A gaze laden with passion and longing. And determination.

"You feel it, don't you, Shamus?" It was a question, but just barely. The desire between them was as heavy as the humid spring air, as sweet as the ripest peach.

Abby parted her lips, emitting a small moan as Nick's mouth moved over her face, kissing her temples, the curve of her jawline, the silkiness of her throat. His hand slid from her chin and rested on her chest, pushing aside the silver shawl as if it were the flimsy tissue that wrapped a precious gift. With a steady arm, Nick cradled her at the small of her back. Taking possession of her mouth, he kissed her greedily, as if satisfying an urgent, long overdue need.

Abby responded passionately, her senses eager for him to fill the hollowness that had gradually grown within her. It had been so long since a man's touch had fanned the fires buried deeply beneath the ashes of past pain.

Nick's hand slid below the neckline of her revealing dress, capturing the underside of her breast, then kneading the sensitive bud already tautened by the chilly air. His rotating fingers sent jolts of electricity through her system, awakening dormant urges, increasing her desire with every stroke.

"It feels just right," Nick murmured in her ear, nipping at her earlobe.

Abby couldn't deny the blatant truth. Cradled against the warmth of his strong body, she was tempted to toss her rule book out the window. Tempted and confused. But she was also not in the habit of behaving impulsively, no matter how good it felt to do so.

"What's the matter?" Nick asked, feeling her stiffen suddenly with hesitation.

"I'm just not ready to plunge into anything right now," Abby admitted. Nick released her as she stepped back.

Nick shoved his hands into the pockets of his trousers **and** stared off into the dark sky. He knew damn well he couldn't claim to share Abby's philosophy on being cautious. His exploits on and off the racetrack had been reported too often, too accurately. How could he explain that his near fatal accident dramatically changed his feelings about almost everything, leaving him unable to take the risks that had once obsessed him? "I can accept your reluctance to rush into intimacy, but now that our folks have reconciled, there's no reason in the world why we shouldn't join forces to recover the jewelry—"

"I don't mix business with romance, Nick."

"C'mon, it wouldn't kill either of us to investigate this thing together, would it?"

A small wistful smile crossed Abby's heart-shaped face. "It could, Nick. Trust me."

"What's that supposed to mean?"

"It means that a good man died while working with me!" she admitted in a burst of emotion. "Mixing business and romance cost a wonderful detective named Roy Stark his life. He ended up in the wrong place at the wrong time because I blundered." Abby shivered, momentarily lost in her memories.

Abby's disclosure jarred him. No wonder she was so insistent upon working alone. "Abby, you'd be doing me a favor by letting me work alongside of you. I'm a rotten detective on my own."

"Now that your father hired me to search for the watch, you're off the hook."

Off the hook with Abby Shay? Not possible. He was rapidly growing obsessed with her. "Don't shut me out." Nick reached for her arms and drew her close once again.

"We can get together when it's over. Maybe go to dinner..."

"Dinner?" he ground out, his temper boiling. It was obvious that his intentions were miles ahead of hers. "Give in to your instincts, Abby. You want me as much as I want you."

"It's too risky."

"Don't school me on risk. I'm already quite familiar with the subject. Just say yes to us and let nature take its course."

Even though Abby's negative response was barely audible, it was the most resounding "no" Nick had ever heard.

He was gone within minutes. The Ferrari's engine stirred, its headlights piercing the dark, tree-lined street. Soon the car was nothing more than twinkling red taillights in the distance. Abby had never felt more alone in her life.

"BUT, MRS. SHAY—YOU MUSTN'T!"

Abby looked up from the paperwork spread across her desk as the inner office door swung wide open revealing Donna's futile attempt at blocking Blanche's path.

"Good morning, Mother." Abby set her reading glasses on top of an insurance claim form she was studying and rested her chin in her hand.

"I tried to tell her you were reviewing a case, Abby," Donna defended her position, while carefully smoothing her blouse, which had no doubt been rumpled during the scuffle. "I tried to stop her..."

"Stop Blanche Shay?" Abby repeated incredulously.

Donna nodded with bruised dignity.

"I'll be satisfied if you stick to screening salesmen, thugs, and vagrants. An eighteen-year-old girl is no match for my mother."

"Now really, you two." Blanche huffily adjusted her forest-green suede dress.

"Coordinated right down to purse and pumps," Abby noted, scanning her mother's petite figure. "You look..."

"Like you?" Blanche said in an ironic tone, eyeing Abby's cream-colored wool dress with a paisley scarf neatly draped over one shoulder.

"Yes, conservatively out of character. What are you up to?"

"Hush, now!" Blanche whispered. Looking back into the outer office she announced in a clear voice, "You can come in now, Verona. Abigal has kindly adjusted her schedule to accommodate us."

A statuesque woman of about sixty glided into the room. Soft gray curls neatly framed a troubled, heavily rouged face. She wore a skirted suit the same shade of gray as her hair.

"Abigal, this is Verona Vickers."

Donna left to answer the telephone while Blanche and Verona sat down on Abby's two molded plastic chairs, which were reserved for visitors.

Verona touched a lacey handkerchief to her eyes and forehead. "I feel as though I already know you, dear."

"Mother's spoken of you often," Abby said graciously. Verona Vickers was one of Blanche's upper-crust Cupid Connection cronies. It certainly explained Blanche's elegant outfit. "Are you ladies lunching out today?"

"Told you she was a great detective," Blanche declared with maternal pride.

Verona nodded. "I fear that is exactly what I need."

Blanche took one look at her friend's anxious expression and launched into an explanation. "When Verona told me her story over a glass of sherry last night, I felt that you should be updated immediately."

"Updated?" Abby leaned back in her squeaky wooden chair and eyed them with polite curiosity.

"I'm talking about the Cupid Connection caper of course!" Blanche cut in. "It was so generous of you to look into it," she added expansively for Verona's benefit, flashing a proud maternal smile.

What a little show-off that woman could be at times! Abby thought with a smirk. It had been a little over two weeks since Abby had been to the dance and had had her confrontation with Nick. She hadn't heard a word from him, but Blanche had been calling regularly to check on her progress. Abby had been purposely cryptic over the phone, not wanting to admit that she had gotten nowhere with the case. "Is there something I can do for you, Verona?"

"Verona was ripped off by someone at the Mazatlan resort, too," Blanche explained, squeezing her friend's hand.

"I lost my diamond bracelet while I was down there three months ago. I gave it to my bellman—a man named Francisco—to have it cleaned. He returned it in a matter of days and I thought that would be the end of it. Well, the clasp broke last week and I took it to my own jeweler in Minneapolis. He immediately spotted the stones as fake."

"Was it the bellman's idea to have it cleaned in the first place?" Abby put her reading glasses back on and pulled a writing pad and a pen to the center of her desk.

"Yes. It seems like a silly situation in retrospect, but Francisco seemed like a very respectable young man...." She trailed off in sniffles and murmurs.

"Why don't you go to the police?" Abby couldn't resist asking.

"For the same reason Charlie and I don't," Blanche fired back, her maternal shine dulling a bit. "We don't want to get bounced out of the dating service for making false, humiliating accusations. The Barones may be entirely innocent."

"Someone from your service is obviously working with people down in Mexico," Abby asserted. "I figure that the jewelry is spotted up here first, copied down there, then switched when the owner arrives at the resort."

"Makes sense," Blanche agreed. "Francisco is one of the bellmen that serves the Cupid Connection guests regularly."

"We must give that charming Phillip Barone the benefit of the doubt," Verona pleaded, a girlish sparkle illuminating her eyes. "He tangos like a dream come true. And his tailored suits hang so well . . ."

"Perhaps it's that cha-cha fool, George Merdel," Blanche suggested.

"Oh, yes, I could live with that," Verona wholeheartedly agreed.

"Put your fears to rest, and go enjoy your lunch. I'll keep you informed."

Blanche and Verona rose to their feet.

"Thank you so much, Abigal," Verona said gratefully, tucking her handkerchief into her purse. "Blanche is so lucky to have such a wonderful daughter. My son is a dentist. He wouldn't know where to begin with a problem like this one."

"Oh, by the way, what is the name of the jeweler in Mexico who handled your bracelet? Maybe I can do some long-distance checking on him this afternoon."

"Why, I'm afraid I don't remember," Verona admitted sheepishly. "When the bracelet was returned to me so promptly, I dismissed the incident. I am so sorry, Abigal."

"It's all right," Abby said, concealing her disappointment.

"Didn't you want to call your son?" Blanche reminded her friend.

"Yes, I did."

"You can use Donna's phone in front." Abby offered.

Blanche closed the door after Verona. "Haven't you come up with a stinkin' thing yet? It's been two and a half weeks!"

"It isn't my fault! I figured once I showed off the diamonds at the dance, the thief would approach me."

"What if Candace Barone is behind it all? That man-eater isn't going to call you for a date." Frowning, Blanche paced the floor.

"I'm doing the best I can. As a matter of fact, the dating service called this morning to set up my first date. I'm having dinner with someone tomorrow."

"Are you telling me this is your first contact?"

A telltale blush crept up Abby's heart-shaped face. "Being the decoy takes a lot of patience."

"What about the Mazatlan trip coming up on May ninth?" Blanche asked. "Surely you're going to sign up for that."

"I was hoping to handle things from Minnesota," Abby admitted, glancing down at the papers on her desk. "Quite frankly, I'm swamped. I have a court appearance scheduled for this afternoon. I'm giving a lecture to a neighborhood watch group in St. Cloud tomorrow. And that Cupid Connection group leaves on the trip next Tuesday."

"This is the last one of the season!" Blanche protested. "You'll lose every chance of finding the Mazatlan contact if you skip it."

Abby knew in her heart that Blanche was right. Although she herself had said that all trails led to Mexico, she'd held a glimmer of hope that she could crack the case without having to leave town. Though Nick had backed off, he never did agree to let her handle the thefts alone. She suspected he'd be part of that last group headed for Mazatlan, intent on doing a little snooping himself.

Abby covered her face with her palms. It wouldn't work between them. The man was simply too much! Too cocky. Too smooth. And too accustomed to wooing women by simply crooking his little finger. Deep inside she wasn't sure she could resist such a powerful, sensuous man under tropical moonlight. But she would have to try, wouldn't she?

"Well?" Blanche tapped her foot impatiently. "Are you willing to admit the trip is the next logical step?"

"You seem to have me cornered. I'll make my reservation today."

"That's my girl," Blanche blew her a kiss and headed for the door. "By the way, what's your date's number?"

"Why? Don't tell me you've memorized them."

Blanche shrugged. "I've always been quick with figures. Just satisfy a mother's curiosity."

Abby flipped through the pages of her desktop calendar. "625749," she said.

"Some Sam Spade you are!" Blanche hooted, placing her hand on the doorknob.

"What do you mean?

"625749 is Charlie's boy." Blanche shook her bright red head merrily. "You're one heck of a decoy."

"How do you know it's Nick?"

"Verona and I just viewed his video this morning. Not bad. Not bad at all."

"Ooo . . . That man!"

"May I suggest you quit playing around with Nick Farrell and get to work."

"I thought you wanted me to find a man," Abby challenged.

Blanche shrugged. "Perhaps you're right not to mix business with romance. Even as a child, you had a hard time doing two things at once. You could never clap and roller-skate at the same time, nor could you chew gum while bouncing a basketball." Blanche opened the door, throwing her daughter a parting smile. "Knock off Nick and the Juicy Fruit during working hours, and you'll get the job done." Abby sat behind her desk, looking chagrined as her mother left the room.

"Donna? Donna!" Abby shouted.

"What is it?" Donna scurried into the inner office just as her boss was leaping out of her chair. "What's the matter, Abby?"

"Find Nick Farrell for me right now!"

"Now you're talking sense," the girl said smugly.

"Track him down somehow," Abby instructed, pacing back and forth across the room, an anxious expression clouding her fine features.

"And then?"

"And then I'll tell you exactly what I want you to do to that amateur sneak."

5

NICK DIVED INTO the Esquire Athletic Club pool, his muscular body neatly penetrating the water. He rose to the surface within moments, breaking into a practiced crawl. The faces of the swimmers in the adjoining lanes were familiar ones. Men like him, who, for reasons of their own, swam laps on a regular basis.

His doctor had steered him toward the pool after the accident, and Nick had gone there as soon as he was physically able. He hadn't swum laps since his high school days on the swim team, but quickly got back into the disciplined regime of his youth. He'd forgotten how revitalizing thrashing through the water could be. It had its healing effects.

The tensions of the last twenty-four hours began to melt away as his arms plowed rhythmically forward. Last night had been a rough one. The nightmare that had routinely plagued him since the accident invaded his sleep in brilliant Technicolor. After cheating death on that fateful day a year ago, Nick had struggled to live, to cope with his new fear of dying on the track. The dreams continued to torment him every night, forcing him to relive that horrifying ride again and again, cruelly reminding him of the weakness that kept him away from the only job he could ever love.

The actual accident had been a rapid series of events. But in the replays, the events were slow-motion horror. The initial rear impact of Doug Peterson's car—skidding and spinning—jerking the steering wheel to no avail—closing in on the concrete wall, the wall he had long ago nicknamed the Wall of Eternity.

He had to admit, however, that there had been some positive aspects to his confrontation with the Wall of Eternity. Though it kept him from racing, it had caused Nick to rethink his values, to reevaluate his life's goals. He wasn't certain he wanted a vine-covered cottage, but he no longer had the desire to flit from one affair to another, either. He now wanted the forever kind of love only a one-woman relationship could provide.

He'd awakened from the nightmare with Abby on his mind.

If only he could explain the Wall of Eternity to her. Perhaps she'd understand him better, even learn to trust him.

Over breakfast he'd decided to place a call to Cupid Connection and set up a date for tomorrow night with Abby Walters, flamboyant divorcée. He envisioned a rendezvous at one of those intimate restaurants east of the Twin Cities. Intimate and romantic, overlooking the St. Croix River. He knew just the place.

Within minutes the arrangements were made. Candace Barone assured him that 761658 would be contacted with his offer of Friday night dinner at Stillwater's River's Edge. No, Candace wouldn't reveal his name if he didn't want her to.

Nick congratulated himself on his cunning as he plowed through the water. Abby would never resist the bait, even without having a name to go on. She would pop into the restaurant, hoping to be confronted with a crook. Wait until she realized who 625749 was! She needed a push in his direction, that was all. She was still hurting over a past tragedy just as he was, and needed to begin again. Talk about a perfect match...

An hour later Nick emerged from the club into the April sunshine, dressed in faded jeans and a red polo shirt, his canvas sports bag slung over his shoulder. The afternoon had grown unusually warm and he was more than comfortable in his shirtsleeves. He crossed the parking lot in the direction of his car, whistling under his breath. He stopped in his tracks as he caught sight of his Ferrari. A female was leaning against it, her head bent over a paperback book. She was wearing some kind of bright yellow mini getup, leaving her long legs provocatively exposed. His heart began to thud as he considered who his visitor might be. He immediately picked up his pace.

"Well, Nick. It's about time!"

"Hello, Donna." Nick flashed the secretary a friendly smile that didn't quite reach his eyes. Obviously Abby had sent a girl to do a woman's job.

"How are you?"

"Wonderful." Nick unlocked his car and tossed his gym bag into the front seat.

"You look . . . wonderful." Donna closed her book and rocked on her yellow high heels.

"What is a nice girl like you doing in the parking lot of a men's club?" Nick folded his arms across his chest and eyed her expectantly.

"Abby sends her regrets for tomorrow night's dinner at River's Edge."

"Oh, I see. On to me already, is she?"

"She's a great detective," Donna praised, her hazel eyes shining with admiration. "Hard for an amateur sneak to outfox her."

"Is that what she called me? An amateur sneak?"

"Oops." Donna's eyes widened, her hand making a slapping sound as she clamped it over her mouth.

"Where is she now?" The challenge in his voice was unmistakable.

Donna glanced at her plastic lavender watch. "Abby's probably just going into the federal courthouse. She's testifying in an insurance fraud case today. She really wanted to come here herself," Donna added.

Nick raised an eyebrow in doubt. "Oh, did she?"

"Absolutely." Donna nodded forcefully. "Said the pleasure should've been all hers."

"Ah . . ." Nick trailed off in understanding. "The woman scorned."

"You shouldn't have teased her. Abby doesn't like it."

"It's not as if I'd slipped a whoopee cushion onto her chair," Nick protested with irritation. "It was her idea to have dinner sometime. I merely set the date."

"A sneaky date."

Nick sighed heavily. "Maybe."

"She sent you a message." Donna pulled a folded slip of paper out of her book and handed it to Nick.

He shook his head with a clucking sound as he read the terse message. "What language!"

"What does it say?" Donna leaned over for a look.

"Not for your innocent eyes, kiddo." Nick pinched the paper shut between his fingers and stabbed it into his shirt pocket.

"Have any reply?"

"Yep."

"Okay, what is it?"

"Not for your ears, kiddo." Chuckling, he ruffled her hair. "You better get back to shopping center headquarters. Do you need a ride?"

"No, that Firebird is mine." Donna proudly pointed to the red vehicle parked several yards away.

"You certainly don't need my assistance." Nick whistled under his breath as he admired her car. "What's your boss using for transportation these days?"

"The bus mostly," Donna answered frankly.

Nick smothered a startled chuckle behind a cough. "Well, good. Waiting for slow city buses raises one's tolerance level."

"Abby is a very special person," Donna blurted out; irritation crossing her young face.

"I know she's special. Stubbornly special."

"Don't judge her too harshly. She's only trying to protect you, you know," Donna assured him. "Crazy, huh?"

"The craziest."

"Maybe after she wraps up this theft business in Mazatlan, you two can make up."

So she was headed for Mexico! Nick fought to keep his expression neutral.

"Gee, I don't think I was supposed to say that, about Mazatlan I mean."

"I won't tell," Nick promised, crossing his heart.

"Are you going along with the Cupid crowd next Tuesday?" Donna grilled studiously, botching up the nonchalant conversational tone the question was surely supposed to have carried.

"I'm not much for group travel," Nick answered with a vague smile.

Nick watched Donna pause in deep thought. No doubt trying to recall if she'd followed Abby's instructions, he reckoned. "Anything else need discussing, as long as we're out here chatting?"

Donna shook her head. "Sure you don't have a message for Abby?"

"No, no, I don't think so."

"Bye!"

Nick watched the girl climb into the Firebird, but his thoughts were with her boss. Imagine Abby sending her regrets by proxy. What a coward! It was clear that she was not above using some very underhanded tactics to evade him. Well, he hadn't gotten this far in life without learning a few maneuvers of his own!

"WELCOME TO THE HOTEL FIESTA, *señorita*."

The bellman set Abby's three pieces of luggage on the plush red carpet of the spacious suite's sitting room, and stood by while she opened the glass door leading to her balcony. Dusk was just settling on Mazatlan. The sun was setting over the ocean in a blaze of yellow and orange, casting a golden glow over the shimmering waters. What a lovely vacation spot, Abby thought, making a mental note to return when she wasn't working.

"*Gracias*...Francisco." Abby moved into the center of the room, pretending to read the name badge on the thin young Mexican's gray lapel. She already knew he was the person who had taken Verona Vickers's diamond tennis bracelet to be repaired. It had taken some quick maneuvering through the crowd of guests in the lobby to secure his services.

"Your flight was good?" Francisco smiled at Abby with innocent brown eyes. She judged him to be nineteen years old at the most, and definitely not the ringleader of a swindling operation.

"My flight was dull," Abby replied with a grin, recalling the boring hours spent on the plane listening to Phillip Barone brag about his art collection. Getting any useful information out of the Cupid Connection people was no doubt going to be at the price of having to sift through a lot of tedious chitchat.

And then there was Nick's position—or lack of it. It seemed that Donna had gotten the facts straight last week at the Esquire Club. Nick didn't join the traveling party of twenty. Had he come to realize that she alone should handle things from now on? Donna claimed he was pretty steamed when she delivered Abby's dinner regrets. Abby quivered involuntarily as she thought back to how sexy he was when his temper was aroused. The pulse at his neck throbbed, his black brows narrowed, that cleft in his chin deepened. And those lean forearms flexed deliciously as he clenched his fists . . .

"If there is nothing else, *señorita* . . ."

Francisco's voice broke into her thoughts, drawing Abby back to reality. She hated to block out the picture of Nick that she'd so carefully created in her mind's eye, but business was business. After going to all the trouble of seeking out Francisco, she couldn't afford to let him slip away in favor of indulging in a hot fantasy.

"Actually, Francisco, this is my first trip to Mexico and I could use some advice." She fingered Aunt Sybil's diamond necklace at her throat, hoping to impress him as a wealthy target. "Do you live in Mazatlan?"

"No, I live in San Rosa, a village along the coast. But I know everything there is to know about Mazatlan," he hastened to assure her.

"Where are the finest places to shop?"

"They are everywhere, *señorita*. There are some just down the road. And there is a nice shop right here in the hotel."

"Is there a secure vault in the hotel for storing jewelry?"

Francisco took the opportunity to openly study Abby's necklace and earrings. "It would be a shame to hide away beautiful stones like those," he protested boldly.

"Perhaps," Abby agreed with a carefree laugh. "I will have to think about it." She picked up her purse and hunted for the Mexican currency she'd gotten at her bank in St. Paul. She handed Francisco a sizable tip and thanked him in fluent Spanish for his assistance.

"You speak our language very well," he complimented. He folded the bills with a look of satisfaction and shoved them into the pocket of his gray trousers. "It will make your visit more interesting."

"I'm counting on you to keep me informed on things," Abby told him with a bland smile.

"I am more than happy to assist all of our Cupid Connection guests. If you need anything, just call on Francisco."

Abby locked the door after the bellman, gathered together her luggage, and headed toward the bedroom. A nice hot shower would be just the thing to revitalize her.

"Evenin', neighbor."

Abby gasped at the sight of Nick Farrell, stretched out on the large bed, holding a huge, stemmed glass in his hand. She immediately dropped the suitcases, the largest one landing on the tip of her open-toed sandal.

"Ouch! Ooo . . ." Abby leaned against the door frame and tore off her sandal to rub her sore toes. "This is all your fault, Nick Farrell!"

"Clumsy me." Nick sipped from the salted rim of his glass, smiling guilelessly into the emerald eye of a brewing storm. A lovely storm dressed in a white eyelet sundress that brought visions of springtime and femininity, of a damsel in distress.

"You know what I mean," Abby huffed, shaking a finger at him from across the room. "You—you have an annoying habit of forcing me into awkward positions."

"Gee whiz." The idea was lighting his face with pride. "I do?"

"Yes, you do!" she snapped, removing her other sandal. "You unnerve me on purpose, force me to speed, make me drop things. I'm normally very good at my job, but you make me look like a klutz.'"

"Oh, so that's why you sent a girl to do a woman's job at the men's club last week." Nick stroked his chin thoughtfully, as if contemplating an insight.

Abby shook her sandal in the air and responded in perfectly enunciated diction. "An employer sent a secretary to deliver a message to the men's club last week."

"I like my tongue twister better. Either way, I did get the message." Nick's expression grew stern. "I never shove anything up there, lady."

"Suit yourself. But I don't care to be made the fool while I'm working."

"What time do you get off then? I can wait."

"It isn't funny, Nick. I was hoping that I had connected with a possible suspect. And it turned out to be you," she added in a disgusted tone.

"Look, no more tricks, I promise. But I am staying. I am going to prove to you that we can work together."

"What am I going to do with you?" Abby's voice took on a travel-weary edge as she shook her heavy mane of hair.

"A little imagination, and who knows?" He looked at her coyly and took a sip of his drink. "The margaritas here at the Hotel Fiesta are delicious. The best in Mazatlan."

Abby's initial thunderclap of shock and irritation wore off as she moved closer to the handsome man on her bed. He looked very at home on a mattress—certainly no surprise! He'd pulled her two satin-covered pillows out from under the colorful handcrafted bedspread and propped them against the ornate mahogany headboard. Abby's pulse quickened as she moved forward as if drawn by a powerful magnet. A virile magnet dressed in nothing but a pair of gawdy floral shorts. She cleared her throat, determined to keep her tone light and steady.

"Love the shorts."

"Just your typical tourist."

"Like hell." Her voice had dropped suddenly to a passionate level as if the two words were weighted with lead. She hadn't meant to betray her true feelings. She had to get rid of Nick before he touched her. Before those trick fingers of his massaged her into oblivion. Before he peeled back her carefully tended professional veneer and sent the investigation right down the tubes.

She'd get rid of him all right, she vowed, now moving more purposefully. She'd get rid of him as soon as she could tear her eyes away from that well-honed body of his.

The answers to some of the many questions Abby often pondered late at night in bed were lying conspicuously before her. Yes, the colour and texture of his hair was repeated on his broad chest and muscular legs. Yes, there were some scars from the accident. A large lightning bolt cut across his left shoulder to his navel. Another ran down the right leg he still sometimes favored with his cane. And oh, yes... He had the power to make her knees weak in a way completely foreign to her.

"How did you get in here?" Abby folded her arms across her chest finding comfort in taking the offensive.

Nick lifted the glass pitcher of lime-green cocktail from the nightstand beside him and refilled his glass. "Actually, Shamus, in a manner of speaking I've already told you." He pointed to a paneled door across the room. "We're neighbors, you see. That door connects our suites."

"How did you manage all of this?" she sputtered in wonder.

"Because I've been down here a number of times, it wasn't so tough to arrange. Just consider me a fellow camper—at a very posh campground."

"This isn't a romp. Our folks are counting on me to track down their jewelry."

"I know. But I'm convinced we'd complement each other perfectly. I know the area and you speak the language. An ideal match."

"No thanks. I work alone."

"Are you afraid that I'll make you look like a klutz for the next four days? I promise to pick you up the moment you trip over any clues."

"I suggest that you stand back and let me do my job," Abby advised stubbornly. "If you cooperate, you'll be on a plane home with the pocket watch before you know it."

"You sound very sure of yourself."

"I'm already making headway."

"You were working pretty heavily on that bellman," Nick noted, wiggling a black eyebrow suggestively.

"Francisco may be some kind of go-between," Abby explained, pacing back and forth across the length of the room. "He took a diamond bracelet from a friend of Blanche's, Verona Vickers, on the pretext of having it cleaned."

"And a duplicate ended up on the lady's wrist."

Abby nodded. "Someone replaced the stones with glass."

"You liked the young fella."

"Yes," Abby admitted, startled by his observation. "How did you know?"

"Oh, sometimes you have a special lilt to your voice that gives you away as an old softy."

"When?" Abby asked guardedly.

"Well, whenever you're telling me to back off, for instance."

"Well, anyway—even though I like Francisco, I'm convinced that he is up to his neck in this mess. Somebody put him up to getting the bracelet. Somebody who had glass stones ready and waiting."

The telephone beside the margarita pitcher began to ring, cutting into Nick's hearty chuckle.

"Keep quiet," Abby ordered, circling the bed. "Explaining a man in my room so soon after my arrival wouldn't be easy."

Nick winked conspiratorially. "You have a lot to learn about playing the loose woman."

"Ms Walters is a *flamboyant* character," she corrected, as she reached for the receiver. "Not a loose one. Hello? Oh, yes, Phillip. I'm quite comfortable... The margaritas?" Abby's expression narrowed into a scowl as she gazed at the man on the bed. "Thank you so much... Yes, I can truthfully say they're going down smoothly, even as we speak."

In response Nick raised his glass in a one-sided toast and drank.

"When? Sounds wonderful." Abby hung up the phone moments later and glared down at Nick. "You bum! You're drinking my margaritas!"

"I'm more than willing to share." Nick patted the mattress obligingly. His voice was full of challenge, his dark blue eyes beckoning with desire.

"You think I won't." The tremor in Abby's voice spoiled her attempt at effecting a cool taunt.

"I don't do much thinking when you're this close," Nick admitted ruefully. "I run strictly on automatic pilot."

Abby sat on the edge of the bed, her thigh angled against his rib cage. She would show him. She would have her case—and her margarita, too!

Nick sucked in a ragged breath as her knee nudged his breastbone and slid along his torso, the nylon of her stocking grazing the coarse hairs on his chest. "Steady as she goes," Nick uttered throatily, struggling to control the glass as his shaky hand betrayed the overpowering desire surging through him. He'd asked for it, he realized, as he grew hard, the tension straining the fabric of his shorts.

Abby steadied his hand in hers, drawing the salt-encrusted glass to her mouth. The tangy combination of lime and tequila brought her mouth to life with a jolt.

Nick set the glass safely on the nightstand, then entwined his fingers in her thick russet tresses. With gentle steady pressure, he lowered Abby's head to his. She parted her lips as she felt Nick's breath against her face. His tongue began to trace a thin circle around her mouth.

"Collecting salt," he murmured huskily, before overwhelming her with a heady passionate kiss. As Abby's hands traveled up Nick's chest, he curled an arm around her waist, drawing her body over his.

"Nice," Nick murmured, planting a trail of kisses down her throat.

"We must stop, Nick," Abby whispered a long, long moment later, tilting her head back as he kissed the roundness of her breasts, exposed to advantage at the V of her sundress. "We must stop before this goes any further."

"Why?" Nick's breathing was ragged.

"Phillip was calling to say that the Cupid Connection crowd is meeting in the dining room for dinner."

"Now?"

"Now."

"Damn!"

"Nick, it's probably for the best." Abby straightened up on shaky legs, smoothing her hopelessly wrinkled cotton dress.

"You can't mean that," Nick shot back incredulously.

Abby's confused feelings for Nick cautioned her to keep him at arm's length. She was too vulnerable to his charm—a charm she wasn't even certain was sincere. Furthermore, she also felt obligated to shield him from the danger that had destroyed her ex-partner.

At any rate, holding him at arm's length was far safer than holding him in her arms—if logic had anything to do with it.

Nick leaped off the bed, his low-pitched growl of frustration knifing into Abby's deep thoughts. "If it's all right with you, I'd like to take our margarita to my suite."

"Certainly," Abby replied in a faraway tone. "I'm going to take a hot shower."

Nick's shower would be cold. But he left without sharing that confidence. If Abby's distressed expression was anything to go on, Nick figured she was being hard enough on herself for both of them.

"AND SO I TOLD HIM, 'Mr. Webster, you can't expect a refund from Cupid Connection just because your date at the opera bored you. We can't guarantee perfect results every time.'"

The Cupid Connection crowd was gathered around an elegantly set table, chuckling over the tail end of Phillip Barone's story, when Abby stepped out into the open-air section of the restaurant.

"Perhaps you should've told him that it really isn't over when the fat lady sings," Abby interceded with delight, drawing a round of laughter away from the host.

A trace of annoyance crossed the vain man's face, but he quickly hid it behind a broad, welcoming smile. He'd obviously planned for her to spend time with him, Abby realized, noting that the only empty chair was beside his. Perhaps he just didn't expect her to steal his thunder while she was at it, she decided wryly.

"Our straggler has arrived." Phillip reached out a smooth, manicured hand to Abby. She accepted it with feigned gaiety and sat down beside him.

"Why, Nick Farrell even made it down here first." Candace said from across the table, flashing Nick a sultry look. "And we didn't even know he was here in the hotel."

Cold showers took a lot less time than hot ones, Nick thought with a grimace, though the sight of Abby in a gold spandex dress did wonders to warm his spirits. Her gleaming auburn hair framed her heart-shaped face and spilled onto her shoulders like a flame atop a curvy golden candlestick.

"Very clever of you, Nick," Abby said, unable to read his inscrutable expression from across the table.

"Pardon me, Ms Walters?"

"I say it's truly amazing how you arrived on your own and have already managed to jump into the thick of things."

"Actually, it was just by chance that I discovered these dinner plans."

Nick had obviously decided to press the issue that she'd foolishly raised, Abby realized, squirming in her chair.

"How so, Nick?" Candace was all ears.

And hands, Abby noted with annoyance. She had five long red fingernails on the sleeve of Nick's white dinner jacket. The red nails glided along the sleeve, over a huge diamond cuff link that secured his crisp white cuff, and settled in the heavy sprinkling of black hair at his wrist. So Nick had come prepared this time with some diamonds of his own. Oh, how persistent he was. Obviously he was determined to join in the hunt.

"I was settled back, enjoying a jumbo margarita when I overheard someone discussing the arrangements."

"I was in the bar," George Merdel said from the opposite end of the table. "But I don't recall seeing you . . ." A puzzled frown crossed his round face.

Abby held her breath, wondering if Nick could handle George.

"But I saw you, George," Nick said, winking slyly at the cha-cha master. "That one waitress was certainly giving you the eye."

George's eyes brightened behind his wire-rimmed glasses. "I know, Nick. Can't dance a step, but what a dish."

Despite his attempt to irritate her, Abby felt proud of Nick. She smiled admiringly. He'd slipped out of trouble as easily as any trained detective. Confidence in your bluff was ninety percent of the battle.

The food was delicious but the dinner conversation brought no useful information to light. During the cold avocado soup George Merdel and a young Minneapolis man named Chris Marshall talked about the thrills of horse racing. During the tossed green salad a young blonde named Joy Feldman, obviously smitten with Chris Marshall, discussed parasailing. And during lobster Candace described her tax problems. A scoop of lime sherbet and Nick's exploits at a race in Monte Carlo rounded off the meal in high style. High style for people like Chris and Joy, who were strictly on holiday to find the perfect Cupid Connection. The young couple drifted off on their own, locked in an embrace. Others began to follow suit, draining glasses, picking up purses.

"Anyone care to track down a good nightclub?" George asked, his eyes scanning the remaining females.

Murmurs of polite refusal circulated the table.

"Abby Walters? How about you?" George stood and painstakingly buttoned his suit jacket over his paunch. "After all, we move together like a pair of doves in flight."

"What a lovely evening," Nick interrupted, inhaling appreciatively. "Weren't you planning to join me for some sight-seeing, Abby?"

"Yes!" Abby said eagerly, standing as Nick pulled back her chair. "That was the plan."

"What about me?" George protested.

"Get yourself another girl," Nick suggested with a grin. "You know how."

"MY FEET THANK YOU for the rescue," Abby said as she and Nick wandered through the front courtyard of the hotel. Walled in from the street, the yard was hushed and pleasant, with a huge spurting fountain, bursts of bright red bougainvillea, and carefully tended palm trees. The evening air was cool and refreshing, scented with a heady mixture of tangy salt air and assorted tropical greenery.

"Your feet ain't seen nothin' yet," Nick assured her, steering her out to the street.

"Nick, what are you up to?" Abby asked as they stood on the street, surrounded by high rises and traffic.

"You should see more than this hotel strip on your first night in Mazatlan," Nick replied, motioning to the driver of a horse-drawn carriage. "This is an *aranas*. Incurable romantics like myself feel it's the only way to tour the city." Leaving no room for argument, he gave Abby a lift up into the carriage and settled her behind the driver.

The carriage followed the coastal road, heading out of the resort area toward the downtown section of the city. Abby turned her head back and forth with interest as she absorbed the sights and sounds around her. Unlike the ordinary buildings at home, the Mexicans leaned toward colorful stucco structures of pink and aqua. High walls lined some areas, the concrete decorated with exotically painted murals.

"I thought you'd enjoy this tour. The slick hotel strip doesn't reflect the native atmosphere at all." Nick pointed to a plaza, which boasted benches, palm trees and pots of tropical flowers. "As we get closer to the downtown area, you'll really pick up on the local culture."

The center of the city proved to be a delightful jumble of shops, markets, and food stalls. The hubbub of activity, the music pouring from wandering mariachi bands, and the bright noisy bursts of fireworks, reminded Abby of a carnival.

"During the day, these food stalls offer an endless variety of fruit—pineapples, mangoes, bananas. And of course all of your important souvenirs—huaraches, shawls, jewelry are all for sale."

"You can even get a shoe shine," Abby said with delight, pointing at a high throne where a man was seated, his shoes being buffed to a high polish.

"Having fun?" Nick asked, tightening his arm around her shoulders.

"Yes, Nick," Abby replied with characteristic honesty. "You really do know a lot about the area."

"Your command of the Spanish language definitely will be a help to you during your stay but it isn't enough to capture all the little things one learns from just experiencing the place."

As they rattled along in the carriage, Abby could feel the pressure of his thigh snug against hers. It was a dangerous reminder of how persistent Nick could be. "Nick, what are your plans?"

"Ah, what do you mean?"

"I noticed your cuff links."

"Pretty big, aren't they?" Nick admitted with a laugh, raising his wrist to show one off. "As you've no doubt deduced, I brought them along to attract our thief. What about you and your pears? Any plans?"

"According to my mother, Phillip, Candace and George are the only three people from the service who regularly frequent Mazatlan," Abby told him. "I plan to concentrate on them and see what turns up."

"I appreciate you taking me into your confidence." Nick squeezed her hand, encouraged when she didn't pull back. "Doesn't it feel good just to smell the ocean air and watch all the commotion?" He glanced up at the velvet-black heavens, sprinkled with stars. "I always feel rejuvenated after a couple of hours here."

"How many times have you been to Mexico?" Abby asked.

"Several," he replied, turning as a band of strolling musicians passed by along the shop fronts.

Abby couldn't help wondering how many other women had taken this particular ride with him. She glanced up at his strong profile, the square chin held at a confident angle, the attractively shaped lips slightly parted.

How could she be so drawn to a man like Nick, who probably had as many women as her Cutlass had lube jobs? So turned on by a man who was a capital "T"? The answer was simple. He was virile with a capital "V"!

She shook her head, forcing the logical side of her mind to supersede her lustful yearnings. Nick Farrell was a shameless womanizer—as her own mother had pointed out with a starstruck grin. And worse, he was poking into one of her cases. A strong second strike against him. Then there was his notorious habit of upstaging her with his pranks and one-liners.

Keeping a safe distance from Nick seemed best. If she was smart, she'd nip things in the bud now. In this *aranas* before she gave in to her desire.

"See how well we get along when we try?" he crooned persuasively, his words a direct contradiction to her thoughts. He tilted his head back as the evening breeze danced over him. Everything seemed possible tonight. Maybe it was the exotic atmosphere. Maybe it was the way Abby's body rested comfortably against his. Ah, the possibilities . . .

"I suppose we should head back to the hotel, now," Abby said regretfully. "We've got a big day ahead of us."

Nick sighed, then nodded. If there ever was a woman who didn't care to be seduced in an *aranas*, it was Abby Shay/Walters.

Ah, the impossibilities . . .

6

LATER THAT NIGHT Abby sat up in bed with a start. Feeling unusually anxious and disoriented, she glanced around the pitch-dark room. Where was she? What time was it?

She groped for her illuminated travel alarm clock on the nightstand and held it up to her face. Three o'clock in the morning in Mazatlan. Suddenly it all came flooding through her groggy senses.

Abby replaced the clock and sat up a bit straighter. She was normally a sound sleeper, rarely waking during the night without cause. As a matter of fact, she recalled having been deeply asleep, in the midst of a very bizarre dream. She had been chasing Candace Barone along the beach, demanding the return of Nick's diamond cuff links. That wouldn't have been so unusual, if Candace hadn't been wearing the large cuff links as earrings while she rode on Nick's back.

Whew! Would a psychologist ever have a field day with that one....

Abby switched on her beside lamp, then sat very still in the silence. What had jolted her awake? What had triggered her adrenaline, causing the hairs on the back of her neck to stand on end? She'd been an investigator long enough to quickly register the signals her body sent her at stressful moments.

Suddenly a muffled groan broke the silence. Then another. It was Nick, Abby realized. Forgetting the cautiousness that had become her creed, Abby bolted out of bed, across the bedroom, and through the door to Nick's suite.

It was dark in there too, but easily identified as his bedroom the moment Abby stubbed her toe on the foot of the heavy dresser against the wall. She groped her way to the nightstand, relieved to find that his lamp was positioned in the exact spot as the one in her suite.

The golden glow of the lamp confirmed Abby's suspicions. Nick was having one hell of a nightmare. His bedcovers were partially ripped from the bed, his long muscular limbs tangled in the rumpled white satin sheets. His features were narrowed in pain, his curly black hair damp and disheveled. As she gazed down at him, compassion overwhelmed her.

So there was an additional piece to the puzzle of Nick Farrell. Abby found the realization quite staggering. The cocky superjock was vulnerable. Behind that enormous ego and crass attitude beat the heart of a fallible human being. She had been so sure that he could never understand the pain that still tormented her whenever she thought about Roy. She had been so sure that he would laugh in the face of fear. But obviously it wasn't so. The man struggled with demons of his own.

The moment of truth had arrived. No matter how strong Abby's philosophy was on mixing matters of the heart with matters of business, one point obscured everything else.

Nick Farrell was simply irresistible.

Abby gasped and pulled back slightly as he groaned and twisted suddenly, kicking free of his shimmering satin covers. It was a night of discovery to be sure . . .

Nick Farrell slept naked.

Her heart began beating a fierce tattoo as she gazed down at his splendid form spread across the bed in unconscious abandon. His face held calmness now and his mutterings had ceased. The only sign that he'd been waging an internal battle was the glistening layer of perspiration on his skin. She felt somewhat like a rabbit in a lion's den; hesitant to stay, but far too fascinated to leave.

Abby's passion began to simmer slowly, a warm sensuous longing spreading through her thighs like heated brandy. What a magnificent lover Nick would be, she predicted, mesmerized by his powerful limbs. What would it be like to be wrapped up in those arms and legs?

It seemed only fair to awaken him. And she would do so soon, she silently vowed.

Sometime soon.

Nick's eyelids lifted slightly as feather light fingers touched his shoulder. He was still dreaming. He had to be! Abby was standing at his bedside, a curvy silhouette in the lamplight. Her partially shadowed features were charged with passion. Her green eyes shimmered under long, thick lashes. Her lips parted like a rosebud. And those thick tresses that he wanted to bury his face in forever fell in a reddish-brown tumble to her shoulders.

From hell to heaven in a split second. The perfect form of celestial travel. Odd that his dreams should take such a sudden titillating turn, Nick thought, a sleepy smile splitting his face. It had never happened before. The disastrous race at Indy always ended with the concrete wall closing in on him. Then the infinite darkness set in.

He'd done a splendid job this time, he congratulated himself smugly. Conjuring up Abby had been an ingenious accomplishment. Dressing her in a teddy of bright fuchsia silk was nothing less than inspired. The lace-paneled bodice was delicate looking, but strong enough to support her full breasts. The lace narrowed at the waist, accentuated its tininess. The silky wisp of fabric rode high on her firm rounded hip and angled narrowly in front, revealing an enticing glimpse of soft curls.

It was definitely time to add some action to the ultimate fantasy, Nick decided. Squeezing his eyes shut, he willed the thin fuchsia straps holding up the works to snap soundly under the heaving pressure of Abby's bosom. The straps would break and the teddy would slip down. Down over her hips to her ankles.

Mind over matter. That was the answer. Nick crossed his eyes with head-splitting concentration. He opened them moments later, fully expecting to find Abby standing in front of him in the nude.

No! The teddy was still firmly in place. Where had he gone wrong?

He tried again, squeezing his eyes shut, concentrating as hard as he could. Snap! Snap, dammit!

"Nick? Nick, can you hear me?"

"Abby?" he murmured huskily in response to the soft tentative voice.

Apparitions didn't cause mattresses to sag under pressure, Nick reasoned. Nor did they exude the sweet aromatic mixture of Abby's trademark perfume and her own natural, heady scent.

"Nick, you were dreaming." Abby was indeed sitting on the edge of the bed, reaching over to stroke his forehead.

"Yeah, I know. Happens all the time."

"The accident?"

"Uh-huh."

Abby's pulse fluttered as she looked into his indigo eyes. His steady gaze had the force to pin her in place and it made her wary. "I suppose you're wondering what I'm doing here." She stumbled over her words, pushing some stray hairs off his forehead with an unsteady hand. It had been ages since she'd behaved in such an uncalculated manner.

"I don't question good fortune," Nick responded thickly. "It's only the bad breaks that I try to sort out."

"Well, you cried out in your sleep and I—"

"I never cry out," Nick cut in gruffly. "You may have heard a groan or two . . ."

"I guess it was more of a macho grunt," Abby conceded softly with a smile.

"That's better." Nick caught the hand stroking his forehead and kissed the palm. His dark eyes never left hers, never gave her a chance to escape their shackling spell.

"I heard you and darted in here without thinking. Thought maybe you were in trouble."

Nick raised himself on his elbow to a half-sitting position, then eased his shoulders back against the pillows. "I relive the accident in my nightmares. Every time—every damn time, I think I'm going to die on that speedway."

"That's horrible," Abby exclaimed tenderly.

"It's as if my life is stuck in neutral, Abby. Because of my injuries I can't go back to the track and there's no path ahead of me that I wish to pursue."

"You need to move forward," Abby whispered in an unsteady voice. Nick had set her hand on his chest and she could feel the thunderous beat of his heart. Could he be nervous, too?

"That's precisely my doctor's advice. He says I need new goals, new ambitions. I know what I need. I need you." Nick's gaze was pointed and possessive, but Abby sensed a genuine uncertainty bubbling beneath the surface.

"I'm not particularly impulsive, Nick," Abby declared.

Nick nodded, acutely aware of the fact. "That's a shame because impulse suits you rather well."

"Really?" Abby wanted him. The truth was impossible to deny.

Abby's mouth curved in a small sensuous smile that held all the promises that Nick had been waiting for. Curling a hand around her waist, Nick pulled her toward the center of the bed. Fuchsia silk rustled against white satin as Abby's bottom slid along the mattress, closing in on the longest distance she'd ever gone.

"You've done it, you know," Abby murmured as Nick gathered her up over his chest.

"Done what?"

"Slipped behind my defenses, crumbled my control. The impossible."

"The longer I know you, darling, the shorter my list of impossibilities." Plunging his fingers into the depths of her russet hair, Nick guided Abby's mouth over his. His lips were hot and hard on Abby's—seeking, provocative, coaxing a response.

Floating in abandon, Abby savored the feel of his tongue skimming over the sensitive recesses of her mouth. She returned his kiss with fervency, teasing his tongue with her own.

Nick pulled Abby closer, positioning her on top of him until she flanked him limb for limb. He was completely aware of every sensation—her silky skin rubbing against his, the lace of her bodice scratching against the coarse hairs of his chest, her triangle of wispy curls pressed against his solid arousal. One hand still anchored in her hair, Nick kissed her face, her throat, the tender spot behind her ears. His other hand massaged her derriere, his fingers kneading her warm flesh.

Abby was totally caught up in the moist trail Nick's mouth traced on her sensitive skin. Eager to touch him, she ran her hands over his broad shoulders and down his chest, her fingers tracing his scars.

"You're the first lover to see it all," Nick admitted against her cheek.

Nick's words weighed heavily on Abby's mind. She had to be his first lover since the accident. "It's been a long time for me, too," she confessed softly. Then frowning in thought she added, "There's something I don't understand, Nick. You had your shirt off this afternoon. It seemed like the most natural thing in the world."

"It wasn't natural at all. I was testing your reaction."

"You beast!" Abby squealed, her nose pressed against his. "How dare you test me that way!"

"I had to know before we got this far—just how you would feel . . ."

"I didn't cringe, did I?"

"Frankly, just the opposite. I thought you were going to devour me on the spot."

"Was my desire that obvious?"

"Yeah. But I could tell you were fighting it. Spontaneous lust doesn't come naturally to a lady like you."

"Who knows what would have happened if the phone hadn't rung."

"I'll show you."

Abby gasped in surprise when, with a swift cradling movement, Nick rolled over, pinning her beneath him. "Nick . . ."

Straddling her, Nick cut off her breathless exclamation with a swift kiss. "I'll show you—after I look at you. I've waited so long for this moment. I want to make certain you're not an apparition."

Abby eyed him with anxious emerald eyes, her heart-shaped face flushed with passion, her lips swollen from his kisses. Her senses throbbed as Nick hooked his thumbs in the straps of her teddy. He tugged the lacy panel down to her waist, exposing her full, white breasts.

"*Magnifico*," Nick uttered in Spanish. "*Maravilloso!*"

"I thought you didn't know the language," Abby whispered thickly.

"A few choice words to set the mood."

"The mood is set," Abby urged seductively. She tried to reach out for him but he had pinned her arms to her sides with his knees.

He hovered over her, savoring the view. To his amazement, her nipples began to harden under his possessive eyes.

"Just one look . . ." Nick teased gently.

"Investigators are trained to respond to the slightest stimulus," Abby returned between short breaths.

Nick dipped his head to nibble at her darkened buds, sending Abby into a luxurious torment with the short rapid strokes of his tongue. He eventually released her hands, shifting to lie beside her on the satin sheet.

Abby kissed the hollow of his throat, inhaling his heady, masculine scent, already so familiar to her. She found his musky scent, heightened by their lovemaking, intensely arousing. Nick groaned in anticipation as Abby's delicate fingertips glided slowly along his rib cage, to the hard flat plane of his stomach, then to the arrow of his black hairline.

"Not yet," Nick cautioned in a raspy whisper, capturing her hand. "I'm progressing at warp speed. You'll need time to catch up, my darling."

Abby sighed, tenderness intermingling with the primitive urges she was feeling. She was profoundly touched by the realization that Nick was a caring, observant lover.

Nick pushed Abby gently back onto the pillows. Then, with a swift sweeping motion, he pushed her teddy over her hips and down her legs. He tossed it over his shoulder like a wispy handkerchief.

"Much better." Pushing apart her legs with his knee, he ran a caressing hand down the smooth inner sides of the thighs he had so long admired. Finally, finally, they were his to touch, to enjoy. And she was opening up to him like an exotic flower, welcoming him into her plush, velvety petals. Abby was everything Nick needed, wanted.

Abby quivered as Nick's fingers and mouth explored her innermost secrets, driving her to a crescendo of pleasure.

"Nick . . ." Abby's voice was a quavering thread as she reached out to touch him in kind with hot, rapid stroking. He pressed hard against her abdomen with the tip of his arousal—liquid fire building within him. Nick had been funneling all his energies into the arduous task of rebuilding his body for such a long time, that to indulge in the physical pleasures of sex was a miraculous tonic to his spirits. His prolonged abstinence notwithstanding, Nick did not allow himself to completely lose his head. The practical question of protection suddenly invaded his hunger, leaving him momentarily uncertain.

"Nick, what is it?" Abby urgently demanded, feeling the weight of his body on hers lighten and shift.

"Abby, are you protected?" he asked huskily against her ear.

"Yes!" she assured him breathlessly. "I've been on the Pill for years."

That was all the encouragement Nick needed. With an urgent thrust, he entered her petaled opening, causing her to gasp with relief and pleasure. They began to move in steady rhythm, savoring the mounting sensations. Rocking together they soared along the edges of oblivion, higher and higher, pressure building, swelling, driving them to the top until they felt they would burst.

The climax was a shattering release. A physical release from the accumulated forces built up during the past minutes of erotic contact. An emotional release from the electrically charged verbal foreplay of the past few weeks.

They rested in each other's arms for a long while, exhausted and content.

"The shingle on your door should indeed read Wildcat." Nick's voice was low, satisfied against her hair. "Nick Farrell's very own henna-haired wildcat."

"Pretty sure of yourself," Abby taunted seductively, cuffing him under the chin with a weary right cross.

"Pretty sure of us," he gently amended, patting her thigh. "The moment I tucked that twenty in the pocket of your blouse—and you shivered with delight—I knew we had a chance."

"About the case, Nick," Abby began in a tone heavy with regret.

"Hush," Nick covered her mouth with a passion-scented hand. "I don't want to hear that I'm not welcome in any corner or crevice of your life—not tonight."

"All right, my love." Abby purred with contentment as Nick caught the underside of her breast in his palm.

"That's it," he groaned as she flicked her tongue around the curve of his ear. "My dreams are once more headed in the right direction . . ."

"MORNIN' NEIGHBOR."

Nick rolled over in bed the following morning to find Abby leaning against the door frame that adjoined their suites. Dressed in a pale yellow kimono, she reminded him of a sweet, delectable confection.

Abby sipped from the cup in her hands, watching him stretch out along the length of the bed. Sunlight streamed through the window, bringing Nick's scars to life with glaring reality for the first time. To her, they were simply a part of him, taking nothing away from his attractiveness, or his distinct masculinity. She was falling so hard for him!

"Hope you didn't dress on my account," Nick mumbled sleepily, rubbing his stubbled face.

"I called room service for some breakfast and thought it best to dress for the occasion."

"Good thinking. Wouldn't want to send some young buck into cardiac arrest." Nick reached down to retrieve Abby's fuchsia teddy from the carpet and drew it to his face. "And you certainly have the power to do it."

"Want some coffee?"

Nick shook his head, closing his large hand over her teddy.

"Eggs?"

Nick continued to shake his head, his midnight-blue eyes gleaming.

"No?"

He tossed the scrap of silk on the empty pillow beside him and crooked a finger at her. "I'm running a Cupid Connection special on whisker burns this morning."

Abby stepped closer, anticipation heating her. "I was about to take a shower," she informed him with coy invitation in her voice.

"All the better." Nick threw back the covers with a flourish. "Ready when you are."

One look at Nick's naked form told Abby that he was indeed ready.

"IT'S YOUR FAULT we missed the Cupid Connection souvenir trip downtown." Abby kicked some of the white sand under her feet as she and Nick walked along Mazatlan's breathtaking shoreline, carefully sidestepping the sunbathers stretched out on the sand. It was a lovely day for the beach. Brilliant sunlight lit the blue sky above them, sparkling down on the high-forming waves. Ships and boats of various sizes, headed for Mazatlan's busy harbor, dotted the Pacific's horizon. Closer to shore, windsurfers skimmed the water's surface, the boards beneath their feet topped with colorful sails. "The reservations clerk said the group piled into a couple of the hotel's pink minibuses two hours ago."

Nick angled an arm down her back and drew her close. "I must have been in the shower when Barone's departure call came through," he confided with feigned regret.

Abby's lighthearted laughter ran through the salty morning air. "That's no excuse. I was planning some heavy buying on that trip."

"I love the sound of that," Nick said, holding her tightly to his side.

"Shopping?"

"No, your unbridled laughter. You're letting go, Abby. Last night's lovemaking. This leisurely stroll. You'd better watch it. You could become one hell of a lazy tourist."

Abby knew any protest would sound hollow. "I haven't felt this relaxed for a long time. I guess mixing business with pleasure can be done—to a certain extent, anyway." She looked out to sea, her expression growing strained.

"I have to warn you, Abby. I refuse to let our relationship stop at the fun and games mark. That's only half of what it's all about. We have to work together on this swindling operation, too."

Abby gazed up at Nick's handsome face. It was full of intensity, the playfulness of the moment before gone.

"You've given me your passion, and now I want the rest. I want your trust."

"I wish it was that simple." Abby slipped into quiet contemplation, gazing out at the choppy blue water, churning along with her emotions.

"Nothing is simple, Shamus." Nick guided her away from the wandering tourists to one of the thatched shelters lining the back of the hotel grounds. She didn't protest when he pulled her into the partially shaded area. "My accident taught me how complicated life can quickly get. I was cruising along, living in high style on the fame I'd achieved and the wealth that I'd earned, thinking it would be forever. But life has a way of tripping up the best laid plans—reminding us of our mortality."

"Yes, I'm all too familiar with the lesson plan on mortality and immortality," Abby assured him with a bitter edge. "It cultivates prudence. Believe me, I have good reason for feeling the way I do," she added.

Nick fought hard to hide his relief. She was ready to confide in him, he could feel the need beneath her defensive tone. He wouldn't blow it with demands and questions, the way he had in the past.

"I don't doubt you think you have valid reasons," he gently prodded, resisting the impulse to rush her or comfort her.

"But I can't believe you caused Roy Stark's death. We seldom have that kind of power over another person."

"If it hadn't been for my carelessness, he would be alive today," Abby finally blurted out. She hugged her knees and dug her heels into the hot sand. "You see, we were partners and I let him down as a result of a tragic error in judgment."

"Tell me what happened."

"Roy and I worked at Compton Investigations together while I was serving my apprenticeship," Abby continued, finally feeling brave enough to disclose the horrible details. "We began building a relationship during that time and when I earned my license, we decided to branch out with an office of our own. In the beginning we seemed destined for success. We had a small office in a Minneapolis high rise and lots of contacts from Compton. And we had each other."

"You were lovers?" Nick couldn't bear the thought of another man having Abby, but he knew he couldn't let his voice betray his jealousy. After all, he'd asked for it.

"Yes, we were lovers." Pain crossed Abby's face as she relived the tragedy. "At the time of his death, we were working on a missing person case. A woman named Elizabeth Crowley had hired us to find her husband. There was a huge life insurance policy over his head." Abby shook her head in frustration. "It was a crazy case with many false leads. To this day I still don't know exactly what happened. But Mrs. Crowley called Roy late one night to say that her husband was prowling around downstairs, collecting his papers from the den, ranting about disappearing for good."

"Abby, I don't see how you are to blame," Nick said calmly.

"I took that call, Nick. I relayed that woman's hysterical cry for help to Roy and he went rushing over to her place at two in the morning, in the pouring rain. I never saw him again." Abby paused, her breathing shaky.

"Take your time," Nick comforted, drawing her close.

"Roy was groggy with sleep when he left the house. His shirt was half-buttoned, his socks mismatched. Don't you see? He never should've gone off in that state. I never should've let him," she added in a voice choked with guilt. "I should've called the police the second she rang off. But Roy didn't want me to. Didn't want to double-cross Mrs. Crowley by exposing her personal problems to the world."

"In the end, Roy and Mr. Crowley ended up dead. As far as the police could determine, they shot each other in the dark. They surmised that Crowley somehow mistook Roy for a prowler and shot him. Roy apparently had a chance to return fire just after he was hit."

"What did Mrs. Crowley have to say?"

"Not much. She gave some vague answers at the inquest and was cleared of any wrongdoing. She eventually collected a sizable insurance policy and is living happily ever after."

"Are you still mourning this man, Abby?" The question had been lodged in Nick's throat for several minutes and he was certain it would choke him if he didn't ask it.

"No!" Abby had been so involved in her litany of self-denigration that Nick's question, posed with such candor, took her off guard. "I believe I proved that last night."

Relief spread over Nick's face as he recalled their love-making.

"Roy's been gone for a few years, Nick. But I feel the lesson I learned from his death should live on in the way I conduct my life."

"You can't punish yourself forever for one error in judgment," Nick consoled. "And Roy sounds like the sort of man who called his own shots."

"We blew it right from the start, Roy and I were too involved in each other to see beyond the surface of the case, Nick. Investigating takes a clear head. I learned that it's best to keep personal and professional relationships separate."

"It's too late for us," Nick asserted. "I'm already involved—professionally, personally. Totally."

"I know." Abby admitted with a soft sigh.

"Abby, it's a case of trusting yourself to make the right moves. And to trust me to do the same. Caution can be carried to a crippling extreme. Look at the torment I've been going through this past year. I've been so consumed with the terrible memories of my accident, that I've stopped building for a future. You've neglected to consider the future too!"

"So what do you suggest we do?"

"Pick up the pieces of our lives and start to build a new dream." Nick proposed, his words impassioned. "Hell, I don't need your protection. I just need you."

"Okay. I'll give your theory a try," Abby agreed.

"If it makes you feel any better, I'll leave the decision making to you. We'll handle the investigation your way,"

"All right," Abby relented. "If you're certain you can keep that promise."

"I will. We all have our fields of expertise. You work out the mental puzzles. I happen to be very good with my hands."

Abby tingled as Nick's fingertips worked soothing magic between her shoulder blades. They sat together on the sparkling sand for a long while, Abby leaning into Nick as he deftly massaged her warm smooth skin.

"Hey, lady! Hey, mister!"

The sound of a voice jolted Abby and Nick out of their dreamlike state. They'd almost fallen asleep wrapped in each other's arms.

Abby opened her eyes and lifted her head off his chest as a young Mexican boy approached from the shoreline. "Nick! Look at that kid. He looks like a one-person department store."

Nick looked over Abby's head. "That, Shamus, is a genuine Mexican hawker."

"But he looks so young," Abby gasped with surprise.

"Peddling is a big business for the poor people of this area," Nick explained. "Often the younger ones are sent out because they can win the hearts of the tourists and therefore make more sales."

Abby watched in amazement as the boy moved closer, balancing an array of items on his slight brown body. Several sombreros were balanced precariously on the top of his head and straw tote bags and purses sleeved his wiry arms. Ponchos draped his shoulders and beaded necklaces encircled his neck.

"Don't settle for his prices," Nick advised. "He'll expect us to dicker him down a little."

"I'm Pablo," he announced in accented English, standing boldly before them. "You like to buy some genuine souvenirs," he assured them in a businesslike tone.

"How about it, Abby? A condensed version of the Cupid Connection shopping expedition you missed is standing before you. No lines, no hustle, no hassle, no Phillip Barone."

"You are so possessive, Nick Farrell," Abby teased.

"Right," Nick growled playfully.

"Well, I'd like to look at those purses," Abby said, sitting up to slide then off the boy's arm.

"I know Phillip Barone. You must be staying at the Hotel Fiesta," Pablo deduced, his large brown eyes shining.

"Yes, Pablo," Nick said, comfortably falling into conversation with the boy. "You sound like a smart young guy."

The boy's narrow chest rose as he threw back his shoulders. "My brother is a big man at the Fiesta."

"Oh?" Abby immediately perked up her ears. "Who is he, Pablo?"

"His name is Francisco," he announced proudly. "He is in charge of suitcases, elevators, and many, many things."

"I've met him," Abby kept her tone neutral, but she was intensely interested in the possible connection between Pablo, his brother, and Verona Vickers's tennis bracelet. She had to find out if this boy knew anything—however inadvertently—about the swindling operation. "Do you and your brother ever work together?"

"How?" Pablo's voice rose slightly and his small face reflected a measure of doubt.

"Surely your brother needs your help now and then," Nick cut in smoothly.

"*Si, si.* Francisco needs me plenty. And when he owns the Fiesta, I'll be his special helper." He beamed proudly over his outrageous prediction.

"That's just fine," Abby assured him, struggling to conceal her amusement over his sky-high plans. Sensing that it would be too soon to press the boy any further, she turned to the items he was selling. "I'm interested in this purse with the sunflower woven into the flap. What do you think, Nick?"

"How much?" Nick asked.

"Three thousand pesos."

"That seems a little steep," Nick declared, rubbing his chin thoughtfully.

Pablo stared at Nick for a long moment, then said, "Hey, mister, are you Nick Farrell, the racer?"

"Yes, I am."

"Francisco told me you were staying here. I'd like to see you drive someday."

"Maybe you'll have the chance."

Dark eyes shadowed with doubt only moments ago, now gleamed like shiny marbles. "Maybe three thousand pesos is too high for you. How about two thousand?"

Nick nodded. "It's a deal. Now, how about a couple of sombreros?"

Skilfully, Pablo lifted two felt hats off the stack balanced on his head and gave them to him. Nick in turn set the smaller of the hats on top of Abby's sunbaked head.

"Hey, lady, maybe you need two purses for all your junk," Pablo suggested. Then turning to Nick he said, "Pretty ladies should get many, many presents from their man, Señor Farrell. Señor Barone always buys his *señora* many, many things. Now, what do say..."

When Pablo finally moved on, Abby found herself surrounded by souvenirs.

"You certainly have a good rapport with children," Abby observed, sorting through her loot.

"I developed a good rapport with them when I was in the public eye," Nick explained candidly. "Being a celebrity has its responsibilities. A thoughtless comment from a sports figure could have a terrible effect on a child."

Abby gazed out at Nick from under the large rim of her sombrero. He had taken his sunglasses out of his shirt pocket and was putting them on. He was made up of so many contradictory qualities; the rough exterior as a result of surviving life's tragedies, yet the tender soul that could tune into a child's sensibilities.

Abby reached out and touched his mouth with her fingertip. She was falling in love with him.

"Why are you grinning, Shamus?" Nick closed in on the finger tracing enticing circles around his mouth. Trapping it between his teeth, he teased it with his tongue.

"The proper investigation should give you the right answer," she murmured, playfully extricating her finger. Abby lay down in the sand, covering her face with her sombrero.

Nick raised her sombrero just enough to reveal her soft full mouth. Pinching her chin between his fingers, he leaned over, intent on kissing her thoroughly.

Abby moaned quietly as the journey began, as his mouth slowly merged with hers, drugging her, driving away all other thoughts and cares. Soon her felt hat was pushed aside on the sand, closely followed by Nick's sunglasses.

Long and intoxicating, the kiss sealed the agreement they'd reached about their futures. When it was over and they lay intertwined on the white sand, Abby's practical side nagged distantly at her sated libido.

"Nick..."

"Hmm?" Nick rested on his elbow, dusting the fine white sand from Abby's back.

"Did you pick up on Pablo's remark about the Barones?"

"No, I don't think so."

"He referred to a Señora Barone."

"I guess he did at that," Nick recalled with interest. "Odd slip of the tongue."

"That much Spanish you do know, right?"

"If you're referring to the difference between *señora* and *señorita*, I can assure you that I picked up on it years ago. It's basic lingo every male American tourist should be savvy to," Nick added, chuckling with great amusement.

"Is it possible that Candace is married to Phillip?"

"Anything is possible," Nick asserted thoughtfully. "But what could they gain from the brother-sister act?"

"I don't know..." Abby's mind spun as she considered the possibilities. "Perhaps easier access to their clients' treasures. They can circulate openly if they pose as singles. I know that Mother and Verona certainly fell hard for Phillip's charm."

"You mean they engage in a little pillow talk before filling pillowcases," Nick tossed back with a smirk.

"Exactly."

"You may really be on to something here," he admitted. "But how can we prove they're married?"

"I'll find a way," Abby asserted.

"*We'll* find a way," Nick amended.

"Old habits are hard to break." She smiled sheepishly.

"How about a dip in the ocean," Nick suggested. "My leg could use a good workout."

"Well . . ." Abby pretended to be thinking about his suggestion as she rose up on one knee. Suddenly she peeled off her terry cover-up and leaped into action. "Race ya!" she hollered over her shoulder. By the time the challenge was out of her mouth, she was already scampering down the sand toward the water's foaming edge.

Nick stood up, momentarily enthralled by the sight of Abby's curvaceous body in her sleek jade swimsuit. "Why, you henna-haired wildcat!" Nick stormed the shore with a good-natured growl, realizing that he'd keel over from old age long before he'd ever tire of this bewitching woman's company.

7

"I CAN'T BELIEVE you're going through with this, Abby!"

Abby paused in the empty corridor on the twenty-sixth floor of the Fiesta Hotel and turned to face Nick's stern expression. "Nick, I thought we settled this whole matter once and for all. Pablo's remark on the beach yesterday morning about a Señora Barone has to be checked out."

"There must be an easier way. Searching Phillip Barone's room seems so, so—"

"Risky?"

"Don't grin when you say that!"

Abby couldn't help herself. Tracking down a hot lead always set her adrenaline flowing and her spirits soaring. "I have a license to snoop, remember?"

"Yes, but this is breaking and entering!" Nick's voice was little more than a growl between clenched teeth.

"I am very disappointed in your change of attitude," Abby scolded calmly. "A couple of hours ago, this plan was perfectly all right with you."

Nick took her by the arm and spoke quietly into her ear. "A couple of hours ago you were sitting on top of me in bed. When a woman is doing all sorts of things to a man..." Fuming, Nick paused to capture the proper words. "He's beyond reason!"

"You seemed lucid enough to me."

"Liar."

"Okay, maybe you weren't in a bargaining position, Nick, but you promised to let me call the shots in this investigation. We are wasting time bickering over something that I have every intention of doing." Abby glanced at her gold watch. "It's already noon. If the Barones took some of the Cupid Connection people out for some sight-seeing, they'll be returning shortly."

Reluctantly Nick released his grip on Abby and she proceeded down the hallway to Phillip's room. When several brisk knocks didn't bring a response, she knelt down in front of the lock and extracted a thin leather case from the pocket of her white shorts.

"What's that?" Nick demanded in a hoarse whisper. He stood over her crouched form, attempting to see beyond the russet ponytail that was swinging in his face.

"A set of picks. I always carry them in my purse."

"I thought you were going to borrow a passkey from a maid," Nick protested, growing more anxious by the minute.

Abby extracted a slender metal instrument from the case and returned it to her pocket. "You suggested I borrow a passkey from the maid. Remember? I couldn't answer you because I was—"

"I remember the moment quite vividly," Nick cut in. Heat flashed through his body like the flame of a butane lighter as he recalled the way Abby's mouth had caressed him with moist tantalizing kisses, catapulting him into an ecstatic frenzy. He fought to push aside his erotic thoughts. He couldn't reason with the woman while visions of her luscious limbs tangled in satin sheets danced through his head. "Are you in the habit of breaking the law?" he demanded forcefully.

Abby slid the pick into the keyhole with a steady practiced hand. "Of course not. But I have no intention of leaving this resort without the watch and brooch. I promised the folks I'd find their heirlooms and I'm determined to follow through on that promise." Abby winced as she thought of the hard time Blanche would give her if she failed. "Breaking and entering isn't as dangerous as it may seem. It would be a much bigger crime for me to fail Blanche. Believe me, we'd never live it down."

"You've got a point there. But there is something I don't understand. If you're not in the habit of picking locks, why is your leather pick case worn to a gloss along the edges? It looks as though it's been carried in many a pocket."

"Because the set was passed along to me by a lovely old man named Lenny the Wire. Of course his last name really isn't Wire. He—"

"Nobody's name is really Wire! It's a nickname somebody gave him for a very specific reason!"

"Shh!" Abby paused in exasperation. "Can we talk later? You're breaking my concentration."

"You can pick and talk at the same time," Nick asserted stubbornly.

"All right," Abby turned back to the lock. "Lenny is a perfectly respectable burglar. When he was paroled last year—for good behavior—he hired me to track down his father. I located him in a Florida nursing home. Since he's totally reformed, he passed along his picks to me as a goodwill gesture."

"Sorry I asked." Nick leaned against the door frame, rolling his eyes.

"I knew you would be," Abby chided. A click sounded moments later and she tested the doorknob to find it turned easily in her hand. "I'm in."

"*We're* in," Nick corrected.

"No, Nick. It's far more important that you watch for the Barones downstairs in the lobby, as planned."

"I've changed my mind. I don't want to leave you up here alone."

"I don't need a bodyguard. I need a lookout. Now let's stick to our original plan."

"All right," Nick conceded with obvious reluctance. "I'll ring twice on a house phone if they show up."

"Perfect." Abby blew him a kiss.

"Get the hell out of there if I call," he said, shaking a finger at her. He started off down the hall, then turned on his heel to add a stern warning. But it was too late. Abby was already closing the door behind her.

There weren't any immediate surprises in Barone's suite. For all intents and purposes, Abby found it to be identical to her own. She crossed the sitting room, looking for personal touches. Nothing. The pottery on the tables and the abstract art on the walls were standard hotel issue. With a hurried step and a watchful eye she proceeded to the bedroom. There had to be something in the suite to establish the man's marital status.

The room was as neat as a pin. Not a sock, shirt or tie lay out in plain sight. She swung open the bifold closet doors to find it full of neatly pressed clothes, all decidedly male. Phillip's dapper image certainly meant a lot to him, Abby surmised as she sifted through the row of linen suits and crisp cotton shirts. He could mix and match himself into the twenty-first century with the clothing right here in this closet!

Abby carefully shut the doors and moved over to the dresser. The top of the dresser, like the closet, was crowded but orderly. She counted five colognes, three pearl-handled brushes, two tubes of sunscreen, a manicure set, and a moustache comb. Phillip was very well prepared for any cosmetic emergency.

Abby reached for one of the brushes and tapped it against her palm. Nick was certainly a sharp contrast to the dating service entrepreneur, she mused, watching herself smile in the mirror. Nick shed his apparel on the nearest chair, and carried only a few basic toiletries in his shaving kit. In short, the guy lived the simple life. Of course anyone who would proudly tell *People* magazine that he hadn't been above sleeping in the back seat of his car to pinch pennies at the beginning of his career, had to be a pretty practical soul. Practicality was a strong point they shared. Abby had also made many similar concessions on her way to successful self-employment.

There was no room for denial. As Nick's personality slowly unfolded for scrutiny, it was becoming increasingly clear that he was a good intellectual match for her. The physical part... Abby tapped the brush with a flush of pleasure. The physical part of their relationship needed no further scrutiny to be judged a perfect Cupid Connection. They fit together exquisitely. He was an excellent lover. She hoped he was an excellent lookout as well, as her thoughts shifted back to business.

At that very moment Nick was stepping off the elevators at lobby level. He crossed the huge red-tiled lobby with its high-domed ceiling, suspended wooden paddle fans and large potted plants, trying to get in the Sam Spade spirit of the investigation. True, the thought of Abby illegally rummaging through Barone's belongings did nearly send him into cardiac arrest, but the situation did have its high points. Abby had finally agreed to give their relationship a try. And in her characteristic all-or-nothing style, she'd drawn him directly into the thick of things. For the first time in a long time, he was exactly where he wanted to be.

Nick stroked his chin, pausing to size up the area. The open-front coffee shop seemed to be as good a place as any to watch the entrance of the hotel for the arrival of the Barones. The moment they stepped through the double glass doors, he could swiftly pick up the phone near the cash register and alert Abby with two rings, as arranged.

With a steadying sigh, he sat down at one of the round wrought iron tables to order a cup of coffee. He had to keep calm. Nothing could possibly go wrong. From where he was seated, he reckoned he couldn't miss a thing. He'd cautioned

Abby to get in and out of Phillip's suite as quickly as possible. He prayed she was making quick work of it.

Abby hadn't moved an inch. She was still in Barone's room tapping the same pearl-handled brush in her hand. She gazed down at it, wondering what was bothering her unconscious. Suddenly it struck her like a thunderbolt. Trapped between the bristles were several mid-length black hairs. By no stretch of the imagination were those raven strands plucked form Phillip's short blond thatch. But the length and color of them reminded Abby very much of the hair on Candace's head. Quickly examining the other two brushes on the dresser Abby found that they held only traces of Phillip's light hair. His and hers brushes.

Abby felt a surge of triumph as she set the brushes back the way she'd found them. Those black hairs didn't prove matrimony. But they did prove Phillip had some company.

Eager to find further evidence of Candace's presence, Abby opened the top dresser drawer. She shook her head with a chuckle. The man even folded his underwear into neat squares! She closed the drawer and opened another.

Pay dirt! she inwardly rejoiced, lifting a flimsy camisole in the crook of her finger. The drawer was full of lavender-scented silk. But did they belong to Candace? The sachet in the corner of the drawer suggested that the lingerie was there for the duration of the trip. Abby tried to recall if she'd seen Phillip with any other dark-haired female, and drew a blank. The pompous host seemed to flirt with all the Cupid Connection women, never homing in on anyone in particular— with the exception of Abby herself on occasion!

Suddenly the jiggle of the suite's doorknob startled her. Her heart crammed the opening of her throat. Was it Phillip and Candace? Would they go away? As if in reply to her question, a key slid into the lock. She was at the mercy of whomever was on the opposite side of the door!

Abby's head spun around the bedroom as impractical options sifted through her mind like grains of Mazatlan sand. There was nowhere to hide.

Damn that Nick Farrell! All she'd asked for was two rings on the phone. Give him one simple little chore and he botches it up. She threw her arms up in the air. Partners were a pain in the neck. She knew it! She knew it! But somehow the satisfaction of being right wasn't especially sweet at that precise moment. She had to think fast . . .

The door swung open moments later and Phillip Barone entered his sitting room in a lightweight powder-blue suit, whistling under his breath. He paused with a frown, obviously sensing that something was amiss. . . .

NICK SHIFTED ON HIS CHAIR down in the coffee shop, growing impatient with Abby's tardiness. She'd promised to join him in the lobby the moment she was finished. So where the hell was she?

Much to his distress the Cupid Connection crowd suddenly burst through the entrance of the hotel. Candace was in the lead and immediately spotted him through the leaves of a nearby potted palm.

"Why, Nick Farrell, shame on you!" Candace broke away from the crowd and clattered across the mosaic tiles toward him in her leather pumps and a black suit trimmed in white. The woman never seemed to be out of dressy clothes and uncomfortable shoes. If she wasn't carrying a bright pink piñata, she'd have looked like a traveling dignitary rather than a dating service hostess.

Nick spared a moment to return her wave, then took the three steps necessary to reach the counter and pick up the house phone. She was quickly approaching and it was imperative that she not see it was Phillip's number he was dialing.

"Here you are, holed up in the coffee shop," she chided, her heavily made-up face set in a pout. "We go to an awful lot of trouble to arrange outings for our members and feel let down when some stay behind."

"Sorry." Nick listened carefully for the two rings, then swiftly broke off the connection. Relief washed over him. He'd done his part. Abby would get out of there safely now. "Did you have a nice time?" He shoved his hands into the pockets of his white twill shorts and looked over Candace's shoulder at the group headed for the bank of elevators.

"So-so. We'd intended to tour the Hilltop Lighthouse in San Rosa. It's one of the historical attractions we normally visit during our stay. Unfortunately, it was closed for repairs. We climbed all the way up the steep embankment only to find the door locked. A sign explained that the wooden staircase inside was rotting and about to be repaired."

"I've toured the tower before," Nick explained truthfully, "I think the climb would've been a bit hard on my leg."

Candace had the good taste to lower her mascaraed lashes demurely. "How rude of me! I should've realized. I figured you and Abby Walters were frolicking on the sands again."

"No frolicking today. Just a lonely cup of coffee."

"Well, I should be going. Phillip drove the minibus around back and is meeting me upstairs. He—"

"Phillip drove around back!"

"It's all on the up-and-up," Candace retorted in a surprised tone. "The hotel often lends us one of the buses."

Nick eyed the bank of elevators with grim urgency. He'd noticed a couple of blond men in the crowd that had come through the hotel entrance but it was now clear to him that neither of them was Phillip. How could he have been so stupid? He was an amateur, just as Abby had said. He'd not looked beyond the obvious. Abby would've been more thorough. Dread gnawed his insides. He had to get up to that suite! "I'm going upstairs with you," he announced abruptly.

"Now?" Candace questioned with a puzzled expression. "I'm headed for Phillip's room. Perhaps later on I—"

"You'll need help with that piñata," he improvised, wrenching the paper animal from her arms. "Hold that elevator, George!"

"Aren't you the masterful one!" Candace declared, scurrying after him. "But I like it," she cooed. "I really do."

ABBY WASN'T AS PLEASED with Nick at that moment as Candace was. Sure, he'd called with the two-ring signal, but it was far too late! Phillip was already standing over her with a very irate expression on his face, his fists opening and closing as if he wanted to use them on her. Nick's timing needed a whole lot of work.

"Ms Walters, what are you doing in my suite?" His gray eyes bored into Abby's with the intensity of a laser beam. His voice cut through the silent room with razorlike sharpness.

"I've been waiting for you, silly." Abby laughed from her perch on the sofa, waving a carefree hand. In a desperate move she'd darted from the bedroom to the living room, hoping to make it look as though she'd been doing nothing but sitting there.

"You've been waiting here for me?" Phillip gazed at her with both lust and suspicion.

Abby cleared her throat, then launched full force into her flamboyant divorcée role. If she was lucky, Phillip would buy her bogus tale of premeditated seduction. If she was really lucky, Nick would show up and rescue her from having to go through with it. "Since when do we stand on formality? Call me Abby."

"I don't know what to call an intruder." His voice was steady as he moved across the room to the sofa. He was interested. But he wasn't hooked yet.

"I should be the one annoyed with you, you know," Abby declared airily, puckering her lips into a pout that would rival one of Blanche's best.

"Really? I can't wait to find out why," Phillip smiled, baring his teeth.

"I came on this trip looking for a hot time, but have since found out that you are already spoken for."

Phillip lifted a tawny eyebrow into an inquiring arch, Abby paused, hoping he'd admit that he was married to Candace. But this guy was a cool one. He was volunteering nothing. If she was going to bluff her way out of this, she'd have to put all her cards on the table and hope her theory was correct. It was a gamble she hated to take. If she was mistaken, Phillip Barone might very well drag her into the bedroom for a Cupid Connection in the most literal sense of the word.

"It's come to my attention that you and Candace are not brother and sister, but husband and wife!" she accused.

"It's true," he admitted nonchalantly. "I'm not available to show you a hot time. But I could come across with a warm one. Candace and I have an understanding about client stroking . . ."

"I couldn't possibly!" Abby jumped to her feet as Phillip zoomed in for a landing on the sofa.

Phillip landed with a humph, bumping his head on an armrest. He appeared dazed, but hardly out of commission.

"Then what are you doing here in that tight sunsuit if you 'couldn't possibly?'" He rubbed his hairline. "You could've phoned in your complaint."

Hitting his head hadn't seemed to cloud his logic, Abby thought with a wince. "I just had to see your face when I exposed you for the phony you really are," she lamented dramatically. "I feel face-to-face confrontation is the only way to deal with problems, don't you?"

Phillip shook his head. "I'm a letter writer myself."

"I want you to know I heartily disapprove of your charade," Abby said haughtily, backing away. "There must be some truth-in-advertising law you've broken or something, so I suggest you try to be more honest in future." With a toss of her head, she turned on her heel. "I must be going."

Phillip's hand shot out, hooking her elbow. "Not so fast. How did you get in here?"

"The door was open," Abby blurted out. "I just made myself at home, thinking you'd stepped down the hall for ice or something."

"I distinctly remember locking it."

Where in the world was Nick? Abby wondered, maintaining a fatuous smile. A little diversion would do quite nicely right now. "I don't know why your door was open. Talk to the maid."

"Hold on a minute." Phillip kept a grip on her arm. "I can't let you go like this."

"Why ever not?" The blood was pounding in her head, but she maintained the offensive. If she showed any weakness, his suspicions would immediately be aroused. And he was already aroused enough in general!

"Look, we're two adults." As his tone dipped to a syrupy level, his grip loosened to a caress along her inner arm. "We find each other attractive."

"Forget it, buster. I prefer single men."

"You say you like me, but you spend all your time with Farrell," Phillip accused, suddenly tenacious again.

"He's single."

"Perhaps if you get to know me better, you'll decide I'm worth a risk or two."

"What do you have in mind?" Abby asked. No longer able to endure his touch, she pushed aside his hand.

"Nothing too wicked. A windsurfing lesson this afternoon. Since it's part of our schedule, most of our members will be on hand."

"All right," Abby agreed. It might be a blessing in disguise, she decided. She could watch Barone without being alone with him.

"Shall we seal the deal with a kiss?"

Abby leaned back as Phillip's mouth homed in on hers.

The door burst open suddenly and Candace glided in. "Just put my donkey on the chair, Nick."

Nick barreled in behind her with the piñata broken in two pieces in his hands. Abby nearly burst out laughing as she met his wild-eyed look.

"What happened to that thing?" Phillip demanded, regaining his composure with ease. During the confusion he had stepped away from Abby and was now straightening the lapels of his suit jacket, brushing the fabric for traces of lint.

"I'm not sure exactly," Candace said, eyeing Abby warily for a brief moment. "Nick apparently doesn't know his own strength."

It was no mystery in Nick's mind. It was all he could do not to shoot up to the twenty-sixth floor under his own steam. The very thought of that wily bastard laying a finger on his woman made him wild with fury. The piñata had borne the brunt of his anger around the time the poky elevator hit the tenth floor. Frustrated, he had split it in two under his flexing arm.

"You've come in at a very opportune moment, sweetheart." Phillip said smoothly.

Candace lifted a penciled eyebrow in speculation. "Exactly what do you mean, sweetheart?"

"Abby Walters has discovered one of our little secrets."

"Which secret are you referring to?" Candace asked, tucking her chin-length hair behind her ears as she turned to confront Abby.

"Our marital status, naturally."

"And we've been so discreet," Candace clucked. "I hope you will try to understand why we claim to be brother and sister."

"Why do you?" Nick interceded, moving past the sofa to Abby's side.

"Romance is our business," Candace explained without apology. "As singles we can circulate freely among our members during parties and trips like this one."

"We feel it's our duty to keep everyone happy," Phillip elaborated. "Offering innocent flirtations to some of our more neglected souls is one of our many fringe benefits."

"Wouldn't want a neglected soul to drop the service because he felt cheated," Nick cut in bitingly.

"Business is business, Farrell," Phillip said with a sniff. "Life is full of white lies and half-truths."

Nick clenched his fists, burning with indignation. His own father could have easily fallen into Candace's grasp if Blanche Shay hadn't caught his attention first. He wondered how many lonely people hung on to the hope that either Candace or Phillip was truly interested in sharing their future. Even if this pair wasn't guilty of theft, they were certainly guilty of using some very underhanded methods. But, he relented, who was he to criticize them for their sneaky tactics when the savvy private eye standing beside him had just pulled a breaking and entering stunt! If he pressed them, they could press Abby. No matter how convincing Abby's alibi had been, Phillip was shrewd enough to know she'd entered the suite illegally.

Nick glanced at Abby, standing quietly beside him in a strapless peach sunsuit. She knew the score, he could tell by her guarded expression. Saying that she didn't have a leg to stand on wouldn't be particularly appropriate considering the luscious limbs in question.

But she didn't have a leg to stand on! They had reached a standoff—for the time being.

"If you two will excuse us," Candace said with curt dismissal. "We have to prepare for this afternoon's activities."

"See you on the sand, Abby," Phillip added, showing them to the door.

"What did Barone mean by that last remark?" Nick asked as they started down the hallway.

"He's giving a group windsurfing lesson after lunch."

"Damn! That's something I'm not up for yet. Have you ever tried it?"

"No." Abby admitted slowly. "But I couldn't turn him down, Nick. I had to show some interest in him when he caught me in his room. It would've looked suspicious if I'd turned the lesson down cold."

"I'm sure you did your best under the circumstances."

"I did! By the time you rang, Barone was stalking me like Jack the Ripper."

"He pulled a fast one and came in the back way," Nick explained apologetically. "I'm ready to concede that there's more to your work than I first thought. It takes a methodical mind like yours to cover all the bases efficiently."

"Ready to give in and let me handle it alone?" Abby asked expectantly.

"And miss all the fun?" Nick shot back with a cynical snort. "Not a chance. I'll just try to be more alert in the future."

"THE FIRST RULE OF WINDSURFING is to accept the fact that you will be falling down—a lot!"

Phillip Barone's opening line brought a round of uncertain chuckles and murmurs from Cupid Connection members clustered around several boards and rigs. Nick shifted his oiled body on the hotel lounge chair that was embedded sturdily in the sand, and tugged slightly at the straw hat atop his head. He appeared to be just another zoned-out sun worshipper, clad only in hat and black nylon trunks. But it was far from the truth. Putting into practice his new vow of alertness, he was monitoring Barone's surfing lesson with an eagle eye. Barone couldn't make a move that Nick didn't register.

In Nick's opinion, Phillip was already making too many moves. It was obvious to any man with a pair of eyes that Abby was a knockout in her jade suit, and Phillip seemed to have excellent vision. His gaze rarely left her to look at either the other six students sitting in the sand, or at his wife Candace, who was hovering over the proceedings in a sturdy tank suit. His hand seemed to drop to Abby's shoulder with the frequency of a persistent bee lighting on the petal of a rare flower. If Barone had any brains, he'd keep his stinger tucked away, Nick thought grimly.

Nick was determined to shield Abby from harm, despite her protests to be given space to snoop. Nick couldn't help feeling a bit uneasy over the morning's events. Abby being caught red-handed in Barone's room had been an incredibly close call. The elevator ride with Candace up to the twenty-sixth floor had been sheer torture. He'd broken through to some very startling revelations during those agonizing minutes. He realized that Abby was now far more to him than just a lovely diversion. His feelings had deepened far beyond fascination, beyond the pulsating excitement her life-style offered. He'd fallen in love with her. And going on without her at his side was unthinkable.

Though his leg wasn't up to exerting the driving force necessary to control a sailboard on the rough sea waters, Nick knew all the ins and outs of operating one. Native Minnesotans couldn't travel far without coming across a lake and catching the windsurfing bug—unless you happened to be a workaholic as Abby was. Nick would've felt a lot better if Abby had had experience on a board. But she hadn't had any and it was up to him to watch over her lesson.

"This is the inhaul line . . ."

Abby forced herself to pay close attention to Phillip kneeling beside a pink and yellow sail, hoping to still the butterflies in her stomach. She was a fair swimmer, but not a water sport fanatic. It would be all right of course. There were other practiced windsurfers out on the water at that very moment, making the sport look like a piece of cake. They were standing tall on their fiberglass boards, holding on to their billowing sails with strong arms.

"It holds the boom to the mast," he continued, pulling the line tautly in place. "It's important to maintain a tight connection without putting undue strain on the mast."

Phillip and Candace assigned sails to everyone and circulated through the group to offer assistance.

"This looks sort of dangerous," George Merdel complained, the girth overlapping his baggy striped swim trunks quivering as he exhaled nervously.

"Not if you've listened carefully to my instructions," Phillip replied with a sharp edge. "Don't make the others uneasy."

"Once assembled, the board and rig must be carried to the water separately," Candace announced brightly over the men's exchange.

Abby stood up, bumping elbows with Candace for the third or fourth time that afternoon.

"Excuse me," Candace said insincerely.

Abby wasn't sure if Candace was playing interference for Phillip's passes at Abby or if she was actually paying attention to Abby's sailboard. Either way, it made Abby wary.

"Ready, Abby?" Phillip asked, insinuating himself between the two women. "Allow me to help you."

"I'll help her, Phillip," Candace protested, tossing her cap of black hair defiantly.

"I need you, Candace," George cut in, pulling her arm.

"So do we!" another couple chimed in.

"Do your job," Phillip hissed into his wife's ear, before turning to Abby. "I'll take your rigging, ah, Ms Walters," Phillip offered, his words underscored with a trace of irony.

Abby didn't care for his tone. Had he checked her out during noon hour and discovered that she was Blanche Shay's daughter? Feeling a trifle vulnerable with this sailing undertaking, Abby turned to gaze at Nick's motionless form several feet away. He'd promised to make sure Phillip didn't try anything. Now, when she turned to him for a judgment, he showed no sign of life under his straw hat. Oddly, she found herself feeling disappointed.

Abby picked up her board and followed Phillip to the shore. Perhaps she was coming to depend upon Nick's assistance more than she'd realized. Perhaps she had blown her experience with Roy Stark out of proportion. Perhaps Nick could fit into her life if she just gave him the chance.

It took all of Nick's self-control to not reach out and grab Abby as she paused to look at him. What had he seen in her eyes? Fear? Disappointment? He couldn't read the message clearly. But she had warned him to stay in the background and he was complying, although reluctantly. He watched Barone assemble the board and the rig on the shoreline and sighed. It would be all over soon. From now on, they would be joined at the hip. Day and night. Nick was determined to see just how sweet their partnership could be.

"Pull yourself up on the board!" Phillip hollered as he stood beside Abby in waist-deep water. "Remember what I told you. That's it," he cheered as Abby rose onto her knees. "Keep cool. That's it. Raise the rig . . ."

With steady pressure, Abby attempted to pull the sail, which was lying flat in the water, up into the air.

"Wide foot position . . . Not so far!"

Abby's board began to rock and she toppled over.

Nick winced each time it happened. Abby would almost get a start into the wind, then would plunge back into the drink. Phillip was on hand to help her back up onto the board every time, his hands lingering on her waist a lot longer than seemed necessary. Others from the group joined the fun, slipping and falling in the same manner.

George Merdel was the first to give up and join Nick on shore. "It's crazy!" he bellowed. "I'm going to stick to dancing. Always sure on my feet out on the floor."

"Good thinking," Nick agreed, pushing his hat up to meet the other man's frustrated scowl.

"Hey, look, Abby finally made it!"

Nick snapped his attention back to the water. Abby was standing on the board with her sail taut, the wind at her back.

Abby felt triumphant as the rig straightened up like a flagpole in front of her. She grasped the boom with one hand as Phillip had instructed, allowing the wind to push her forward. She skimmed across the water into deeper waters, being careful to maintain the proper stance on the board. She realized that she was rapidly picking up speed, but felt confident and steady with her back straight and knees flexed.

Suddenly Abby heard a snap and felt a jolt that knocked the air from her lungs. The sail was no longer attached to the board! She lost her footing and began to fall backward. The sail was loose in her hands, whipping wildly in the wind. The swinging boom was the last thing she saw before falling dizzily into the sea.

NICK'S HEART STOPPED DEAD as he watched the tall aluminum mast collapse in Abby's hands with a jerk, causing the rig to whip out of control and fly over Abby like a huge tarp. She fell into the water, quickly disappearing beneath the sail.

Nick had already hit the water by the time her board shot up into the air.

8

WHEN ABBY OPENED HER EYES, the glaring blue brilliance of the Mexican sky filled her vision. What was happening to her? she wondered with a growing sense of dread. She remembered the shock of holding the loose mast in her hands, the boom swinging at her head. She remembered falling into the water.

Abby paused to think, to feel. She was still in the water. Her head was above the surface and her limbs were floating free. She wiggled her fingers and her toes to find they still worked.

Had she died? She surely hoped not! Her ears were ringing and her temples throbbed. Heaven had to be more comfortable than this. And after catering to Blanche's exploits over the years, she was a cinch to make it past the pearly gates! But how . . . Why . . .

"Rest easy, Shamus. I've got you."

Nick. Nick was speaking to her in calm, steadying tones. His arm encircling her chest was snugly hooked under her armpit. He was keeping her afloat. He was rescuing her. He obviously hadn't been snoozing under that hat after all! They were moving now. He was pulling her along with a strong, smooth stroke.

"Relax," he coaxed. "Swimming is one thing I'm still pretty good at."

Abby shut her eyes against the sky, realizing that it had been a good long time since her life had been in someone else's hands. A smile crossed her lips as she thought just how much those hands had come to mean to her.

As Nick reached shallow water with Abby, three anxious people rushed forward to help.

"Release her, Farrell," George Merdel urged. "C'mon, man, you can't do it all!"

Nick reluctantly loosened his hold on Abby, and George and Phillip proceeded to transfer her to a blanket, which had been laid out on the sand. He dashed up the beach on their heels, kneeling beside her on the blanket with heaving breaths. "Abby?"

At the sound of Nick's voice Abby raised her lids once more. He was hovering over her this time, looking wild and worried and extremely wet.

"You're safe, honey," he assured her, stroking her forehead with a feather light touch.

Safe? Abby looked beyond Nick to the curious faces poised over his crouched figure. Phillip was fingering his moustache with an inscrutable expression, Candace's face was a study in uncharacteristic concern, and George's complexion was pasty with dread. Fear crept up her spine. Had one of them sabotaged her sailboard?

"Dreadful accident," Candace cooed. "I knew I should've checked her rig, Phillip."

"Shut up," Phillip snapped with a tight smile. "She's alive and well, and that's the main thing, isn't it, darling?"

"Yes, darling." Candace mimicked.

"Perhaps we should take her to the hospital, Nick," George suggested solicitously.

"No!" Abby startled the bunch with her squealing refusal. She lifted her head and snuggled into a sitting position. She had to take action before it was too late.

"Are you sure, Abby?" Nick asked. He stretched his legs out on the blanket and settled Abby against him.

"Positive. I'll be fine in a little while," she assured him, resting her head against his hairy chest. "I just want to rest here. Please go back to your fun, everyone." She dismissed them with a weak, grateful smile.

"Let me take you upstairs to the suite," Nick urged as the threesome drifted off. "This heat is murder."

"Oh, no, not yet!" Abby protested in an agitated whisper.

"This accident has clouded your senses. You need rest."

"I don't think it was an accident," Abby rasped, her body shuddering on his muscular chest.

Nick's expression narrowed in uncertainty, his arm tightened protectively around her shoulders. "I don't know Abby... Preparing a rigging can be tricky, especially for a beginner. If your inhaul line wasn't secure, it would cause the whole works to come tumbling down the way it did."

"That line snapped, I tell you," she insisted with a frustrated murmur. It was horrible to feel so weak, so helpless in tracking down a lead. "I need your body, Nick," she hissed urgently. "This instant."

Nick raised a heavy black eyebrow in horrified amazement. "Abby, you're bouncing from attempted murder to attempted whoopee! Maybe I should have you checked out at the hospital."

"No, you've got it all wrong!" she insisted. "I need you to take investigative action for me, to physically check out that rigging. It would look extremely strange if I, a nearly drowned divorcée, was seen crawling out to the water to look at that rope." She raised her head with her last ounce of energy to meet his gray eyes squarely. "Please."

Nick gazed out to the ocean. He saw George Merdel attempting to push the pieces of the sailboard onto shore. This would be his chance to inspect the line without arousing too much suspicion. "Okay. We'll settle it one way or another." He scrambled to pick up his straw hat lying a few feet away and set it on Abby's head. "Sit tight," he directed with half-hearted sternness. "And if you begin to feel woozy, holler."

Abby tucked her knees under her chin and watched Nick slosh out into the foamy waters to assist George with the rigging. She noted that George tried to offer Nick the fiberglass board, but Nick aggressively reached for the mast with its loose line and floppy sail.

Had George begun to collect the rigging himself? Did he want to remove any evidence of tampering? she wondered. Had he deliberately tried to push the board at Nick, rather than the line, in order to hide his dirty work? He seemed so harmless . . . Oh, damn, but it was hard to think when your head was pounding, Abby moaned to herself.

Nick immediately carried the rigging up to Phillip's makeshift school in the sand and joined Abby once again. "Bad news, Shamus," he muttered, dropping down on the blanket. "Your inhaul line snapped just as you suspected. And it had a little help, a clean slice into the rope."

"Someone wants me dead," Abby whispered hoarsely, gripping Nick's arm.

"Let's not jump to conclusions," Nick said consolingly, stroking her cheek. "There are surer ways to murder someone." It tore him up to see Abby so fragile, so vulnerable. He had wanted her to back down, soften up to him—but only if she chose to! Certainly not by a knock into the drink!

"What a great setup for accidental death! Maybe somebody knows who I really am." Panic choked her for a moment. Her life had never been threatened before. And then there was Nick's life to consider, too.

"The Barones would've been fools not to check you out after that little 'B and E' adventure this morning," Nick deduced as calmly as he could manage, "if they're the guilty ones . . . I couldn't have stood it if something had happened to you today, Shamus," he continued with rough emotion. "We'll have to play it a lot closer to the chest from now on. No more break-ins, no more water sports."

No more partnership, Abby added silently, allowing Nick to gather her in his arms. Death could also threaten the man she cared for. Nick would not end up as Roy did, she vowed, burying her face in the wet hollow of his shoulder. If only she'd met *him* in the supermarket. Things couldn't have been so different.

WHEN ABBY AWOKE the following morning, her headache was little more than a dull throb. Certainly nothing to keep her bedridden, she decided gingerly as she sat up and stretched. Her muscles felt a bit stiff with the movement, but she felt pleasantly alive. And she intended to stay that way! Keeping Nick safe and sound was at the top of her list, as well. She gazed down at him, sleeping soundly at her side, his long muscular body curled up on a sliver of the mattress. No doubt he'd been concerned about jostling her aching body. With a light push she rolled him into the center of the bed and covered him with the satin sheet. She wondered just how long he'd actually been asleep. Probably only an hour or two, she guessed. He'd been so concerned about her well-being that he'd most likely kept a late-night vigil.

Abby moved around the room quietly, picking out her clothing. Most of her things were now in this room—his room. It felt good to shift through a closet that smelled of Old Spice and man. She pulled her sundress of muted pastel flowers off a hanger and headed for the bathroom to dress.

Abby switched on the overhead light, chuckling when she discovered her Lycra swimsuit in a wet heap in the bathtub and Nick's navy nylon briefs dangling from the curtain rod. Nick must've stripped them both off in quite a hurry and tossed them in the most convenient spot. Well, there was no time to rinse them out now, she thought as she ran a brush through her hair. She had work to do. She had to set a trap for the weakest link in the swindling chain: Francisco.

"But I cannot help you, *señorita*." Francisco flashed Abby a puzzled look from behind the reservations desk thirty minutes later and slid Abby's pear-shaped pendant back across the polished mahogany surface.

"Of course you can," Abby insisted. She slipped some pesos under the diamond and slid it back to him. "Verona Vickers told me you helped her out a few months ago."

"Verona who?" Francisco picked up his dust cloth and began to rub the desk with concentrated effort.

"Verona Vickers," Abby enunciated the name carefully, struggling to hide her impatience. Nick could awake at any time and find her gone. She had to make some headway in the case before he caught up with her. "She came with the Cupid Connection dating service a few months ago. She's tall, thin, in her sixties."

"I am always willing to help out anyone from Cupid Connection," he said in a rehearsed tempo. "But I don't remember no Verona Vickers." He rested a gray-sleeved arm on the desk and tipped his head toward Abby's.

"What is it, Francisco?" she asked with urgency.

"I don't know this Verona Vickers," he insisted. "And I don't ever handle jewelry for guests. *Escusa*. I have to work." He straightened up and adjusted the black tie at his throat.

Abby snatched back the money and pendant in frustration. Trying to trap the jeweler with her diamond obviously wasn't going to work. Either Francisco was as innocent as he seemed, or he knew she was an investigator setting him up and was on his guard. Abby's instinct told her the bellman was totally honest. But Verona claimed he'd taken the bracelet to be cleaned and had brought back a phony. She would have no reason to lie, would she?

"*Buenos dias!*"

Abby turned to find Pablo entering the lobby from a seaside entrance. He was dressed in a worn T-shirt and shorts, and his unruly thatch of black hair wasn't burdened down today with hats. Leather belts draped his small shoulders and purses hung from his thin brown arms. In his hands he carried a drawstring canvas bag.

"*Hermano!*" The reprimand in Francisco's tone would've broken any language barrier. "You do not belong inside."

"But I saw the *señorita* through the window," Pablo explained defensively. "Where is the racing man named Nick?" he quickly asked. "I have a wonderful deal for him. A belt just right." Pablo pulled a finely crafted belt from his shoulder.

"I could lose my job," Francisco hissed.

"I'll take responsibility," Abby assured the bellman with a smile. "I'll buy the belt later, Pablo, I promise."

"I also have some very wonderful jewelry." Pablo loosened the drawstring on his sack and dumped its contents on the reservations counter. Colorful stones set in silver covered the wooden surface, twinkling under the fluorescent lighting.

"*Ese niño es muy malo*," Francisco lamented mournfully, covering his eyes.

"I am not very bad." Pablo retorted. "Am I, *señorita*? Am I?"

Abby was barely listening. With shaky fingers she was picking through the pile of stones. So far she'd extracted three brooches identical to her mother's.

"*Señorita*, you have the finest taste," Pablo babbled confidently.

Abby continued to pick through the treasure trove, finding six brooches in all. She turned them over in her hands, carefully examining each one. Each was a forgery. None of them had an inscription.

"You like? You buy?"

"I'll buy. But I want to know where these came from, Pablo."

"Oh, that is easy. A jeweler in San Rosa—near our farm— makes them. Isn't that right, Francisco?"

"That is right," Francisco snapped. "Put that stuff away before a manager walks by."

"If you want more, *señorita*, I will bring them tomorrow," Pablo offered.

"I want to see this jeweler for myself," Abby said, struggling to keep the urgency from her tone.

"But I give you a good price. The best price."

"I have a good deal for you," Abby told him with a smile. "I am going to pay you very well for what I'm buying now, and I want the name of the jeweler."

"His name is Carlos Alvarez," Francisco supplied, tossing the jewelry back in the sack. "He has a shop in San Rosa."

"I must go there." Abby appealed to the elder brother.

"There are several hotel minibuses, *señorita*. They often tour the town."

"No, no. I need a car now. One of my own." Abby bit her lip in concentration. "How do you get to work every day?"

"Francisco drives us in his very own car," Pablo contributed proudly. "He's a big man here at the Fiesta."

"Francisco, let me borrow your car."

"But San Rosa is twenty-five miles away. Twenty-five miles of rough road."

"I'll pay you well," Abby coaxed.

"Okay." Francisco fished in the pants pocket of his uniform for his keys. "I will call to the parking attendant and tell him you are coming."

"Thank you so much." Abby crushed some bills into the palm of the bellman's hand and rushed toward the glass doors.

SHE HADN'T EVEN left him a note.

The woman couldn't be trusted. Nick had stormed through both suites in search of her, a naked, angry panther on the prowl. Then, realizing that she'd left him behind, he returned to his bedroom.

She was a crafty temptress. And he was a doting fool. Why had he chosen to fall in love with her? Nick pulled fresh underwear out of the dresser then yanked his royal-blue polo shirt and tan slacks out of the closet. Why not chase a model or a secretary? Why not find a woman that would not only love, but honor and obey as well?

Why not indeed! Hell, he didn't know why! He sat on the bed and shoved his legs into his pants. Abby Shay was one of nature's little wonders that defied explanation. She could prick like a thorn, open and close like a rose, warm him like the sunshine. He'd never been so enraptured by a female— and he was thirty-five years old! Thirty-five and a seasoned veteran of the dating game.

Nick ran a hand over his whisker-roughened face. He needed a shave, but he didn't dare take the time. The practical PI would no doubt be putting every second of her borrowed time to very good use.

"GOOD MORNING, EVERYONE," Nick greeted the tableful of Cupid Connection members in the dining room minutes later.

"Hello, Nick. How is Abby today?" Candace looked up at him over the rim of her coffee cup, her expression inscrutable.

"Is she resting?" Phillip asked, carefully dabbing the corners of his mouth with a snowy white napkin.

"Actually, she's already up and about," Nick informed them lightly. "I'm looking for her. Anyone seen her?"

George Merdel swallowed and raised a thick forefinger in his direction. "I was crossing the lobby a minute ago and saw that Francisco fella handing her some car keys. Then, that kid that's always peddlin' ran after her waving a map."

"Thanks, George." Nick turned on his heel, nearly colliding with a waiter carrying a tray. Nick quickly steadied the slender young man and moved him aside.

"Aren't you going to eat?" Candace clucked in disappointment.

"Aren't you going to shave?" Phillip chimed in with a sneer that Nick would have gladly twisted from his face.

"I'll be back." He said it in a way that was both a threat and promise, and then he darted out of the dining room.

"Francisco!" When Nick spotted the bellman at the entrance, peering intently out the glass doors, he broke into a run. "Where is she? Where is Abby?"

Francisco took one look at Nick's smoldering expression and pointed out to the courtyard at a battered old blue car. "She's out there. In my Chevy."

Abby spotted Nick charging down the red-carpeted stairs of the Hotel Fiesta as she guided the Chevy around the courtyard's circular paved road. Her knuckles whitened on the chipped blue steering wheel as she sized up the situation. She was literally trapped on the road that ringed the large spurting fountain gracing the entrance. She couldn't leave the grounds without passing by the doors—and Nick. It was quite simply a race for time.

He flew down the stairs. She sped round and round, pressing hard on the accelerator. It looked like she had a chance, she realized with a sense of triumph. Then suddenly, coming from the opposite direction, a pink hotel minibus rolled up under the awning, and stopped dead in her path. With a cry of dismay and a fleeting prayer that they were in decent condition, she slammed on the brakes. She missed the bus's fender by inches.

"Gotcha!" Nick's large hand reached into the open window and clamped the steering wheel.

"So you do."

"Not bad for an amateur sneak, eh, Shamus?" Abby looked so damn cute with her sunburned nose in the air, a yellow cotton hat atop her flowing russet hair. But Nick knew if he showed any mercy she'd tromp on the gas pedal and leave him in a cloud of exhaust fumes. "I've won this round. Slide over."

"No, thank you." Abby kept her eyes focused out the windshield at the passengers disembarking from the bus.

"I'm not offering you a cup of tea. I'm giving you an order."

"And I'm trying to save your life!"

"I believe you have that confused. I'm the lifesaver around here. I pulled you out of the drink yesterday, remember?"

"You know what I mean," Abby argued, still not looking at him for fear she'd relent. "You're not going to end up like Roy. I've already decided that. Our partnership is severed. As of now!"

"Like it or not, you need me, Shamus." Keeping a steady arm on the wheel, he lowered his mouth to her ear. Hoping to intimidate her, he spoke in a forceful tone. "Trying to drive this heap may be more of a challenge than you think. The play in the wheel needs expert handling. And so do the brakes. You didn't exactly stop on a dime a minute ago."

"Handling my Cutlass for ten years should qualify me for something," Abby claimed.

"It qualifies you for either the poor farm or the funny farm—depending on your reasons for driving that dangerous heap into the ground."

"You know it was a matter of economics."

"Okay, okay. I get a little crazy over inferior vehicles. Let's stick to the point. I'm better qualified to drive this car than you are. You're obviously on a hot lead and would like to get going. I have no intention of letting you drive on without me. Clear?"

"Why do you have to play boss all the time?" Abby finally turned to face him. His royal-blue polo shirt and tan slacks were neatly pressed, but the rest of him could use some work. His coarse black hair was mussed and his face was darkened with the beginnings of a beard. "Whatever happened to our equal partnership?"

His patience exhausted, Nick jerked open the creaky driver's door and shifted the gear into park. "You said we're no longer partners, so I can be as bossy as I want to be."

"Whatever happened to your razor? Whatever happened to your comb?"

"Slide over."

"You'll be in my lap in a minute," Abby gasped.

"Thanks for the invite, but I don't like any major distractions when I drive. Now, move over."

The driver of the minibus was now backing up, waving at them to continue on. A taxi was on their rear fender, honking for them to move. With a resigned sigh, Abby slid across the cracked vinyl seat as Nick eased in behind the wheel. "Try to keep a guy out of trouble . . ." Abby trailed off in a grumble.

"Now, that's enough."

"So, where are we headed, big shot?" Abby challenged, straightening her hat.

"Don't get sassy, Shamus," Nick warned. He scanned the dented dashboard with a frown, shifted into gear, and eased around the minibus. "If you've got a lead, you'd better spill it. All hell is liable to break loose if your cover is blown." He cast her a hard, impatient look as he guided the Chevy through the hotel's plush grounds.

"Pablo got me started on the trail again," Abby admitted, reaching into her purse. "He had six of these in the canvas bag of tricks he was peddling this morning." Abby handed Nick one of the brooches.

"Well, I'll be." Nick rested the brooch on the wheel and turned it over in his fingers. "Not a bad replica."

"Apparently the jeweler lives in San Rosa." She unfolded the map Pablo had given her.

"That map won't be necessary," Nick claimed, dropping the brooch back into her purse. "I've been to San Rosa several times. It's a rustic coastal town popular with celebrities trying to get away from the madding crowd."

"Francisco said the ride is pretty rough."

"It is. And traveling it in this bucket of bolts isn't going to improve it any."

"We'll get there eventually," Abby declared with conviction. "I always get my man."

Yes, Nick silently agreed. *But what do you do with him afterward?*

THE SCENERY ALONG THE ROAD to San Rosa was a sharp contrast to the luxurious hotel strip and hectic downtown Mazatlan. To Abby, it seemed like a path to another world. The Chevy rumbled along, leaving the dusty arid city for a lush, tropical forest. The surroundings were riveting, peaceful. Dense, hushed jungle flanked the road, with streams flowing surprisingly close to the roadside. Colorful birds soared through the clear cobalt sky, lighting on marshy flats and mangroves. Thatched huts were scattered along the wayside, and an occasional native could be spotted beside a stream washing clothes.

"Why, there's someone…" Abby's voice dropped off at the sight of a man taking a bath in the stream. He didn't even look up as the Chevy ground by.

"You expect him to wear clothes while bathing?" Nick teased. "You don't."

By the rules of fair play, Nick's last statement shouldn't have sent a current of desire down her spine, Abby decided, biting her lower lip until it stung. But those two words held that certain husky edge of his—the powerful edge which easily reduced her to a meek, cuddly kitten, willing to accept him as a partner in all her endeavors. Oh, he knew just how to bring her around. And he *knew* he knew! But he didn't belong in the middle of this case, no matter how sensuous his tone, no matter how inviting his mouth, no matter how much she longed for those strong hands of his to roam every inch of her body.

"Take it easy on that lip."

"Huh?" Abby glanced at him, startled by his request.

"Your lower lip. You're biting the hell out of it and it's turning purple."

"So what?"

"So, when we kiss and make up, it'll be too tender to touch. Half a mouth just won't do."

"No, half of anything is never enough for you," Abby grumbled resentfully. "A person loves you enough to keep you from harm and what do you do? Charge right in like an angry bull."

"I wouldn't be here if you didn't need me," Nick shot back.

"Sure, sure, I know. You'll ring twice at the first sign of trouble."

"I knew you were going to throw that at me again!" Nick fumed. "There's more to your work-alone attitude than Roy's demise," he accused, unable to curtail his temper. "You like to be in total control, all the time. You don't want to rely on anyone else for help. Not your mother. Not me. Not anyone!"

"What makes you such an expert on me?"

"A lot of studying," Nick replied confidently. "I think about you day and night. And I think I know you better than you know yourself."

"Oh, really." Abby folded her arms across her chest, burning with indignation.

"I believe you began your solo act because of Roy, but I think you grew to enjoy being in total control. I think you've forgotten how to share. How to trust. Abby Shay, you are in a rut."

"I am not!"

"In a rut—like a doddering old woman, who talks only to her plants and herself."

"I go out. I'm a success."

"You go out—on stakeouts. You're successful—at solving other people's problems."

"And you! You're an arrogant poop who's angry because women don't chase him anymore!" Abby squealed.

"I *used* to be an arrogant poop who was angry because women didn't chase him anymore," he corrected. "I've been so busy chasing you lately, that I've given up feeling sorry for myself."

"Congratulations. You're cured."

"With a little work you'll be cured, too."

"What makes you think I'm willing to change?"

"Deep in your heart you must be wondering if it would be worth it to do some attitude adjustment. You want me as much as I want you. You're just not sure how to handle us as a couple, yet."

"I think we should call a truce," Abby suggested fretfully.

"Why, because I'm winning this one?"

"No, because someone is after us," she answered, pointing her thumb out the back window.

"We're being followed?" Nick glanced in the crooked rearview mirror. "Are you sure?"

Abby shot him a wry look. "Positive. I've been tailed by the best, as you well know."

"Why thanks, I'll take that as a compliment." Nick's eyes flicked from the road to the mirror. "A pink minibus from the hotel."

"It's been keeping its distance for a couple of miles. Who knew I was leaving the Fiesta?"

"Everybody. The Barones. George Merdel. Francisco. Pablo."

"This could get sticky." Abby's voice betrayed her trepidation as she gazed up the narrow two-lane road. "What are we going to do?"

"Our options are limited on this bumpy obstacle course," Nick said, turning the wheel to avoid a crater-sized hole in the road.

"We could end up in the ditch." Abby knew she'd read his mind as her words hung in the air between them. His jaw visibly tightened under his half-shadowed skin and his mouth thinned to a hard grim line. She glanced out her window, down the steep bank so near to the side of the car. Dense mangroves flanked the stream, their damp gnarled roots curling up to the road. The Chevy wouldn't fare well plowing through the muck and trees.

"Hold on to your hat," Nick warned. "They're making their move."

Abby turned to find the minibus openly approaching. "Step on it! Lose them!"

"Are you crazy?" Nick shouted back above the din of the engine. The Chevy grew louder as he pushed it to the limit. He knew something could burn or blow at any time.

"You're the expert driver. The champion who's won all sorts of prizes and things! Surely you can make some fancy maneuver!"

"Abby, Darling." Nick struggled to control both his temper and the vibrating car. "A driver is only as good as his machinery. This Chevy is an eggbeater on wheels. The steering is wild, the tires are bald, and the engine is backfiring. Winning 'prizes and things' doesn't qualify me as a miracle worker."

"It's show time!" Abby sucked in air as the bus swiftly overtook them. The bus reduced its speed to run parallel with the Chevy. Nick gripped the wheel, bracing himself for the jolt the gawdy pink menace would deliver when it struck their car.

"I wonder what's going on?" Nick asked, as the bus rolled alongside them in the opposite lane.

"The driver is toying with us," Abby muttered, her hands gripping the door handle for dear life.

Suddenly the bus shot ahead and swerved into the lane in front of them.

"Now what?" Nick growled.

As if in response, the back window of the bus lowered several inches and the tip of a gun nosed out over the edge of the tinted glass.

"Oh, my God," Abby uttered, hypnotized by the blue barrel glinting in the sunlight as the bus bounced along. "We've got nowhere to go."

"Almost nowhere." Nick slammed on the brakes, hoping the element of surprise would confuse their assailants. It worked to an extent, the gap quickly widening between the vehicles. But the gunman was swifter than the bus driver. A snap crackled through the air before the bus peeled away. Its target was immediately obvious as the right front tire of the Chevy quickly started to deflate.

"We've been hit," Abby shouted as the Chevy began a crippled thumping roll toward the embankment.

Cursing, Nick maneuvered the car to a stop on a precarious strip of shoulder overlooking the ditch.

"Be careful getting out," Nick cautioned as Abby opened her door.

Clutching the car for support, Abby stepped out onto the top of the embankment. The ground was soft, covered with oyster-encrusted mangrove roots. "My shoes will never be the same," she grumbled, gingerly picking her way up around the car.

"A dart." Nick pulled Abby up to the road, then held a miniature aluminum arrow with a feathered end.

"I'm glad that ended up in the tire," Abby said, inspecting its pointed tip.

"It could've smarted in a more tender spot," Nick agreed.

"Think we're dealing with killers, or someone intent on simply scaring us off the trail?"

"That was no simple scare." Nick set the dart on the roof of the car and leaned against the front fender. "Abby, if this car had barreled into the jungle, I don't think we'd be on our feet right now."

"You're right," Abby conceded with a grateful grin. "It's thanks to your prowess and not their mercy that we're unharmed."

Nick eyed her as she leaned against the car beside him. "Say that again."

"Say what again?"

"What you said."

"Thank you?"

"No! That I'm right." Nick's face glowed with satisfaction. "It sounded so sweet. So—so right."

Abby pulled the brim of her yellow hat lower over her face and gazed down the deserted road. "I guess you're right about a few things."

"Oh, really?" Nick put a hand on the back of her neck and kneaded his thumb into her soft skin.

"I guess I do like to be . . . in control of things."

"You probably never would've succeeded in your work had you not been single-minded," Nick pointed out in a softer tone.

"Wildcat Investigations has been my only focus for a long time. I put all my energies into it, and I guess I am in kind of a rut. But I don't talk to plants or myself," she added, turning to shake a finger at him. "I have Donna to talk to. I pay her just enough to garner her rapt attention."

Nick threw back his head in hearty laughter. "She admires you so much, I'm sure she'd listen for free."

Abby laughed along with him. "I don't know about that!"

"My only objection to your life-style is that there seems to be no room in it for me," Nick admitted with passion. "Your accident yesterday afternoon brought out some very heavy emotions in me, Abby. I've come to realize just how much I love you."

"I left without you this morning for exactly that same reason," she explained, tracing a finger along his lips. "I love you and want you to stay safe."

"It was your safety that was at risk this morning," he confided ruefully. "When I woke up and found you'd cut out, I could've strangled you with my bare hands." With a growl he closed his hand around her throat.

"Falling in love has been the easy part, Nick."

"Are you nuts? I feel like I've been through the wringer these last few days."

"I'm saying that the trust part is going to be the most difficult obstacle in our relationship."

"Oh, I see." Nick paused in thought. "We'd better get to work on that one. No more decision making without the other's approval. Total trust in each other."

"Equal partnership," Abby agreed with a nod.

"Fifty-fifty all the way down the line, no matter what," Nick promised solemnly.

9

"A HINT OF LEG, ABBY," Nick stood in the middle of the road an hour later, surveying Abby with a critical eye. "We agreed to stop a driver with a flash of flesh."

Abby laughed from her perch on the trunk of the Chevy, adjusting the skirt above her crossed tanned knees. "We agreed this was the only way. Two buses and one Volkswagen passed us by without as much as a wave."

"But you're defeating our purpose." He approached the car, his hands on his narrow hips. "A man spying that much thigh could lose control of his vehicle," he patiently explained. "Could end up plunging headlong into the jungle."

"What a sweet thing to say!"

Nick carefully draped the full hemline of her pastel sundress over the upper part of her legs, taking the opportunity to close a loving hand over a stretch of tender flesh. Streaks of warmth swiftly spread through her body from the pressure of his touch, bringing back the sensations that Nick had aroused in her during their lovemaking.

"I hear a hum," Abby giggled.

"It'll be an ear-piercing whine before I'm through," he predicted in a low, seductive tone.

"I'm talking about an engine, Nick. Someone's coming—from the direction of San Rosa."

Within seconds a battered green truck came into view. Nick straightened up, pulling the skirt down to Abby's ankles.

"Coward," Abby teased.

"Just call me selfish."

The truck slowed as it passed by, revealing the driver to be a middle-aged Mexican dressed in a wrinkled white shirt, a straw hat on his head. The back of the truck was full of chickens stacked in wooden crates, squawking over the clatter of the engine.

Abby quickly requested a ride in Spanish, attempting to raise her voice over the racket. The man scrutinized her carefully, then beckoned her closer.

"Un minuto, por favor." Abby reached into the Chevy for her purse. "I'm going to offer him some money," Abby told Nick. "And please, Nick, let me try to win his confidence alone."

Nick reluctantly stood near the Chevy, keeping a watchful eye on the exchange between Abby and the farmer. He couldn't follow everything the man was saying, but it was easy to pick up the warning in his tone and his refusal to take the bills offered him. "Exactly what's the problem, Abby?"

"None as yet," Abby replied cheerfully, smiling at the driver. "He says he's on his way to Mazatlan with his chickens. He's a bit on the crabby side and has offered to take us back the way we came—for a price."

"Maybe I should try to convince him to turn around." Nick suggested. "Use the man to man approach."

"With your broken Spanish?" Abby gasped. "We'd no doubt end up plowing his fields." She opened up her purse and extracted more money. "Just leave it to me."

"Very well," Nick invited expansively. He wandered around the area, rubbing the perspiration from his forehead. From what he could translate, the man wanted more pesos. *Mucho mucho pesos.*

"He now says that for a few thousand more pesos, he'll not only turn around, but he'll throw in the chickens as well."

"Tell him what he can do with his chickens," Nick urged, smiling charmingly at the man. "The way you did in that note you sent me at the Esquire Club."

"But I'm not trying to irritate him the way I was you, my love," Abby returned with a smirk.

The driver listened carefully to Abby for several minutes, then turned to scrutinize Nick. *"Sí, sí, señorita."*

"Then we're set?" Nick interpreted with hope.

"He's agreed to take us to San Rosa," Abby affirmed.

"We're riding up front, I hope," Nick said, casting a doubtful look in the direction of the chickens.

Abby's mouth dropped over the prospect of joining the Mexican's feathered friends.

"Frente," Nick said, pointing into the cab of the truck.

The driver looked at Abby and replied with a flat no.

"I suppose the sneaky old coot wants you up front by yourself," Nick concluded. Hands on hips, he eyed the driver suspiciously through the cracked windshield.

"Calm down," Abby advised, her smile never wavering. "Let me get to the bottom of it." She turned back to the cab to speak to the man again. To Nick's surprise, her tone grew lower and more anxious. Finally, the Mexican nodded and accepted Abby's money.

"All set," Abby announced with relief.

"It had better be enough," Nick growled.

"He's happy," Abby assured him, closing her purse. "I don't expect him to hold out for my Visa card number."

Nick couldn't help but wonder about all the hushed negotiating that had gone on at the end, but climbed up into the cab without question, pulling Abby onto his lap.

The driver made a clumsy U-turn on the narrow road and headed back in the direction of San Rosa.

"What are we going to do about Francisco's car?" Abby asked as they bounced along on the bumpy road. "If someone wants it badly enough, they'll tow it away."

"Don't worry, Shamus. I'll buy him a whole new car if I have to," Nick assured her.

"Hmm, you've never offered to buy me a new car," Abby complained.

"Curb your sassy ways and you might get lucky," he murmured in her ear.

"Thanks a lot."

The driver dodged potholes as they bounced along, and jabbered at them a mile a minute.

Abby could feel Nick's arm tighten around her waist. "It's nothing to be concerned about, Nick. Honestly."

The driver suddenly reached over, poked Nick in the arm, then gripped the steering wheel with a laugh.

Nick felt a rush of frustration over the language barrier. "Abby, I demand to know what this man is babbling about!"

"All right! All right!" Abby folded her arms across her chest, her face screwed up in disgust. "The pesos weren't enough. To get the ride I had to tell him that you're a famous racer."

"Racer," the driver repeated excitedly. "Veroom, veroom *amigo*." He pounded on the steering wheel, accidentally hitting the horn with a sharp honk.

Nick shook the squat hardened hand extended to him in friendship. "I'll be damned. Pleased to meet you." He looked from the driver to Abby's grim profile. "So what in the world happened between the two of you?"

"This farmer from the ends of the earth recognized your name and insisted that his 'veroom, veroom *amigo* sit up front there in the cab." Abby admitted.

"So?"

"He wanted me to sit in back with the chickens!"

Nick threw back his black curly head, his deep, rich laughter filling the cab.

"Are you satisfied?" Abby asked, stiffening on his lap.

"Take it easy," Nick murmured in her ear, tugging at the brim of her hat. "You know I'd never have thrown you to the chickens, even if I had to give him both our Visa card numbers."

It was late afternoon by the time the truck rolled into San Rosa.

"See if he knows anything about Alvarez," Nick instructed as he jiggled the loose door handle.

"Good thinking."

The driver responded with animated gestures, circling the truck to open the passenger door from the outside. As Abby and Nick stepped down out of the cab, he pointed down to the end of the street.

"What is he saying?" Nick asked.

"He says that Carlos Alvarez is a respected craftsman who makes fine jewelry," Abby replied. "He has a shop at the far end of the plaza."

"*Gracias,*" Nick said, slapping the man on the back.

With a laugh the Mexican tipped his hat, climbed back into his truck, and started back in the direction of Mazatlan.

"It sounds like we may have your jeweler," Nick said hopefully.

"Do you recall ever being in his shop?"

"No, I never did much shopping during my visits here. Just hung around the beach for the most part."

"Let's check it out," Abby said, slipping the handle of her purse over her shoulder.

"Watch for the pink minibus along the way," Nick added, linking his arm through hers.

As they joined the people walking along the cobblestoned street, Abby found herself being caught up in the charm of the rose-scented plaza. Palm trees swayed in the breeze along the well-kept thoroughfare, exuding an exotic, tropical atmosphere. Tourists and natives alike smiled pleasantly and appeared totally relaxed. "There is a certain kind of peace here that I didn't feel in Mazatlan," she murmured with fascination.

"Yes, life moves slower here in San Rosa," Nick agreed, scanning the street with a satisfied nod. "It has a sleepy small-town atmosphere. And the fact that it's surrounded by dense jungle gives you the feeling of isolation. It's an ideal spot for rest and meditation."

"A love nest," Abby blurted out in a burst of jealousy.

"Not for me," Nick disagreed, giving her a squeeze. "Not so far, anyway. I may have boogied down in Mazatlan, but the only person who ever accompanied me to San Rosa was Charlie. The harbor here is an excellent fishin' hole for a couple of Minnesota anglers."

"How's the leg?" Abby asked, as he absently rubbed his thigh.

"It hurts a bit," Nick admitted with a frown, pausing to flex his sore muscles in an effort to relieve the ache.

"We passed a café called the Three Frogs several yards back—"

"Let's see about our jeweler first. We've lost so much time already."

"All right." Abby cast him a reluctant look, but complied as he tugged at her arm.

"The church is the central structure here." Nick pointed to a quaint brown adobe structure surrounded by huts. "Religion means a lot to these people."

"I wonder if stealing goes against Señor Alvarez's religious beliefs," Abby speculated dryly.

"We'll soon have the chance to quiz him on the subject," Nick assured her.

"What's on that hill?" Abby asked, pointing to a white stone structure in the distance.

"That's the Hilltop Lighthouse," Nick supplied. "It's the tourist attraction that the Barones took the Cupid Connection crowd to yesterday."

"It looks ancient."

"San Rosa was a busy port in colonial days. In its heyday that lighthouse guided many a sailor."

"I'd love to see it sometime."

"Candace mentioned that it's closed for repairs. Someday, when my leg improves and we're not tracking crooks, we'll take a hike up there."

They continued on through the plaza, passing small touristy shops offering clothing, jewelry and a wide assortment of craft items for sale.

"Here's the place, Nick," Abby said, stopping in front of a large building, second in size only to the church. The storefront was colorful and rustic, as all the neighboring structures were, but Abby noted that the side of the building was of relatively new brick construction.

A bell jingled as they opened the door of the jewelry shop. A quick inventory of the room told Abby that this store wasn't as exclusive as Richters back in the States. There were shelves and shelves of souvenirs—everything from seashells to lizardskin belts. The decor exuded a touristy atmosphere. The ceiling was low and lined with rough wooden beams. The walls were a creamy cracked stucco. Merchandise was displayed on wooden counters and shelves—stacked, squeezed and jammed together.

Abby moved around the shop, searching for jewelry among the huge assortment of novelties. She eventually found some trays of colored glass arranged along a counter spanning the back of the room. One of the trays was literally overflowing with brooches.

"Nick, I've hit the jackpot!" Her exclamation brought not only Nick, but a heavyset woman from somewhere in the back of the store. Her bulky frame now filled the curtained doorway behind the counter.

"*¡Buenas tardes!*" the woman greeted, pulling the elastic neckline of her ruffled blouse up over her plump shoulders.

"Buenas tardes," Nick responded with a friendly smile. "Is the owner here?"

"No English," she replied, phrasing her syllables carefully, smoothing some salt-and-pepper strands of hair back from her face.

"Proprietario," Abby put in. "Carlos Alvarez."

"Espere un minuto," she answered, disappearing between the curtains.

Moments later a short, stocky man in a twill apron drew back the curtains. His round face was pleasant, the smile beneath his bushy gray moustache unassuming.

"Carlos Alvarez?" Nick swiftly asked.

"Si. ¿Permitame que le ayude?"

"We hope you can help us," Abby said hopefully. She reached into her purse and handed Alvarez one of the brooches she'd bought from Pablo.

Nick was prepared to detain the jeweler if he tried to get away, but the man merely shrugged and continued to speak in quiet calm phrases.

"He says that he's made many copies of this particular brooch," Abby translated, as the man pointed to the tray of green stones. "He wonders if we wish to buy more."

"He isn't exactly cringing with guilt is he?" Nick uttered in confusion.

"No," Abby agreed. "And I don't think we'd get any straight answers by hurling accusations at him."

"Tell him we're interested in the original," Nick directed.

Abby complied, raising a russet eyebrow over his answer. "He says that the owner would have no wish to sell. That the piece has sentimental value."

"There must be some kind of mistake!" Nick protested, gazing at the jeweler. *"Equivocacion."*

"Sentimiento," Carlos insisted. "Carlos."

"Cupid Connection," Nick tossed back to test his reaction.

The jeweler's head bobbed. "*¡Si! ¡Si!* Good job. *Mucho money.*"

"Now we're getting somewhere," Abby said, her excitement growing.

"I wonder who he works for," Nick pondered. "What's the Spanish word for head man? *¿Jefe?*"

Abby tried to phrase the question properly, but got nowhere. "He insists that he's self-employed."

"Hold on a minute. I believe I have a way to get through to him." Nick fished into his pants pocket for the copy of the pocket watch that Charlie had given him.

"You have that with you?" With open delight Abby eyed the silver timepiece resting in his palm.

"Sure. It's a fake, but it keeps perfect time." Nick set the watch beside the brooch on the counter. "*Reloj. Padre.*"

"Carlos!" Carlos Alvarez exclaimed. "*¡Padre!*" Carlos circled the counter and enveloped Nick in a huge hug. "Carlos! Carlos!"

"Abby, why is he saying his own name?" Puzzled, Nick looked over the stout man's shoulder.

Abby burst into gales of laughter, triggering the same measure of merriment from the others. "Don't you see, Nick?"

"No!"

"As you know, *padre* means father. Well, Carlos means Charles," she added significantly.

The answer hit Nick squarely in the gut. "He knows Dad."

"And likes him, too," Abby added with a smirk.

"Welcome," Carlos said jovially, patting Nick on the back.

"IT DOESN'T MAKE a damn bit of sense!" Nick pounded his fist on the wooden table in the Three Frogs and lifted a beer can to his lips. After a long talk with Carlos and Maria Alvarez, they'd left the shop and headed for the café down the street. It was a cheerful place with orange tablecloths, brick arches, and lively Spanish music flowing from a large square radio. There were tourists and farmers occupying the tables around them, laughing and chattering over their food.

Abby drained the second beer she'd had in the last ten minutes and shook her head in response to Nick's confusion. She hadn't realized how hungry, thirsty, and tired she was until she felt the dark local beer trickle down her parched throat. It felt wonderful to relax in the dim mellow café.

"I can't figure it out, either," Abby admitted with frustration. "But some things are clearer than others."

"Our parents' heavy hand in this is fairly easy to decipher," Nick muttered. "They set us up like a couple of lovesick high school kids. They hired Carlos Alvarez to make phony copies of the jewelry, then sent us here on this merry chase."

"Why, even that stakeout on the first day was choreographed down to the last detail."

"Yeah, the old coot figured that with my interest in cars, I'd swiftly take an interest in your heap out in the street."

"And my mother figured that I'd never be able to resist a puzzling case."

They paused while their waitress set a basket of rolls and steaming plates of food before them.

"Everything smells wonderful," Abby said, inhaling appreciatively. "It was probably smart to order the specialty of the house."

"Though I believe any food would look wonderful to us at this point, I have found that the simple dishes prepared in small places like this are often as tasty as the fancy cuisine you get in a hotel," Nick explained, immediately lifting his fork to spear a sample. "This is *chilaquiles*," he said swallowing. "A casserole made from tortillas, chicken, cheeses and chilies."

"And tomatoes," Abby noted hungrily.

Nick broke open a roll and pushed a piece into Abby's mouth. "These are called *boililos*. Mmm . . . Fresh."

They ate in companionable silence for a while.

"You know, I'm totally convinced that Blanche and Charlie engineered our fantasy fling, but I can't believe they'd put us in danger." With a contemplative look he picked up the slice of lime from the edge of his plate and squeezed it over his beer can, then added a sprinkle of salt as the locals were doing around him.

"Except for the snapped line and the gun, Blanche's little thumbprints are all over this caper," Abby agreed. "Mother's not heavily into realism. She prefers to drift along on cloud nine."

ABBY AND NICK LINGERED in the café for a while longer, enjoying the dark beer as well as the sweets the waitress insisted they sample. Conversation turned away from cloak-and-dagger details to intimate murmurs of contentment. There was little more they could do until they talked to Blanche and Charlie. And that would have to wait until morning.

By the time they emerged from the café, dusk was hovering on the horizon in streaks of gray and deep purple.

"Where to now?" Abby asked, hooking her finger into one of Nick's belt loops.

"Let's stop in a shop for some toiletries, and a razor for me!" he added, rubbing a hand across his rapidly developing beard.

"And then?"

"We'll spend the night in my favorite hotel along the beach. If we hurry, we can watch the sun set over the ocean."

"How far away is the water?"

"About a mile. Let's catch a taxi. We'll be there in no time."

The sun was just beginning to dip below the horizon, turning the sea a rich molten gold, when Abby and Nick wandered out onto the back terrace of the Twin Palms Hotel. Nick gave Abby a boost up onto the stout stone wall overlooking the sand, then hopped up beside her.

"What a majestic sight," Abby remarked in awe. "I never watch the sunset at home. To me, usually it's just a signal that the evening is on the way."

"We'll have to remedy that bad habit," Nick whispered, his lips nuzzling her hair.

"Oh?" Abby's heart picked up tempo as Nick's lips pressed against the hollow of her throat.

"Mm-hm. As your new partner, I intend to be on hand to supervise all the fringe benefits offered at Wildcat Investigations. Sunsets, extended lunch hours, paid holidays, and lots of tag team stakeouts."

"You sound so—so permanent!"

"You are a crackerjack detective, aren't you," Nick chuckled. "Whew, what a business we'll share."

"You really want in?" Abby searched his face intently, absorbing the gravity of his words.

"I want in." Nick's words held a double-edged meaning, Abby realized, reading a combination of desire and commitment in his tender, shimmering eyes. "All the way. For always."

THE TWIN PALMS WAS extraordinarily simple compared with the Hotel Fiesta, but it was clean and comfortable. Their room was small with rough, whitewashed walls, two overstuffed chairs, and an ancient creaky bed with a marshmallow-soft mattress.

"So this is the place where you usually stay." Abby threw her yellow hat on a chair and wandered around the room.

"Yeah, you like it?" Nick sat down on the edge of the bed and kicked off his shoes.

"It's quaint," Abby replied with a grin. "I guess I expected it to have more creature comforts."

"It has a john," Nick tossed back with amusement.

"As every celebrity haven should," Abby returned dryly.

"If it had everything, it wouldn't be a hideaway anymore." Nick stood, unbuckled his belt and dropped his khaki slacks unceremoniously. Though the gesture was obviously not intended as an act of seduction, the sight of him in scanty black underwear set her aflame. "Put in television and whirlpool tubs, and everybody would come down here," he continued, peeling off his royal-blue polo shirt. "Pretty soon you'd have another Hotel Fiesta full of *Cupid Connection-ites* slinging arrows at each other."

"You would, huh?" Abby said in a sultry, faraway voice.

Nick set his clothing on one of the worn chairs. "Yes, you—" He cut himself short when he turned to discover Abby wearing a most wanton expression, her green eyes openingly combing the length of his tanned, muscular body.

"Aren't we the busy fella," she murmured. The full skirt of her floral sundress swished with the sway of her hips as she shortened the distance between them on the scuffed green tile floor. "Preparing yourself for me."

Any weariness that Nick might have felt dissipated the moment Abby's fingers touched his chest, forging through his dense bed of coarse hair, rubbing his nipples until they tingled. Her mouth followed her fingers, nipping the brown circles rapidly into erectness.

Nick's hands moved across the exposed skin of Abby's back until he found the zipper of her dress. The scratching noise it made as he drew it down bounced off the rough walls of the tiny silent room, heightening his anticipation. The dress fell in a frothy heap at her feet, leaving Abby in lace panties and leather flats.

"Leather and lace," Nick uttered against her ear, running his hand over the satiny skin of her back, over the curve of her bottom. Abby melted into him as Nick dropped to his knees to move his half-roughened face over her creamy skin.

He glided and explored at his leisure, leaving a trail of pink burning skin behind. Eventually he stripped her of her sandals and panties, stood up, and scooped her into his arms.

"Where to?" Abby asked, tipping her head back with a startled laugh.

In answer Nick dropped her on the bed. She landed in a heap on a mattress that was so soft, it seemed to swallow her whole.

"You may lose me to this marshmallow trap," Abby cried.

"I'm right behind you." With a husky moan he climbed over her, pressing her even deeper into the bed. He shuddered slightly, his body suddenly tautening.

"What's the matter?" Abby gingerly eased out from under him, discovering that his face was etched with pain. His eyes shimmered with need, but the lines around them were creased with stress.

"Don't move another inch!" Nick hooked an arm around her waist to still her. "It'll be okay. . . Give me a minute."

"It's your leg," she realized immediately with a wave of guilt and concern. "You never should've lifted me. You never should've—"

Nick curtailed her protests with a hard thorough kiss. "Hush, woman. I'm not dead. I'm just going through a period of adjustment." With that he dropped back onto a pillow and squeezed his eyes shut.

"I'll help." Abby crawled toward the foot of the bed and began to run her hands along the length of his hard, corded leg.

Nick groaned in pleasure and pain as Abby's strong fingers glided along his hair-dusted skin, cleverly kneading his stiff muscles. She paused at the sound of his voice. "Don't stop, sweetheart. I'm not complaining."

"But I'm hurting you."

"Often the purest levels of pleasure lie just beyond a barrier of pain," Nick philosophized with a coaxing growl.

"Dwelling on our relationship again, are you?" Abby teased, resuming the motion of her fingers.

"If my theory holds up, we should be acing a lifetime partnership agreement any time now. Oh! Ah . . ."

"Just relax and enjoy," Abby tempted.

Nick's head moved on the pillow in a short nod. "You're the therapist." The shooting daggers of discomfort melted away as the steady pressure of Abby's fingertips rotated across his leg.

"Better, darling?" Abby asked, her voice striking an odd, off-key note to Nick's ears.

"You're an angel," he mumbled from his cocoon of contentment. Never had such a loving hand relieved his misery. Hospital therapy and swimming would never seem quite as beneficial again. "You're an angel," he repeated softly. "A naughty angel!" he added suddenly in a hoarse growl.

Seeing that Nick was in a far better state of mind, Abby's firm touch on his leg had changed pressure and direction. Feather light fingertips had taken a right turn at the center of his inner thigh and were now climbing up and down the tender sensitive skin of both his legs. Nick's nerve endings came to abrupt attention, his breathing grew shallow with anticipation as he followed the course of her journey. Her fingernails skimmed along his thighs like confident skaters on thin ice, deftly edging under his navy briefs. She hooked the fabric, and then with a steady pull, tugged the underwear off him.

He was hers. Abby could feel the power as she straddled him, pinning him between her silky soft legs. She leaned over to flick her tongue in his navel and close her hand over his arousal.

Nick found himself lost in ecstasy as Abby loved him with moist kisses and fevered stroking. When he realized he was about to lose control, he gripped her forearm suddenly, then effortlessly hoisted her over him. Holding her poised in the air he kissed her throat and breasts, urging her nipples to firm peaks in his mouth.

"Nick . . ." His name became an adoring pant on her lips as he drove her to the quivering brink. With a swift thrust she suddenly bore down on him, taking him deeply inside her.

"Abby! Abby. . ." This woman always managed to catch him off guard, to amaze and delight him. Nick arched his back to meet her, desire charging through his system like liquid lightning. She began to move on his hips, picking up a hot plunging rhythm. Nick anxiously matched the pace. He gripped her hips with helping hands, greedily soaring to new, yet unexplored planes of pleasure. He savored it all, every moan of encouragement from Abby's throat, the way she clung to his back with grasping fingernails.

She gasped as sweet sensations overtook her. She pressed on and on, addicted to the exhilarating flight of frenzy. Heat seared within them till they finally found their sweet release.

Abby trembled and collapsed on Nick's chest, burying her face in his hair-roughened skin. His hand raked through her tumbled mane of hair. His lips pressed against her temples.

"You give new meaning to the word partner, Partner," Abby murmured thickly.

Nick sought her mouth and consumed it with the last ragged ounce of energy he possessed. He'd been waiting a long time to be addressed with that one magical name. She'd called him many things, but "partner" was a first.

10

A SERIES OF SHARP RAPID KNOCKS on the door awoke Abby and Nick the following morning.

"I wonder who it is," Abby mumbled groggily, scanning the room for her sundress. Unfortunately it was still in a heap on the floor where she'd left it the night before.

Nick swiftly yanked on his tan pants. "It sounds like a damn woodpecker." With a noise between a grunt and a yawn, his bare feet hit the linoleum floor with a slap. "Ready?" he asked, pausing to buckle his belt.

Abby pulled the floral dress over her head and smoothed it the best she could. "I guess so."

Nick crossed the room with Abby on his heels. "What annoying so-and-so would want to knock so relentlessly?" Nick wondered, turning the lock and throwing back the chain.

Abby shrugged. "Who indeed?"

Nick swung open the door with a flourish, prepared for whatever menace might be on the other side.

"Oh, Mother!"

"Oh, Father!"

"Oh, children!" Blanche gushed beside a beaming Charlie Farrell. "You managed to make a Cupid Connection despite it all."

"Don't get teary-eyed, honey," Charlie said, his pale blue eyes gazing at Blanche with tenderness.

"But I've finally straightened out Abigal's life!" Blanche sniffed, drawing a tissue from her purse. "Haven't I, Abigal?" Blanche's mischievous gaze passed from Abby to lie significantly on Nick's bare-chested form. "I've hooked you a hunk and we don't have any difficult in-laws to deal with. There's only Charlie!"

"Please come in, Mother," Abby invited in a deceptively quiet voice. She grasped at the silky bow of her mother's white blouse. "We want to thank you properly."

"Now, Abigal, easy on the bow," Blanche cautioned, as Abby led her into the room by the collar.

"You too, Dad." Nick clapped a heavy hand on his father's back, guiding the smaller man inside.

"We checked into the Fiesta first, hoping to find you there," Charlie explained. "Francisco told us that you'd set out for San Rosa in his Chevy yesterday. He was quite concerned. Said he found his car along the road with a flat tire last night on his way home from work."

"Yeah, we owe him a new tire," Nick muttered, securely closing the door.

"I remembered that this hotel is one of your favorites, so here we are," Charlie explained, shaking his silver-haired head.

Blanche disengaged Abby's fingers from her blouse and took a deep breath. "You won't believe our story, children. Not in a million years."

"Oh, I don't know, Mother," Abby protested dryly, folding her arms across her chest. "I try to keep an open mind where you're concerned."

"Hold it," Nick interrupted, thrusting a finger in the direction of the lumpy brown couch near the window. "Blanche. Charlie. Sit."

"But Nick," Charlie objected, raising his hands in the air.

"We have some things that need to be cleared up immediately," Nick insisted. "You owe us some answers."

Blanche and Charlie exchanged a look of frustration and sat down together on the old couch.

"Go ahead," Blanche invited loftily. "Chew us out for tricking you. Holler at us for making you the happiest couple south of the border."

"The second happiest couple south of the border," Charlie corrected, squeezing Blanche's knee below the hem of her red culotte skirt.

"Oh, Charlie, you big tease," she laughed.

"Fun and games!" Abby scolded. "You two never stop, do you?"

"If you'd only listen to us for a minute," Blanche begged.

"You'll get your chance," Nick assured her, pulling his royal-blue polo shirt over his head.

"You sent us down here on this merry chase," Abby scolded. "And don't try to shade the facts with excuses. Carlos Alvarez told us that you ordered the duplicate watch and brooch personally—as a joke!"

Charlie nodded. "We saw a daughter and a son who had no fun left in their lives."

"We felt you needed a relaxing vacation," Blanche chimed in.

"Why didn't you simply pass out airline tickets?" Abby asked.

"Abigal, you know darn well you'd never have agreed to another one of my brilliant matchmaking schemes. I knew the only way to bring you around was to bait you with a crime-in-progress, give you a juicy mystery to sink your teeth into."

"What about me?" Nick demanded, pacing the room. "Why draw me into an elaborate charade?"

Charlie fished a cigar and lighter out of the pocket of his bold Hawaiian print shirt. "You were turning into one hell of a dud, lad. You were limping around the house, choking on my smoke, dreaming about dying all the time. It seemed high time for a diversion." He set the cigar between his teeth and lit it. "A diversion that would blot out all your personal struggles."

Nick met Abby's flashing green eyes with a look of confusion. "Well, I have to admit I haven't had a dream since my first night in Mexico."

"See, we were right!" Charlie gloated, twin streams of smoke flowing from his nostrils.

"Another Cupid Connection in the family," Blanche said blithely, homing in on the rumpled sheets.

"How did you manage it all?" Abby asked, lifting a russet eyebrow wonderingly.

"Well, let me tell you, Abigal, you certainly didn't make things easy," Blanche complained, wrinkling her turned up nose. "We expected you to leap into action, take Mazatlan by storm. Instead, you let all of your inhibitions concerning the death of Roy Stark hold you up. According to Donna, you avoided Nick like the plague, fearing for his safety."

"According to Donna?" Abby repeated. "She was in on your scheme?"

"Yes, and don't you dare chastise her for being disloyal. She loves you as much as I do."

"Another meddler!" Abby moaned, leaning against Nick's shoulder. "A meddler who loves me!"

"Steady, Shamus," he whispered, kissing her forehead. "We can handle this pair of dating service delinquents."

"Anyhow, when I couldn't get you to budge, I called in Verona Vickers to run that bracelet story by you—jump start you onto the trip."

"That was all an act?" Abby's mouth dropped open. "Of course it had to be if you invented the entire crime. No wonder I couldn't trap Francisco into revealing the identity of the crooked jeweler. He was totally in the dark. He couldn't even remember meeting Verona."

"Verona's never been to Mazatlan," Blanche explained. "She's afraid to fly."

"And I'm afraid that in all the hubbub, we neglected to call Francisco and warn him that we'd made him a suspect in a crime," Charlie tossed in, flicking ashes into the chipped ashtray on the small table beside him.

"We decided to keep nearly everyone in the dark about things so that they wouldn't act in an unusual way on the trip," Blanche added. "Abby, you are a shrewd judge of character, so I feared you'd see through a lot of amateur performances. George Merdel, Phillip and Candace Barone, none of them knew what was going on. We figured we'd give you a few days of adventure and pop in and tell all of you the truth."

Charlie nodded. "Now you can see why we insisted you not call in the police. There really was no crime committed, so we didn't want anyone to land in the pokey by mistake."

"At least we thought there was no crime committed," Blanche lamented, a fiery show of temper surfacing on her face in a pink flush.

Abby looked at Nick with trepidation. "What do you mean, Mother?"

"I mean that our heirlooms are really missing!" Blanche cried indignantly.

"It's true," Charlie affirmed. "Sometime during our final stay here in Mexico, the brooch and pocket watch were actually switched."

"We were so occupied with obtaining the copies, that we paid little mind to the genuine articles." Blanche rolled her eyes with regret. "Except for the short time Carlos Alvarez had them, Charlie kept them in a velvet pouch in the hotel safe."

"For how long did he have them?" Abby asked.

"For only an afternoon," Charlie recalled thoughtfully. "We came down to San Rosa with the Cupid Connection group on one of the minibuses. While we explored the town, Carlos took measurements and pictures. Folks on the bus knew we were obtaining the copies, but they didn't know why."

Abby's green eyes hardened in thought.

"Abigal, I want you to understand that Carlos Alvarez is completely innocent," Blanche warned. "When he returned the pouch to us, it contained the real thing. And we put the real thing back in the hotel safe that afternoon."

"All right, let's assume Carlos is innocent," Abby conceded. "The thief still had to get the copies from him. No one else had time to produce them and Carlos was making a quantity of them—even sending them out with peddlers!"

"It will be impossible to track down the person who bought copies for criminal purposes!" Nick muttered. "Half the people on the beach probably own copies of your jewelry."

"Oh, no they don't," Charlie disagreed with a shrewd glint in his eye. "Carlos may have made additional copies of the brooch, but he had no interest in mass-producing my watch. The timepiece was far too intricate to work with."

"All we have to do is question him about who ordered the extra watch," Blanche proclaimed, snapping her fingers. "Then we rock'em and sock'em!"

"Slow down, Blanche," Nick instructed firmly. "We're dealing with some very rough players."

"What do you mean, Nick?" Charlie demanded.

"For one thing, that flat tire on Francisco's car was no accident. Someone trying to deter us punctured it with a dart," Nick informed the pair. "It could've been fatal, had that old wreck crashed into the jungle."

"And someone tampered with my sailboard yesterday," Abby continued over their gasp of concern.

"It's all gone wrong!" Charlie thundered in a cloud of gray smoke.

"Our only motive was to see you together—and happy..." Blanche trailed off, gazing up at them apologetically.

"CUT LINES, dart gun blowouts," Blanche shook her bright red head over the rim of her coffee cup. "I'm astonished that our harmless little plan grew to such dangerous proportions."

With a meditative frown on her face, Abby poked her fork into the runny egg on her plate. The foursome had gathered for breakfast in the Twin Palms' small restaurant, but Abby found she had no appetite whatsoever. Nick had expressed the same feeling a short time ago, leaving his plate untouched and going back to their room for some rest. "Think back, Mother, Charlie. Did anyone have the chance to pull the switch?"

"We did retrieve the velvet pouch from the Fiesta's safe the night before we left for home," Charlie recalled. "I remember it clearly. We were at the reservations desk and the night manager turned the pouch over to us."

"Yes, and the Barones popped up behind us all of a sudden," Blanche added.

"Insisted we have a nightcap in the Fiesta's lounge with George Merdel," Charlie continued. "We tried to beg off, but they were so insistent."

"I put the pouch in my handbag right in front of them."

"And . . ." Abby prodded anxiously.

"And we tied one on." Charlie admitted with a grin.

"I still don't understand it," Blanche insisted with a self-righteous lift of her chin. "We each had two margaritas and ended up on stage singing with the mariachi band." She pointed her finger to her head like a gun. "Bang! Instant humiliation. Acted like a couple of drunken fools."

"Someone doctored your drinks," Abby guessed.

"Most likely," Charlie agreed. "We were so zonked out, they could've stolen the socks off our feet without us knowing it."

"It never occurred to me at the time to examine the jewelry with care," Blanche admitted. "We were in a hurry to get to the airport the following morning. I peeked inside and saw a watch and a brooch. I packed the pouch in my carrying tote and the rest is history."

Nick returned moments later, taking his place at the table.

"Feeling better?" Abby asked, thinking that Nick looked just as drawn as when he'd left them earlier.

Nick shrugged and pushed aside his plate of cold food. "I won't feel better until this matter is cleared up."

"Remember, Nick," Charlie said, jabbing a finger across the table. "We've agreed to question Carlos about any copies he made of the jewelry, but it must be done without a hint of accusation, we became fast friends a few years ago when you and I began fishing down here. I trust him completely and don't want to offend him."

"We still don't want the cops informed," Blanche added.

"They would give Carlos a hard time, treat him like a suspect." Charlie's face narrowed over the prospect.

"There's no sense in involving the police yet." Abby gave Charlie's hand a consoling pat. "We still have no proof of anything. When the time is right, we'll notify the proper authorities. Right, Partner?" Abby added, winking at Nick.

Nick responded with a shrug, not acknowledging Abby's attempt at levity. The entire episode totally frustrated him. What he'd thought was going to be a joyous battle of the sexes had turned so completely sour that he could taste the bitterness in his mouth.

"I'll pull our rental car up to the entrance," Charlie announced, rising from his chair. "Carlos should be open for business by now."

"Yes," Blanche agreed, popping up enthusiastically. "He'll give us the proof we need to make any charges stick."

Nick tossed some money on the table to cover the meal. "Will you settle up the hotel bill, Shamus? I don't have enough cash left."

"Shamus?" Blanche repeated with undisguised amazement as Nick followed his father out of the restaurant. "And you called him *partner*. Things must be pretty cozy."

"You were right about this match, Mother," Abby replied, her heart-shaped face beaming with pleasure. "Nick and I are meant for each other. We've grown to trust each other completely. So completely that we're going to team up, make Wildcat Investigations a joint effort."

Blanche squeezed her daughter's hand, beaming with pleasure. "Good news like this will make losing the jewelry tolerable."

"Don't even think negative," Abby chastised with a grin. "It's not over yet. Not by a long shot."

"BUT WE DON'T WANT to go back to the Fiesta!" Blanche twisted around in the front seat of Charlie's rented Buick to confront Abby with a ferocious glare. "Carlos will set us straight and we'll all go for it!"

"No, Mother," Abby repeated firmly.

"But who knows what Carlos will tell us!"

Abby broke contact with Blanche's stubborn green eyes in favor of the tropical splendor outside her window. The huge colorful flowers growing amongst the lush greenery were breathtaking yet fragile, reminding Abby of her mother. Abby could understand Blanche's eagerness to get involved, but she herself was only human. Abby had already taken on one partner and that was her limit!

"What if Carlos wants Charlie and me to handle things?" Blanche pursued. "What if he won't talk to you?"

Abby shrugged evasively and gave the purse on her lap a light pat. The note in her purse was her guarantee that Carlos was more than anxious to deal with her. When she'd paid the hotel bill, the clerk had handed her a message from the jeweler. The English was rather rough, but his message came through loud and clear. The moment Blanche and Charlie were safely on their way back to Mazatlan, she intended to share its contents with Nick.

"Mother, no matter what happens at Carlos Alvarez's shop, I want you and Charlie to let us handle things from here on in. Right Nick?"

"No matter what happens," Nick repeated flatly, immersed in thoughts of his own.

"Humph." Simmering with frustration, Blanche turned to Charlie in the driver's seat. "Well, Charlie?"

"Let's give Abby space to do her job."

"Oh, who asked you!" Blanche exploded, throwing her hands in the air.

"I think we've interfered enough," Charlie stated clearly. He guided the car off the narrow winding coastal road and into the plaza. The cobblestone street was already alive with activity. Tourists roamed the walkways with cameras and suitcases. Mexican mothers emerged from various storefronts with squealing toddlers clinging to their skirts.

Charlie turned onto a side street a short distance from the shop and halted the car.

"Now, why on earth didn't you just pull up in front of the shop?" Blanche inquired anxiously. "We're in a hurry!"

"There was another vehicle parked in there," Charlie explained, unbuckling his seat belt.

"He has company?" Blanche demanded.

"A pink minibus?" Abby wondered.

"A police car," Nick supplied. He sat up straight and faced the three sets of hard eyes suddenly trained upon him. "I'm guilty, I wasn't resting at all during breakfast. I was at the reservations desk calling the Mazatlan police. They promised to dispatch a car to the shop immediately."

Bursts of shock and anger greeted Nick's announcement.

"You had no right!" Blanche yelled, shaking a red-tipped finger at him.

"I had every right," Nick shot back, on the verge of exploding. "Your cloak-and-dagger game nearly got us killed!"

"But we didn't mean any harm," Blanche objected. "I wouldn't put my own daughter in danger."

"Not purposely," Nick conceded. "But it's happened and we have to take precautionary measures."

"But Carlos is right in the middle of this mess and he doesn't deserve to be," Charlie ground out, slamming his hand on the dashboard. "He'll have a hell of a time clearing himself with the cops."

"We'll clear him, Dad," Nick assured him, forcing himself to rein his anger.

"The authorities down here don't give a man a lot of slack," Charlie said grimly. "At the very least they'll close up his shop and drag him in for questioning."

"Abby. . ." Nick turned to the woman at his side for support.

"I thought we were going to discuss all our moves before making them," she sputtered. Feelings of utter betrayal welled up inside her, fueling her anger. "You're the one who has pushed so hard for mutual trust—right from the start!"

"Abby, the stakes are so high now—"

"You betrayed me, after all the promises we made!" Abby pushed aside the hand Nick set on her shoulder. "A fifty-fifty partnership is what you wanted, remember? You couldn't keep the agreement for twenty-four hours—much less a lifetime! You tell me, Nick, which of us is guilty of wanting to control everything?"

Nick looked into her burning green eyes and realized he'd pushed Abby over the edge. "I'm trying to protect you from harm, Abby. Can't you accept that?"

"Go to hell."

"I think you're underestimating the police," Nick said stubbornly.

Charlie intervened with a grunt. "What's done is done. We're accomplishing nothing by sitting here and bickering."

And they would accomplish nothing at the shop, Abby knew with a rush of satisfaction. "Go on without me," Abby said, jerking open the car door. "I'm bailing out!"

"Hold on." Nick's arm coiled around the waistline of her wrinkled sundress.

Abby jerked free, the handle of her purse slipping off her arm unnoticed.

Nick made a move to follow her, but Blanche put a restraining arm over the seat of the car.

"Let her work off her anger alone," she advised with a sage nod.

Nick leaned over and picked up her bulky leather handbag from the floor of the car. "But she doesn't have anything without this," he protested, holding up the heavy purse. "Not as much as a peso."

"She doesn't need anything to storm through the plaza." Blanche pointed beyond the windshield at her daughter, marching along the cobblestones with the ocean breezes lifting her russet hair and billowing the floral skirt of her dress. "She'll simmer down and join us in the shop. She has nowhere else to go."

"Blanche knows best, son." Charlie put in. "After all, no one's been a thorn under Abby's collar more often than she has."

Blanche wrinkled her nose. "You always seem to agree with me, Charlie, but somehow...you get the better of me as well."

Charlie chuckled. "No mystery why we're the perfect match."

"CARLOS! BLANCHE!" Maria Alvarez rushed out from behind the back counter of the shop the moment the threesome walked in the door. Nick stood in the background as the sturdy woman enveloped Blanche in a hug and launched into an emotional outburst in Spanish. A Mexican policeman leaned against the wall near one of the counters, watching the scene intently.

"You are Señor Farrell?" he asked, moving toward Nick.

"Yes. I called you about a theft."

"Very strange circumstances." The policeman stroked his narrow chin. "A theft. And a disappearance."

Blanche nodded at Nick. "Carlos is gone, Nick. Maria says he left for the shop at the regular time this morning, but apparently never opened for business. Maria arrived several minutes ago to find the door still locked and the policeman waiting outside!"

Mayhem unfolded before Nick's eyes during the next ten minutes. Maria, Blanche, and Charlie chattered in high-pitched unison at the policeman, leaving him with little insight into the problem. When they were forced to take a breath, Nick took the opportunity to suggest that Charlie and Blanche accompany the policeman to Mazatlan to file a stolen property report. They agreed, on the condition that Carlos be listed as a missing person.

"Don't worry about a thing, Dad." Nick felt a huge weight lift off his shoulders as Charlie handed him the keys to the rental car and climbed into the policeman's vehicle with Blanche. Knowing that the parents would be safe and sound back at the Fiesta was a great relief.

"Explain things to Abby," Blanche said, poking her head out the open window. "Tell her we hated to leave you two on your own. Tell her we're sure she can come up with some answers once she cools off."

Nick watched the dusty car roar off through the plaza. He would tell her those things and more. But first he had to find her.

A thorough search of the plaza left Nick standing alone and confused in the center of the cobblestone street. He'd gone into each and every store, questioning anyone who knew a syllable of English. No one recalled having seen her. And no one knew as well as he how memorable Abby was! She couldn't have left town, not without collecting her purse!

After some deliberation Nick decided to return to Charlie's rental car. It made a lot of sense: Abby would eventually return for her purse and Nick could stretch his leg out on the back seat in the meantime.

A bright sun was beginning to heat the plaza as Nick inserted a key in the Buick's lock. Because the interior of the car was already growing stuffy and stale, Nick opened all the car's windows. For all he knew, he might have a long vigil ahead, considering that Abby had left in a very unforgiving mood.

Nick climbed into the back seat, propping his right leg across the plush upholstery. His muscles were already stiffening from his walk around town. Add to that the soft mattress he'd shared with Abby at the Twin Palms and his lack of physical therapy, and he was asking for a wheelchair.

Abby's purse was still there on the floor, he noted. He took the heavy bag into his hands, wondering if she carried any aspirin along with her many belongings. He unzipped the center pocket and found an assortment of female items jammed inside. A person would have to dump the works out to find anything, he thought with a dissatisfied grunt. He dipped into the jumble with his index finger, hoping to jab a bottle. The yellow slip of paper wrapped around a stick of gum would've eluded his scrutiny had he not noticed the double palm letterhead printed in the corner of it.

"The Twin Palms," he uttered under his breath. "What the . . ." He swiftly unfolded the small sheet, wondering who could've left Abby a message at the hotel. The message was brief and addressed to both of them. Come to lighthouse. *Urgente.* Carlos.

So that's where she had so eagerly charged off to! Nick eased out of the car and, shielding his eyes form the sun with his hand, gazed up at the Hilltop Lighthouse off in the distance. Was she at the top yet? Was she all right? Normally a stream of tourists would be combing the steep dirt path leading to the historical attraction, but Candace had mentioned that the lighthouse was closed for repairs.

It was the perfect spot for an isolated meeting. Or an isolated assault.

Apprehension climbed Nick's spine with the touch of a stealthy spider, causing him to shiver involuntarily. There wasn't a moment to lose. Nick opened and slammed car doors, turned the ignition, and roared off toward San Rosa's historical monument.

Gravel sprayed behind the rear wheels of the Buick as Nick sped into the parking lot at the foot of Lighthouse Hill. The lot was deserted, Nick noted as he locked the doors of the rental car. But it was evident from tracks in the lot that another vehicle had entered the lot with spinning tires. And oddly enough, the tracks didn't swing into a loop to leave again. The deep grooves headed right into some dense bushes across the lot. It appeared that the vehicle had stopped dead on the edge of the gravel and disappeared. Nick crossed the lot and pulled aside some of the tangled leafy branches. He was confronted with a wall of pink.

He'd found the hotel minibus.

11

THE WALK DOWN THE RUTTED ROAD and the scramble up the hill to the lighthouse left Abby breathless and quite disheveled. She stood on the windblown bank overlooking the ocean and inhaled a dose of salty air in an effort to steady herself. It was a sheer drop to the water on that side of the hill, a long, long way down. The ocean was crashing into the rocky cove below, its roaring rhythm echoing up the incline, scattering in the sky.

Abby instinctively stepped back a foot or two, not trusting her rubbery legs or her rattled nerves. She had a right to feel a little dizzy and confused, she consoled herself, massaging her temples. And it wasn't simply the altitude! The last confrontation with Nick over his decision to call in the police had made her feel like a coiled wire crackling with ten thousand volts of electricity.

The man couldn't be trusted. Give him an inch and he took a foot—a leg, an arm, of her precious business! He had a lot to learn about partnership. There was no doubt in her mind that Nick believed man and woman were created equal. He'd shown her time after time in bed. But the business end of their relationship was another story altogether! He thought nothing of pinning a tin star on his shirt and proclaiming himself Sherlock Holmes's smarter brother. How could she love such an arrogant rake so deeply?

From a loving point of view, however, their fight couldn't have come at a better time. Nick was in no condition to climb the hill she'd just conquered. It had been rough in the best of conditions. It was best for all concerned that she check out this lead alone.

Abby glanced down to discover that the trip hadn't left her in the best condition. Her sundress was stained and torn and her hair a snarled mess. She pulled a hand through her russet mane, stopping short with a squeal when she snagged a broken twig. She carefully untangled the twig and tossed it aside, thinking how handy her purse would be right now.

Her purse! She'd left the purse in the rental car. And the note from Carlos was inside! How could she have been so careless?

Abby circled the lighthouse and gazed down the steep path for any sign of Nick. Nothing yet. If Carlos was inside, she was prepared to confront him.

The entrance to the lighthouse was roped off, with no trespassing warnings in several languages posted everywhere. According to other signs, the wooden stairs were rotting and were to be repaired within the weeks to come.

Abby slipped under the ropes and tried to open the heavy oak door to the lighthouse. The brass knob turned easily in her hand. With a rusty creak, the door swung wide open.

The only light in the tower was filtered sunshine streaming through high dusty windows. Abby stood on the wooden floor, charmed by the quaint, homey atmosphere of another era. The lighthouse had been well tended to preserve its colonial atmosphere. There were two rooms on the first level on either side of a spiral staircase. A kitchen was on the right with a black wood-burning stove, a baby's high chair, and a dinner table with only one chair. A small study with a painted desk, bookcase, and rocking chair was to the left. Both rooms were partitioned off with a waist-high fence to discourage hands-on tourists from entering.

"Señor Alvarez? Carlos?"

Abby started up the winding wooden staircase, stepping gingerly on the white wooden planks. They squeaked under pressure, making Abby flinch. She paused midway, suppressing the urge to call out again. If Carlos was as innocent as Blanche and Charlie professed, why wasn't he answering her? And why set up a meeting in such an isolated location? His shop would've been far more convenient.

She was a fool! She'd been so set on getting the jump on Nick that she hadn't clearly weighed the meaning of the note. Her pride and bullheadedness may very well have landed her in a very dangerous predicament.

She rested her hand on the cold rail to steady herself. A chill passed from the steel in her hand through her system, making her body shiver. The fine hairs on the nape of her neck rose to attention as well. Now she could actually smell the danger in the musty darkness of the tower.

She stood immobile as she assessed the situation. She could proceed or she could retreat. If only she had a weapon, if only...

"Welcome, Ms Walters. Or should I say Ms Shay?"

Too late. Abby looked up to find Candace Barone's smug face gazing down at her from the next landing, the dart gun in her hand.

"So you're the marksman." Abby said in the level voice she used on those occasions when she found herself on the barrel side of a weapon. Keep them talking. Keep them calm. Two rules Abby never broke while facing a gunman.

"Target shooting is a hobby that I've been putting to very good use of late. Don't think of running," she added, second-guessing Abby with a shrewd grin. "I can nail a bull's eye at fifty feet."

Abby was tempted to bolt, but after reconsidering the odds of a successful escape, she climbed the final twist of stairs. There were two bedrooms on the second level. Candace waved the gun in the direction of the nursery. "Climb over the fencing."

Abby obeyed, clumsily raising her weary legs over the picket barrier. Carlos was already in the room, tied to a wooden chair that had been set among a cradle, dresser, and rocking horse. His mouth was covered with a wide strip of tape. His eyes were round with fear, and his gray hair was disheveled. It appeared that he had put up a struggle. A narrow stream of blood trickled down his chin.

"Lie down on the floor, Abby, while I'm climbing the fence." Candace ordered. "On your stomach. Do it now!"

Abby reluctantly complied, flattening out on the wooden planks. She was in position no more than a minute when Candace, dressed in white slacks and pale yellow sweater, gingerly lifted her long, strong legs over the fencing.

Carlos was now struggling in his chair, desperately trying to communicate through his taped mouth.

"He's trying to tell you that he's innocent," Candace said pleasantly, her brown almond like eyes trained on Abby in a hard stare. "I forced him up here at gunpoint so that he couldn't tell anyone who commissioned the extra watch."

In Spanish, Abby told Carlos that she understood.

The jeweler nodded vigorously, his gray hair falling over his eyes.

"*You* left us the note at the Twin Palms, Candace," Abby said conversationally, slowly rising to her feet.

"Yes, I did that. Took me a while to track you down." Phillip had appeared on the landing, looking the dapper tourist in white cotton pants and a plaid shirt, a pair of binoculars hanging from his neck. "No sign of Farrell on the path."

Candace frowned. "Perhaps she actually did climb up here alone. It would seem that your foolproof lure wasn't as brilliant as you thought," she retorted. "You assured me that we'd round up the three of them with this ploy."

"How was I to know Abby and Farrell would separate?" Phillip said with a peeved look. "They've been together for most of the trip. They came to San Rosa together, spent the

night together. Odds were that they'd end up here together."
Phillip turned to Abby, giving his thin tawny moustache a
twist. "What happened, Abby? What happened to spoil the
works?"

"You know what they say about the best laid plans . . ."
Abby trailed off regretfully.

"Where is Nick Farrell?" Candace demanded harshly.

Abby shrugged and shook her head. That certainly was the
question of the hour. "Last time I saw him, I told him to go
to hell. Maybe he went."

A FATE WORSE than the fires of hell.

The tropical sun was blazing down on the steep hillside
with relentless intensity as Nick picked his way upward
through the rocky undergrowth, using a tire iron from the
Buick's trunk as a makeshift cane. He paused regularly to
wipe sheets of sweat from his forehead and to gaze at the
white stone lighthouse in the distance. Several yards back he'd
left the fairly rugged dirt path for the impossibly rugged ter-
rain of the steep hillside. Chances were that he was walking
into trouble and he figured it would be best to have the element of surprise on his side. At this point, it was about all he
did have on his side.

Even Abby was against him.

Pain shot through his leg like the touch of a hot poker, in-
tensifying with every step. Nick's attitude toward Abby's
defection was in sync with his pain. He grew more irritated
with her with every step.

Sure, sure, he'd been wrong to call in the police without
consulting her first. Her words on the subject still singed his
eardrums. Accusations of betrayal, banishment to hell. She
minced not a word.

So he'd flunked one test of trust. Nick bent over and tossed
aside a jagged rock in his path. He'd saved her ornery, stub-

born hide, hadn't he? He'd loved the living daylights out of her, hadn't he?

Maybe she was more trouble than she was worth!

With a ragged breath, Nick paused to rest on a particularly uncomfortable bush. Yeah, she was a bundle of trouble all right. But she was worth it. Every fiber of his body sang a frenzied tune of erotica when she touched him. Every inch of his soul yearned for her gentle murmurs of love and support. She completed him as no other female ever had.

But he filled her up quite nicely too, didn't he? he countered defiantly. It wasn't a one-sided affair at all. Each filled the other's needs, which certainly was a good basis for a lasting partnership. She had no right to storm off on her own— not with the jewelry and their safety at stake. He pushed some stray locks of damp black hair from his forehead and eased up on his stronger leg. Abby needed a firm, steady hand directing her. His hand. He continued with fresh purpose, fervently hoping that Barone's hand hadn't beaten him to the punch.

"PLEASE TAKE A SEAT near Carlos," Candace directed.

Abby could see they were fully prepared. There were two empty pine chairs positioned back-to-back near the jeweler. It was clear now why the kitchen table downstairs lacked seating. "I may as well tell you, Nick has notified the police," she announced evenly, not moving an inch.

Phillip and Candace exchanged a surprised look.

"I don't believe it, Candace," Phillip decided after some reflection. "It's obvious that Charlie and Blanche sent the pair down here to do some unofficial sleuthing. They had no proof to connect us with the theft and hoped to get some." Phillip shook his blond head and leaned against the fence smugly. "That's why she searched my suite." Phillip turned to Abby with a chastising look. "Which, by the way, Abby my sweet, aroused our suspicions about you. I must say, I was bitterly disappointed to discover you were flying under false colors."

"And so you arranged my windsurfing accident," Abby surmised. If she stalled long enough, perhaps Nick would make his way up here with the cavalry. He'd get around to looking in her purse, wouldn't he? He'd explored every nook and cranny of her. Under the circumstances, dipping into her handbag didn't seem like an invasion of privacy.

"I took the liberty of slicing into your line," Candace interceded cattily. "No matter who you really were, I was sick and tired of your flirty ways. Now sit down!"

Abby stood her ground, wanting to be on her feet when help arrived.

"Don't be stupid, Abby." Candace took a shooter's stance. "You saw the puncture in the Chevy's tire. Imagine a dart piercing the smooth skin between your eyes."

"Now, Candace, there's no need for crudeness," Phillip reprimanded. "Give me the gun and help Abby into the chair."

Abby chose to sit down on her own as Candace approached her with a vicious gleam in her almond-shaped eyes. She was beaten for the time being. Candace was three or four inches taller than she was and outweighed her by twenty pounds.

"Put your arms behind the back of your chair," Phillip instructed, keeping the barrel of the gun trained on Abby. "That's a good girl."

"Quit treating her like one of your playmates." Candace's voice was sharp behind Abby's ear. She pulled Abby's hands together behind the wicker back of the chair and wound the rope around her wrists with a yank. Abby groaned in pain as the twine cut into her skin.

"Weave it through the legs of the chair as I did with Carlos," Phillip instructed pleasantly, as if overseeing a macramé project.

The rusty creak of the door below drifted up the spiral staircase. Abby inhaled to cry out, but was caught with a lungful of air when Candace slapped her palm over Abby's mouth.

The four of them remained motionless as a pair of feet thumped around on the level below. Phillip held up his index finger, smiling with relief at Candace. There appeared to be only one visitor below. The footfall moved to the staircase, taking one step at a time, with an unidentifiable intermittent thud.

Air streamed out of Abby's nostrils as the step-step-thud rhythm grew stronger. What could she do? she wondered, her deductive reasoning slipping into high gear. She didn't want to interfere if a passerby had wandered into the tower. A cry could send an innocent person tumbling down the stairs—or set him up as a convenient dart board.

But what if it was Nick? He'd appreciate some advance warning, wouldn't he? Surely he would already be on his guard. She had a gut feeling that it was him. But why...

It was the mysterious thud of course! Abby was drawn back to the day they'd met, their confrontation in her office parking lot. When Nick had followed her into the office, he'd stomped behind her in his snakeskin boots. Stomp-stomp-click. His cane had created the extra rap on the blacktop! Nick, being an inventive soul, must've found something to serve as a cane for his climb up the hill.

There were only seconds left. Abby was momentarily paralyzed, emotion clouding her reason. Her last partner had died because of one of these sticky decisions. But maybe Nick was right about her. Maybe she had grown far too cautious. He'd expect her to take the risk for him. Abby squeezed her eyes shut, raised her head for momentum, then with a downward jerk, sank her front teeth into Candace's fingers, biting down viciously.

"Oww!" Candace screamed a loud outraged squawk, slapping Abby smartly across the cheek. A string of nasty curses spurted from her mouth, making Abby extremely grateful that the woman no longer held the dart gun.

Nick charged up onto the landing, pausing to get his bearings and size up the odds. He'd taken the last few steps in a bound, not giving his pained leg the attention it deserved. He first spotted the women and Carlos, looking ludicrously out of place in the historical nursery. Then from the corner of his eye, he spotted Phillip, hovering behind the door. Barone stepped forward, raising his gun to take careful aim.

Nick twisted sharply into position, raised the tire iron and drew it downward toward Phillip's hand, knocking the gun away with a clang.

The gun fell and skittered across the planked floor. Nick made a grab for it. His fingers were within inches of the weapon when Phillip, nursing his wrist with a whimper, gave Nick a swift hard kick in his right thigh.

"Nick!" Abby watched in horror as Nick's leg collapsed under him.

12

NICK GRUNTED IN PAIN, reaching out to cushion his fall. The tire iron flew from his hands and bounced down the spiral staircase, clanging against the rail somewhere below. Abby rocked on her chair, desperately wanting to help him. She found she could do nothing. The ropes that were stretched and pinched at her ankles and wrists held her fast.

"So much for the big rescue attempt," Candace taunted Abby. "Your threat of police intervention was mighty scary."

"Help him over the fencing, Candace." Phillip snapped, still nursing the hand that had held the gun. Abby shuddered as she imagined the condition of Nick's leg.

Abby's eyes locked with Nick's for a brief moment before Candace shoved him into the chair that was butted up against hers. She flashed him a message of apology, but she wasn't certain by his pain-hazed face if he really had her in focus.

"Tie Farrell's hands behind him," Phillip directed. "Then tie the backs of their chairs together. Make it tighter!" he added peevishly. "He's not one of your boy toys!"

"It's plenty tight," Candace shot back with a withering look.

"Maybe we should kill them and be done with it." Phillip calmly paused in thought, as if deliberating over selections from a wine list. If the situation wasn't so grim, Abby thought she might burst into giggles over his appearance. Abby couldn't believe that this sweaty, bleary-eyed creature with the grubby suit and tie askew, was the same tidy peacock with a dresser top full of colognes.

"Go ahead and kill them," Candace invited with challenge.

Abby could suddenly feel Nick's roughened fingertips squeezing her own between the chairs. The small gesture of comfort triggered all the welling fear, frustration, and guilt she'd been fighting to suppress. She tried to swallow, finding that her intense emotions had closed her throat. It was crystal clear to her that she still loved Nick.

"Sure, sure," Candace continued in a sarcastic tone. "Kill them and we'll both spend the rest of our lives running from Charles Farrell and his executive son. They'll spend every last penny of their fortune tracking us down."

"But, he hurt me!" Phillip waved the gun at Nick. "Bruised my hand."

Nick sat still, not giving Barone the satisfaction of seeing him flinch. "I could've knocked you over the head with that tire iron." And he was rapidly beginning to wish he had.

Candace tied a final knot on Nick's chair and moved toward her husband with syrupy murmurs that made Abby want to throw up. But, Abby rationalized, the woman was fighting for their lives, so any phony, artificial tricks she wished to play on Phillip were certainly fine with her.

"We discussed all of this after we found out Abby was an investigator," Candace purred, stroking his forehead. "Any death would have to look accidental. A sailboard accident. A tire blowout in the jungle."

"If Farrell wasn't such a damn good driver, they'd be dead now," Phillip snapped.

"No use fretting over past failures. We can't make this look like an accident, pet," she said, casting a sardonic look around the room. "Let's pick up our marbles and get out of here!"

"All right," Phillip relented. "Get the marbles."

Abby and Nick watched as Candace moved over to a pine crib in the corner under the window. With her back to them, they saw her flip up the mattress, then heard a sharp rip of fabric. When she turned around she was holding a small black velvet pouch embroidered with the letter "F."

Nick's expression sharpened with recognition. It was Charlie's pouch. The pouch that the Farrells' pocket watch had been kept in for many generations.

"The jewelry's been here for weeks," Candace said, sliding the watch and brooch out of the pouch. "Since tourists aren't allowed to actually come inside these rooms, it seemed like the ideal hiding spot."

"We knew it would only be a matter of time before Blanche and Charlie discovered they'd been taken to the cleaners," Phillip added in a raspy voice. "So we didn't dare keep the pouch in our possession."

Abby couldn't resist asking for some answers. Knowing from experience how proud criminals were of their deeds, she decided to encourage their boasting. "Why go to all this trouble for two pieces of jewelry?"

Candace and Phillip exchanged a cunning smirk.

"The brooch is certainly a fine piece," Candace replied. "As a matter of fact, I intend to keep it for myself."

"But it's the pocket watch that will enrich our lives, so to speak," Phillip put in, handling the timepiece with reverence. "Your father, Farrell, was an idiot not to realize this watch could be sold for a fortune."

"Charlie knows the watch's worth," Nick ground out, the insult to his father biting more deeply than the ropes on his wrists. "Because he already has all the money he'll ever need, he chose to enjoy the watch's rich history and fine old craftsmanship."

"Unfortunately, we are short on both cash and sentimentality," Candace snapped. "We've been waiting months for the opportunity to lift the pieces."

"Seemed like years the way you nagged me about the damned brooch!" Phillip chastised his wife with a sniff of contempt. "As if I could just go rip it off the old woman's dress!"

"Hah!" Candace's eyes flashed with indignation. "And what about Mr. Witherspoon?" She turned to Nick and Abby, anxious to tell her side. "He's a former Cupid Connection member who happens to be an antique dealer—and an expert on Abraham Lincoln." She stabbed a finger at her husband. "When Phillip learned what that pocket watch was worth to a private collector . . ." She shook her head in disbelief. "There hasn't been a moment of peace in our home since. Phillip became obsessed with stealing it! Even had Witherspoon put us in touch with a buyer!"

"How did you stop Witherspoon from telling Charlie about all this?" Nick asked, amazed at their confession.

"That's the real corker!" Candace shouted, throwing her hands in the air. "Phillip took some pictures of Witherspoon and me in some very compromising positions. Made me seduce the old coot!"

"Money doesn't grow on trees, darling," Phillip lectured, shaking his blond head. "I've told you over and over again. Modern families require two breadwinners."

"Well," Candace continued in a huff, "Witherspoon didn't want those photographs to go public. He'd taken a shine to one of our members by then . . . We suggested he leave the service for good."

"Then we waited for our chance," Philip proudly continued. "We heard Charlie and Blanche commissioning Carlos here to make those copies around Christmastime and realized our silver opportunity had arrived. We didn't know what they were up to, but it really didn't matter. We hoodwinked Carlos into believing that we were playing a prank on the over-the-hill lovebirds, and he provided us with an extra set of phony jewelry. When Blanche and Charlie picked up their copies last month, we switched *our* copies for the real thing, covering our tracks in the confusion."

"And then you two showed up and started poking around in our affairs," Candace reproached.

"We simply could not tolerate your interference on this trip," Phillip chastised. "We intend to use it as our springboard for our new life abroad. Our buyer is meeting us in Germany, and then it's off to greener, more permanent pastures."

No wonder Phillip's closet was jammed with clothing, Abby reflected. It was his entire wardrobe! She couldn't believe the irony of the situation. In their matchmaking fever, Charlie and Blanche had accidentally tossed them into a real crime-in-progress.

"So we'll say goodbye," Candace said, slipping the jewelry back into the pouch. "I'd like to leave on a positive note, but you've been annoying and tiresome. Yes, you've been a couple of real pests."

"You're just huffy because Farrell turned down your advances," Phillip goaded, following her out the door. Her heated response echoed along with their footfalls on the staircase.

"Are you all right, Nick?" Abby asked anxiously.

"I'm stronger than I appeared a few minutes ago." A frustrated growl rumbled from his chest as he strained his arms to test the ropes binding him. "If Phillip hadn't thought to kick my bum leg, I'd have made a much better showing."

"Don't blame yourself," Abby consoled. "Where are our folks?"

"They're safe and sound. I sent them back to Mazatlan."

Abby released a breath of relief. "So what on earth happened to the police? I thought if we stalled the Barones long enough, they'd come charging in here."

"Excuse me?" Nick said incredulously.

"The police," she repeated. *"Policia."*

Nick couldn't believe his ears. "The *policia* I wasn't supposed to call, you mean?"

"The very same," Abby asserted matter-of-factly.

"You didn't want the police, so you didn't get the police!" he thundered.

"I didn't say I didn't want the police," Abby fumed, struggling to keep her temper in check.

"Oh, no? Then what was our fight about? What caused you to go storming off in the middle of our first case together?" Nick laughed grimly. "One minute we're in bed together, in business together, then the sight of a cop spoils it all!"

Abby exhaled to gain strength and patience. "If you recall, I merely said that I wanted to have a say in all the decisions. You bullheadedly called the police on your own. That's not the way a partnership is supposed to work, is it? Well, is it?"

"I've come to believe we're not very good at teamwork, Shamus," Nick said regretfully. "I'm sorry, but it's the way I feel."

"How can you say such a thing after all we've been through?" Abby demanded, her pride wounded.

"It's not easy," he admitted. "But the Barones, with all of their warts, have outdone us here—outdone us working as partners."

"How can you compare me with that oversexed viper?" Abby cried out defensively.

"I don't condone their methods, but they stuck together when it really counted."

"Sure," Abby retorted, "he held the camera and she tickled Mr. Witherspoon's fancy."

"No, no, I'm talking about today. They never could've captured us had they not worked together. Had we stayed together, we probably wouldn't be tied up with poor Carlos over there."

"I guess you've got something," Abby relented on a sigh. "Those two crooks outsmarted us. But I still think we belong together," she added passionately. Nick's plan to join her agency had really become something to look forward to. The idea of sharing her personal and professional life with him had seemed better by the minute. It had certainly given her a lot of comfort during the past hour. "Let's give it another chance, Nick."

Nick didn't answer, but suddenly Abby felt her entire chair begin to wobble. "What are you doing, Nick?"

"Giving it another chance. Abby, by rocking from side to side and tipping over I think we've got a chance of breaking apart this ancient pine. But we have to do it as a team. Rock with me, and on the count of five, swing hard to the right. One, two . . ."

On the count of five, Abby leaned with all her might. Nick leaned with all his might. Unfortunately they leaned in opposite directions. The ropes holding them together pulled taut, making Abby scream and Nick curse.

"Abby!" he roared in disbelief. "You went the wrong way!"

"I thought you meant to your right, so I pulled to my left," she explained feebly.

"To your right, not mine," Nick corrected in a low, controlled voice. "I prefer to land on my strong leg. Understand, Partner?"

"Oh, it's no good," she lamented. "We can't even fall off a chair together."

"Yes, we can," Nick assured her in a softer tone. "C'mon, we move together very well when we put our minds to it. Take last night for instance . . ."

They rocked together in unison, crashing to the floor in a heap of limbs, twine and knotty pine. As she lay crouched on the wooden planks, Abby tried to work at the ropes holding her, still without luck.

"I think I've done it," Nick uttered with a grunt, twisting and turning in the tangle. "Yes! A leg broke on my chair." It took time, but Nick managed to break free of his ties. He rose to his knees and pulled aside the pieces of chair and rope. Within a couple of minutes, he had Abby free and on her feet.

Abby wound her arms around his neck. "We did that rather well, didn't we," she said with a sniff. "Thank you for coming to my rescue."

Emotion welled within Nick and he pulled her against him for a short hard kiss. "There will be more time for that once we wrap up this mess!" He set her back on the ground. "Let's untie Carlos and get the hell out of here."

"Do we have a vehicle?" Abby asked anxiously, gently peeling the tape from Carlos's mouth.

"Dad's rental car," Nick replied, swiftly working to untie the jeweler's ropes.

"One break in our favor. But how will we ever catch that pink minibus?" Abby wondered.

"Have a little more faith in your partner, Partner," Nick said, wiggling a black eyebrow.

NICK AND ABBY PASSED THROUGH San Rosa's main street to drop off Carlos at his shop. Once they were out of the plaza and back on the narrow jungle-flanked road, Nick hit the gas pedal.

"That pink minibus has so much horsepower," Abby remarked as they sped along. She cringed as she relived the moment yesterday when it overtook them and the barrel of the gun appeared out the back window.

"You have to remember we're not in that crummy old Chevy anymore, Shamus," Nick returned confidently. "We're moving along at a pretty good clip this time around."

"But will it be enough?" Abby wondered. "If Mother loses her brooch, I'll never ever hear the end of it."

"Not to worry," Nick consoled, reaching for his sunglasses on the dashboard.

"Nick, those are three little words I already hear enough!"

"Sorry," he murmured, amusement tugging at the corners of his mouth. "I just couldn't resist."

They drove on a little farther to find the pink minibus edged onto the narrow shoulder of the road. "Look, Nick," Abby pointed ahead excitedly. "It's the bus!"

"So it is. And there's a police car parked directly in front of it." Nick slowed down and eased the car onto the shoulder behind the two vehicles. They scrambled out to the road just in time to watch two policemen ease the handcuffed Barones into the back of the squad car.

Hands on hips, Abby shook her head in amazement. "But how did the authorities know to detain the bus?"

"Oh, children!" Blanche's bright red head suddenly popped up from the jungle side of the bus. "Thank heavens, you're safe! The Barones have been a trifle stubborn about disclosing your whereabouts. Charlie? Charlie, it's the kids."

Charlie immediately appeared at her side. "You got here just in time to watch the last roundup," he announced, his pale blue eyes dancing merrily.

Blanche circled the bus and enveloped Abby in her arms. "When we got back to the hotel and discovered the Barones had cleared out, we knew they had to be the culprits. With the help of these nice policemen, we began looking for the minibus."

"Found it stranded here on the side of the road," Charlie put in, fishing in his pocket for a cigar.

"So you've recovered your jewelry," Nick assumed with a sigh of relief.

"Yes, we have," Blanche said, gazing from Nick to Abby. "We've managed to bring this whole thing to an end. Thanks anyway for trying to help, dears."

Abby couldn't believe the cavalier way Blanche was dismissing their efforts. "*Thanks anyway*? Is that all you have to say, Mother?"

"I think that says it all, Abigal," Blanche insisted, holding up Charlie's pouch. "Proof positive is right here."

"But—"

Blanche put a crimson-tipped finger to her daughter's lips. "Now Abigal, who cooked up the original phony scheme about the jewelry?"

"You did, Mother."

"And who pushed you down here to investigate?"

"You did, Mother."

"And who discovered the heirlooms were really missing?"

"You did, Mother."

"And who—mind you, this is the whopper—handed the Barones to the cops on a silver platter?"

"You, you, you, Mother!" Abby exclaimed in defeat.

"Well then, it's clear that we held the key to everything!" Blanche smoothed Abby's disheveled russet mane. "Let's haul it back to the Fiesta for a celebration. Margaritas for everybody!"

Nick gave Abby's shoulders a squeeze as the foursome headed back for the car. "Is she always like this, Shamus?" he asked with concern.

"Oh, yes," Abby assured him solemnly. "Always."

Dread clouded his face. "Good Lord."

"You know, Nick," Abby ventured with a sly gleam in her eyes. "I realize we opposed their relationship in the beginning, but I think we should take a fresh, more liberal view of the situation. I think Mother belongs with Charlie. I think they should live together under the same roof."

"Really?"

"Absolutely," she affirmed with a playful smile. "He has just the right kind of temperament to listen to her sage advice. And he's retired, free to join her wild-goose chases any time of the day or night."

"Yeah, yeah." Nick nodded his head with fresh insight. "She's available to sit around all morning in her skivvies and drink coffee laced with Irish whiskey. She doesn't seem to mind the cigars too much. And she hasn't heard all his stories a thousand times, either," he added joyfully.

"We'd really be off the hook, wouldn't we?" Abby said with a chuckle.

"Yeah, free to concentrate on each other," Nick murmured, covering Abby's mouth with his own.

The car's horn began to beep in short demanding toots.

"I believe we can ignore that pretty easily," Nick whispered, kissing her temples.

"What if they leave us stranded?" Abby asked, nibbling at his ear.

"They can't." Nick replied with certainty.

"Why not?"

"Though your mother believes she holds the key to everything, she is mistaken. I have the most important key of all at the moment."

"The car key," Abby said with a laugh.

Nick pulled her closer and buried his face in her hair. "Exactly."

Epilogue

"LOOK ALIVE, SHAMUS!"

Abby opened her eyes to find Nick moving up the beach in her direction, dodging the foamy waves that were inching up the shore. He looked handsome and relaxed in an orange shirt, scandalously short shorts and his favorite reflective sunglasses.

"I must've fallen asleep," she confessed feebly, as his long shadow fell over her.

Nick's mouth opened in amazement. "Snoozing again?" he demanded, appreciatively scanning her oiled body on magnificent display in her jade swimsuit. "You're so damn lazy these days! I'm beginning to wonder if you're planning an early south of the border retirement."

Abby shrugged with a laugh. They'd stayed on at the Fiesta an extra week with Charlie and Blanche and Abby had fallen into the routine of beachcombing, shopping, and napping with surprising ease. "I'm still reeling from the conclusion of the Cupid Connection caper," she said in her own defense. "Besides, now that I have a partner, I can afford to slow my pace."

"Such goldbricking," he said with mock reproach in his voice. He folded his arms across his chest. "Will I ever get another day's worth of detecting out of you?"

"I'll be ready to board a plane Sunday morning as planned. Then it'll be back to the old grind. I promise."

Nick looked out at the breathless blue horizon, clear and endless as his future with Abby. "I talked to the Mexican authorities this morning. I'm happy to report that the Barones are being extradited to Minnesota today."

"Whew! That's wonderful. When I think of how close they came to escaping..." Abby shook her head. "Mother would've been crushed had she lost her brooch forever."

"Charlie, too," Nick declared, sinking into the warm sand beside her. "Dad claimed he would've been satisfied with the fact that we'd found each other, but I know he was just being gallant. Showing off that watch has given him priceless pleasure."

"It was a stroke of fate that the Barones ended up with car trouble on the road back to Mazatlan. Neither of them knew the first thing about changing that flat tire on the minibus. And the police—under Mother's direction—were already looking for them. The Barones literally fell into their hands."

Nick pulled his sunglasses down to the tip of his nose and scrutinized Abby with doleful amusement. "C'mon, Shamus. Still sticking to that stroke of fate theory?"

"You have a better one?" Abby inquired with surprise. "If you do, you've never mentioned it."

"I never said anything because I had implicit faith in your well-honed tools of the trade," he explained, running his hand along the slippery curve of her oil-glistening thigh. "I figured you'd make further deductions, ferret out the truth with wildcat enthusiasm."

"You did?" Abby sat up with a startled gasp.

"Yes. But it appears you've shut down your generators. The only thing you've snooped for this week is the hotel bartender's latest tropical drink."

Abby threw her hands up in the air. "I guess I just considered the case closed."

Nick clucked regretfully. "Let me ask you this. How many times has fate intervened in one of your cases, wrapping it up with a neat ribbon?"

"Rarely," Abby conceded, growing curious. "But a flat tire is a flat tire, isn't it?"

"Certainly not! Take it from an expert, there are many kinds of flats. You've got your bald blowout, your broken bottle pop, even your dart or bullet tear."

"And?" Abby asked, prompted by Nick's sly, expectant grin.

"And the most annoying to all commuters, the slow leak. A slow leak in the Barones's case caused by a long slender decorator's nail."

"Supplied by you?" Abby wondered with pride, her green eyes gleaming.

"Actually, you supplied it, Shamus. Found a package of the things at the bottom of your purse. I was in too great a hurry to tamper under the minibus's hood, but I did pause long enough to pound a couple of the nails into the rear tire with my trusty tire iron."

"I bought those to hang some prints at the office," Abby recalled thoughtfully. "I just never got around to giving them to Donna."

"Speaking of Donna, she called a while back," Nick reported casually. "Says there's a desperate client clamoring for your attention."

"Really?" Abby's voice picked up tempo, along with her professional instincts.

"Yeah," Nick shrugged nonchalantly. "Donna was all worked up, but she is just a kid—relatively speaking. Everything is dramatic at her age."

"I trained her myself," Abby begged to differ. "She's pretty sharp."

"Don't worry. As a member of the agency, I spoke for both of us. All it took was a firm reminder that you're still on a well-earned vacation."

"You did what?" Abby blurted out with shock.

Nick balked at her reaction. "It's only Thursday. You wanted to stay until Sunday, right?"

"True, true." Abby began to chew her lip, her mind humming into action.

"More than anything else in the world, you said you needed a good rest, right?"

"Right. Did she say anything else? Who is the client? What's the case about?"

Nick pushed his sunglasses back up his nose and paused in thought. "She was very vague, and naturally I didn't press the issue."

"Dammit, Nick." Abby sighed hard with frustration. "You have scads to learn about the business. Scads to learn about me, as well. Detectives are on call all the time!"

"Sorry, honey. I'll learn."

"Forget it," she murmured, patting his knee. "If it had been really important, Donna wouldn't have let you put her off. She would've given you the dirt. All of it!"

"We talked only briefly," Nick assured her.

"I'm happy here," she declared, patting his knee. "This is living."

"Sure beats chasing around in search of a missing will," Nick remarked dismissively, stretching his arms over his head with a yawn.

"A missing will?" Abby repeated in a squeal. "Did Donna mention a missing will?"

Nick smiled sheepishly. "Guess she did. It seems our adventure down here made the St. Paul papers. The woman read about Wildcat Investigations playing a key role in the case—"

"You said woman!" Abby pounced on Nick's lap.

"I did?" Nick steadied her on his thighs, lifting an eyebrow above his reflective lens.

Abby nodded vigorously, her heart-shaped face alight with excitement. "First you said you didn't know anything." Abby wiggled back off him and began stuffing her sandals, bottle of oil, and paperback into her beach bag. "Then you said there was a will. Then you said the client's a woman!"

With an amazed expression on his face, Nick ran a hand through his thick black hair. "I did at that."

"See what a person knows without realizing it?" Abby jumped to her feet and dusted the sand off her swimsuit. "Are you coming?"

"Huh?"

"Are you coming?" she repeated, casting an impatient look down at his blank face. "To pack? To hop on a plane? To get to work on our second case?"

"Well, what about your naps? What about those tropical drinks with the umbrellas?"

Abby began to tug at the beach towel under him. "I've changed my plans!" When Nick didn't budge, she yanked at the towel with a grunt, sending him off balance into the sand. "Flexibility is important in our business," she informed him with a beckoning hand. "Once you sink your teeth into a couple more cases, you'll understand. Private investigating becomes a passion."

"Oh, I see."

"You'll learn the ins and outs," Abby assured him airily, fumbling to balance all her gear. Backing up in the direction of the hotel she said, "Are you with me on this one?"

Nick responded with the thumbs-up signal. "Go ahead," he called after her. "I'm right on your heels." He stood up at his leisure, a huge secretive grin crossing his face as he watched her scamper off in the sand. "Always one step behind you, Shamus," he murmured, patting the airline tickets in his shirt pocket. "One step behind."

H·I·S·T·O·R·I·C·A·L
Christmas
S·T·O·R·I·E·S 1·9·9·0

Once again Harlequin, the experts in
romance, bring you the magic of Christmas
—as celebrated in America's past.

These enchanting love stories
celebrate Christmas made extra-
special by the wonder of people
in love....

Nora Roberts	**In From the Cold**
Patricia Potter	**Miracle of the Heart**
Ruth Langan	**Christmas at Bitter Creek**

Look for this Christmas title next month
wherever Harlequin® books are sold.

"Makes a great stocking stuffer."

ARE YOU A ROMANCE READER WITH OPINIONS?

Openings are currently available for participation in the 1990-1991 Romance Reader Panel. We are looking for new participants from all regions of the country and from all age ranges.

If selected, you will be polled once a month by mail to comment on new books you have recently purchased, and may occasionally be asked for more in-depth comments. Individual responses will remain confidential and all postage will be prepaid.

Regular purchasers of one favorite series, as well as those who sample a variety of lines each month, are needed, so fill out and return this application today for more detailed information.

1. Please indicate the romance series you purchase from regularly at retail outlets.

Harlequin	Silhouette	
1. ☐ Romance	6. ☐ Romance	10. ☐ Bantam Loveswept
2. ☐ Presents	7. ☐ Special Edition	11. ☐ Other _____
3. ☐ American Romance	8. ☐ Intimate Moments	
4. ☐ Temptation	9. ☐ Desire	
5. ☐ Superromance		

2. Number of romance paperbacks you purchase new in an average month:

12.1 ☐ 1 to 4 .2 ☐ 5 to 10 .3 ☐ 11 to 15 .4 ☐ 16+

3. Do you currently buy romance   13.1 ☐ yes   .2 ☐ no
series through direct mail?

If yes, please indicate series: _____

                                           (14,15)   (16,17)

4. Date of birth: _____ / _____ / _____

        (Month) (Day) (Year)
        18,19   20,21   22,23

5. Please print:
Name: _____
Address: _____
City: _____ State: _____ Zip: _____
Telephone No. (optional): (_____)

MAIL TO: Attention: Romance Reader Panel
             Consumer Opinion Center
             P.O. Box 1395
             Buffalo, NY 14240-9961

Office Use Only   TDK

Take 4 bestselling love stories FREE

Plus get a FREE surprise gift!

PASSPORT TO ROMANCE
SWEEPSTAKES RULES

1. **HOW TO ENTER:** To enter, you must be the age of majority and complete the official entry form, or print your name, address, telephone number and age on a plain piece of paper and mail to: Passport to Romance, P.O. Box 9056, Buffalo, NY 14269-9056. No mechanically reproduced entries accepted.

2. All entries must be received by the CONTEST CLOSING DATE, DECEMBER 31, 1990 TO BE ELIGIBLE.

3. **THE PRIZES:** There will be ten (10) Grand Prizes awarded, each consisting of a choice of a trip for two people from the following list:
   i) London, England (approximate retail value $5,050 U.S.)
   ii) England, Wales and Scotland (approximate retail value $6,400 U.S.)
   iii) Carribean Cruise (approximate retail value $7,300 U.S.)
   iv) Hawaii (approximate retail value $9,550 U.S.)
   v) Greek Island Cruise in the Mediterranean (approximate retail value $12,250 U.S.)
   vi) France (approximate retail value $7,300 U.S.)

4. Any winner may choose to receive any trip or a cash alternative prize of $5,000.00 U.S. in lieu of the trip.

5. **GENERAL RULES:** Odds of winning depend on number of entries received.

6. A random draw will be made by Nielsen Promotion Services, an independent judging organization, on January 29, 1991, in Buffalo, NY, at 11:30 a.m. from all eligible entries received on or before the Contest Closing Date.

7. Any Canadian entrants who are selected must correctly answer a time-limited, mathematical skill-testing question in order to win.

8. Full contest rules may be obtained by sending a stamped, self-addressed envelope to: "Passport to Romance Rules Request", P.O. Box 9998, Saint John, New Brunswick, Canada E2L 4N4.

9. Quebec residents may submit any litigation respecting the conduct and awarding of a prize in this contest to the Régie des loteries et courses du Québec.

10. Payment of taxes other than air and hotel taxes is the sole responsibility of the winner.

11. Void where prohibited by law.

COUPON BOOKLET OFFER TERMS

To receive your Free travel-savings coupon booklets, complete the mail-in Offer Certificate on the preceeding page, including the necessary number of proofs-of-purchase, and mail to: Passport to Romance, P.O. Box 9057, Buffalo, NY 14269-9057. The coupon booklets include savings on travel-related products such as car rentals, hotels, cruises, flowers and restaurants. Some restrictions apply. The offer is available in the United States and Canada. Requests must be postmarked by January 25, 1991. Only proofs-of-purchase from specially marked "Passport to Romance" Harlequin® or Silhouette® books will be accepted. The offer certificate must accompany your request and may not be reproduced in any manner. Offer void where prohibited or restricted by law. LIMIT FOUR COUPON BOOKLETS PER NAME, FAMILY, GROUP, ORGANIZATION OR ADDRESS. Please allow up to 8 weeks after receipt of order for shipment. Enter quickly as quantities are limited. Unfulfilled mail-in offer requests will receive free Harlequin® or Silhouette® books (not previously available in retail stores), in quantities equal to the number of proofs-of-purchase required for Levels One to Four, as applicable.

OFFICIAL SWEEPSTAKES
ENTRY FORM

Complete and return this Entry Form immediately—the more Entry Forms you submit, the better
your chances of winning!
- Entry Forms must be received by **December 31, 1990**
- A random draw will take place on **January 29, 1991**
- Trip must be taken by **December 31, 1991**

3-HT-2-SW

YES, I want to win a PASSPORT TO ROMANCE vacation for two! I understand the prize includes
round-trip air fare, accommodation and a daily spending allowance.

Name_____

Address_____

City_____ State_____ Zip_____

Telephone Number_____ Age_____

Return entries to: **PASSPORT TO ROMANCE**, P.O. Box 9056, Buffalo, NY 14269-9056

COUPON BOOKLET/OFFER CERTIFICATE

Item	LEVEL ONE Booklet 1	LEVEL TWO Booklet 1 & 2	LEVEL THREE Booklet 1, 2 & 3	LEVEL FOUR Booklet 1, 2, 3 & 4
Booklet 1 = $100+	$100+	$100+	$100+	$100+
Booklet 2 = $200+		$200+	$200+	$200+
Booklet 3 = $300+			$300+	$300+
Booklet 4 = $400+	_____	_____	_____	$400+
Approximate Total Value of Savings	$100+	$300+	$600+	$1,000+
# of Proofs of Purchase Required	4	6	12	18
Check One	_____	_____	_____	_____

Name_____

Address_____

City_____ State_____ Zip_____

Return Offer Certificates to: **PASSPORT TO ROMANCE**, P.O Box 9057, Buffalo, NY 14269-9057

Requests must be postmarked by **January 25, 1991**

--✂--------

 ONE PROOF OF PURCHASE   3-HT-2

To collect your free coupon booklet you must include the necessary number of proofs-of-purchase
with a properly completed Offer Certificate

See previous page for details